HOME
BY THE
SEA

ANN M PRATLEY

BY ANN M PRATLEY

Power Moore Investigation Tales
Hoonigan
Resolution of Happiness
Home by the Sea
Tiger in Our House

Forbidden Conflicts Series
Amethyst of Youth
Ruby of Law
Diamond of War
Sapphire of Prejudice
Emerald of Wisdom

Freedom of Flight Series
Christian
Brandon
Trinity

Golden Desires Series
The Golden Desires
The Golden Supremacy
The Golden Unity

Chisholm Manor Series
Alessandra

CHAPTER 1

Jordy Simpson sighed as his eyelids opened to the sliver of sunlight that had just touched them. Every morning that the sun shone brightly, and the small level of rays slipped through the boarded-up window to the right of his bed, he was reminded of days gone by.

As always at that time of day, he lay in his bed, unmoving. His body told him it was time to fully wake up and go to the bathroom. He fought the urge. First thing in the morning was the only time of true peace in his life now. Not even a demanding bladder would make him want to ruin or rush that.

Despite all that he'd lived through, he'd managed to stay alive for sixty-seven years. He wouldn't say that he felt old, exactly, but he certainly felt time passing. One day soon would likely be his last in this world. Was he sad about that? It was hard to say, given his current circumstances. Generally, he didn't believe in giving up on life. No matter what life had thrown at him, he'd fought and done whatever he'd had to in order to stay alive. He didn't regard life as fickle and something to throw away. As a general rule, he wanted to live. He'd *always* wanted to live. Some mornings now, he wondered if living was even a choice for him.

He turned his head away from the rays of sunlight. To the left of him, in the next bed over, was George Jones. It had taken a long time to get used to sleeping so close to old George. Jordy wasn't unfamiliar with sharing sleeping quarters with others. Hell, when he was in the military, he'd slept in one room with twenty or so guys on exercises away from the base. No, it wasn't the sharing that had taken time to get used to; it was the snoring. Even that, Jordy was used to, to a degree, but if ever there was some kind of record to be awarded for snoring *volume*, surely George Jones should be the selected winner for that!

As the sounds coming from George grew even higher in volume, the variety of the grunts that were intermingled with more traditional snoring sounds made Jordy smile. It wasn't really funny, having so many sleepless nights, but he knew it was good to seize an opportunity to find a little joy in something. Each day, each month, each *year*, it got harder and harder to smile. It wasn't how he'd thought his life would turn out when he'd lived almost seventy years.

Had he even expected to live as long as he had? He took a moment to play that question over in his mind as his eyes automatically shifted to the sunlight again. He didn't think he'd ever had any such expectations. There had been a short time when he'd been on the frontline in a war zone. He hadn't expected to die during that time, but it had certainly been a time when he'd considered that he might not return home. Soldiers died every day, somewhere in the world. He'd not liked his odds on that mission, but something had been on his side and protected him. He'd made it home safely that time, and the next, and the one after that.

The first time he'd returned home, it had been to a bachelor pad. In his twenties, the thought of getting married, having kids, and committing to a mortgage that would have him tied to one place forever, just hadn't seemed like any kind of a good time to him. After he'd been on a second mission, what he'd seen and experienced had changed his thinking somewhat. That had opened up his mind to the possibility that it might be nice to have someone to come home to after all.

He hadn't gone out of his way to meet someone. It

had been fate that had stepped in and made that decision for him in the end. Two weeks home from his second away mission, he'd run into a young woman at the supermarket - literally.

He smiled as he remembered that first moment. He'd only needed cigarettes. It had been a habit back then, and a bad one. Now, whenever he thought about smoking, it didn't evoke any desire to buy a pack of cigarettes. Instead, it evoked a feeling of nausea. He could still remember the taste, and that wasn't a good memory. So many years on, he didn't even know why he'd indulged in it for so long, but it had calmed his nerves when he'd needed that most.

The day he'd run into Missy Hargest as he rounded the corner by the confectionery aisle in the grocery store, he would never have guessed he'd ever give up his bad habit. He'd been smoking since he was in high school. Almost all of his friends had done it then. Almost all of his colleagues had done it throughout his time in the military. That was long before the days of discouragement for it as a habit, and giving up was definitely something he just never gave any thought to.

Once he'd recovered from the surprise of the large brown eyes he was looking into at that moment in the supermarket, he'd was a goner, that was for sure. Those big brown eyes had looked startled as the young woman comprehended what had happened. Then she'd giggled. Oh, what a beautiful sound that had been. After the horrors and noises of war, there had been nothing so sweet as the giggle of Missy. Whenever she got something in her head that she found funny, she could giggle for a good thirty minutes. Not only that but when she did it, everyone around her would start too.

Jordy laughed softly to himself. Tears threatened as he thought about his past. Part of him wanted to hold onto those memories. Part of him wished his mind would give up being so clear and let the memories fade. There was joy in the past. Remembering it had the potential to pour over him incredible sadness. The comparison of his life then to what it had become in recent years was unbearable at times.

As he rubbed his eyes to keep the tears at bay, he let his mind jump back into the memory again. It wasn't easy, but as much as he wished he didn't feel the sadness that came from thinking about his earlier years, he equally couldn't let the images of joyful moments leave his mind. Not yet, anyway.

That day, after the initial surprise about what had happened, Jordy had almost let Missy walk out of the supermarket doors and out of his life forever. Almost. They'd both moved on and done whatever shopping they were there to do. They'd both gone through checkout, paid for their purchases, and left through the large exit door. By that time, Jordy had suspected that the young woman wouldn't be giving him another thought. It was purely unintentional that when he walked around the exterior corner of the large building, he walked into her a second time.

It was a small thing, but it felt like a sign. He was already taken by those big brown eyes and that delightful sound of laughter she gave off. Running into her twice - literally - left no doubt. He was meant to act, so act he did.

She hadn't looked surprised at all by his question when she'd said yes to the two of them going to grab a bite to eat at the diner down the street. Not much had been said between them as they'd walked, but it hadn't felt uncomfortable. Jordy knew it was corny to say that it had felt like he'd known her for years, but that was exactly how he'd felt on that day.

Once they'd sat and begun talking, something magical had happened. He knew that he only had a couple of hours before he had to be back on base and report for duty that day. He'd extended that time out to the absolute final minute he could, not wanting to leave. Their parting on that first day had ended with a promise to meet up again the next day. The next day had ended with a further promise to meet up the day after that.

Those first few weeks had comprised only meeting and talking. Jordy had received news that he would be going away again on another war bound mission. He knew from the stories he heard among the men that it was pretty usual for them to use going to war as a reason to bed young women. He wasn't interested in that. It was something more than a physical attraction that kept him intrigued and interested in Missy. He liked her, and he respected her. As his respect for her only grew stronger, he was resolved that it wouldn't be right to make any promises to her before he left. He wouldn't do anything that might affect her future in any way. He was heading to a dangerous part of the world. A future was something he could promise nobody.

As he lay in his bed, his mind awash with the few select but happy memories, he felt a chill come over him. He knew that feeling. Although he had long ago stopped knowing what day it was, or how many days were passing, when the coolness came, soon would follow the shadows on the walls. When he'd first experienced them, he'd dismissed the shadows as nothing to fear. It hadn't taken him long to understand that the shadows that came to him and the others who lived alongside him, should never be dismissed.

Never be dismissed, and *always* be feared.

CHAPTER 2

"Moore!" Special Agent Tim Moore heard his supervisor call out to him as he walked down the sterile white corridor in their headquarters.

Immediately he turned around and walked back to look into the office where Sarah Johnson sat.

"Hey, boss," he said to her, attempting to smile at her even though he knew the only look he ever received from her was as cold and sterile as the corridors outside her office.

"I have a case for you and your partner," Sarah said as she nodded at him. "Where's Power right now?"

Tim held back from shrugging his shoulders, even though that was his instant response. He hadn't touched base with his partner, Special Agent Ashley Power, for a few days. That wasn't unusual for them. They worked well together on cases, but they certainly weren't joined at the hip when cases had been solved and there was a little downtime.

"I am not sure," he replied. "Do you want me to summon her here?"

The look he received from his supervisor was one he was well used to. Even without words spoken, it clearly said a very sarcastic, *'Yeah*, I want you to summon her here!'

"On it," Tim said, not waiting for any verbal confirmation. One look was quite enough.

As he walked out of the office, he pulled out his mobile. He wasn't sure Ashley would answer. Whenever they finished a case, she liked to go into hiding for at least a few days before interacting with anybody again. Tim didn't completely understand it, but he'd grown to respect it. Ashley was a good agent. She had what almost seemed like a sixth sense at times. That had come in handy on many a case they'd solved together.

Dialing her number, he wondered what level of solitude she was currently in. If still needing absolute removal from everyone, he suspected she wouldn't answer her phone. If she was coming out of that need for solitude, she might answer the phone. If she was ready to come back to work, she could possibly already be putting on her work clothes.

He let the call ring three times. The game he played in such times was that he'd let it ring five times, and then he'd hang up. He knew she'd see the missed call. If she wanted to talk to him when she saw that, all good. If not, that was fine too.

The fourth ring passed. One more to go, and then he'd hang up…

Behind him, he heard the distinct ring tone. Not a usual or common choice, the musical jingle was apparently from an old Atari game Ashley had played with her father when she was a kid. In Tim's opinion, the jingle was annoying as hell, but he couldn't deny that it was certainly recognizable.

As he turned and saw her walking toward him, he hung up the call.

"Looking for me?" Ashley asked as she approached him. That her partner had called her mobile just as she was making her way to talk to her supervisor didn't surprise her as much as it might have someone else. In their time as partners, slightly weird coincidences had become a little bit normal. Weird, but true.

Tim stood still and waited for her to reach him.

"The boss is," he said, grinning at her. "I think she wants to fire us," he went on to tease. "Too good, I reckon."

Ashley couldn't help but roll her eyes and then smile. Tim thought he was funny. Even though he so often wasn't, she couldn't help but find amusement in his efforts and the belief he had that he *was* funny.

"Best we go and face the news then," she said as they began walking together. It felt good to be back in the workplace again. It had become a pattern with her, to avoid everyone after a case ended. She didn't know why she needed it. She just did. It had become such a routine now that everyone expected it and left her to it - until the next case came in, that was.

As the two of them entered the office of their supervisor, silently they were directed to sit down.

"I have a case for the two of you," Sarah said. "Now, this one might not turn out to be anything, but I've said we'll see what we can find out, at the very least."

Ashley and Tim both nodded, patiently waiting for details to be provided. They watched as Sarah lifted a plain buff-colored manila folder and pushed it across the desk toward them.

"It's a missing person case," Sarah continued as she watched Ashley pick up the file. "This isn't the usual type for us to take on, but hey, I've been asked to look into it, so now I'm asking *you* two to look into it."

As Ashley opened the folder and began speed-reading the first page, she leaned closer to Tim, allowing him to look and read too. It was a familiar pose.

The two partners browsed the initial pages before Tim looked at Sarah.

"Is there anything more that we know about the disappearance of Mr. Simpson before we head to the airport?"

"No airport today, Moore," Sarah said, scoffing. "You two are driving to Compton."

Tim, being the one never too afraid to express whatever he was feeling, showed surprise on his face.

"That's a good six hours away by car," he said.

Although he didn't expect his boss to show any sympathy or change her mind about any such trivial matters, he never failed to enjoy trying to get a response.

"Yep," Sarah said as she nodded. She didn't smile, but she didn't mind Special Agent Tim Moore trying to sway her in decisions. She refused to show it, but inside she might have been smiling ... a little bit. "Get yourselves sorted and get going," she continued as she handed them a travel folder with a map and motel details. "I told them you'll be there tonight."

Ashley looked at Tim. Already she could see his usual excitement. It always began at the same time on any case. The moment they were told they were off to solve something - anything - his countenance took on a level of anticipation that was infectious.

"On it," Ashley said, turning to face Sarah again. "We'll touch base when we're there and know more about what's going on."

Sarah nodded but didn't reply. She sat quietly as she watched the agents stand, look at one another, then negotiate who was going to walk through the doorway first. That was always a fun thing to watch. Tim Moore was a bit of a player when it came to women, but he knew all about chivalry. He would always try and hold back and allow a woman to pass through a doorway first.

In contrast, Ashley Power was a strong, independent woman. Although she dressed femininely and took pride in her grooming and presentation, she emanated a strong determination to always be treated like an equal to anybody, regardless of gender. There was a staunchness about her that demanded respect. Watching Tim react to Ashley sometimes made for very interesting viewing indeed.

Today, Ashley allowed Tim to be a gentleman and let her go first. Sarah smiled and shook her head before the agents left her office completely.

CHAPTER 3

"Must be my turn to drive today," Tim said, knowing full well what Ashley's response would be. While he suspected that one day she *would* let him be the driver, and he *did* enjoy pretending he wanted to be, deep inside, he was just teasing her. Truth be told, he didn't mind at all being able to sit back and read case notes while Ashley drove when they had to travel long distances on the road.

"In your dreams, Special Agent Timothy Moore," Ashley quipped back, making Tim chuckle. When he looked at her, he saw her grin at him in response. The same back and forth banter was just one of their well-established routines. "Go home, get ready, and I'll pick you up in forty minutes."

Tim nodded as he pushed open the outer door of the large building. No more words needed to be said. Towards the east side of the large carpark, Ashley walked, while he headed toward the west side. While walking, his mind did a double check of everything he'd need. He knew it wasn't required. He kept a bag packed and ready to go for last-minute trips all the time. Regardless, it was always good to do one last inventory check, even if only in his head while he was driving home.

As Ashley made her way home, her mind was already processing the little information she'd managed to read in the office. She'd had five days of solitude since she and Tim had finished their last case. She was now ready to work again. Being assigned to a case at almost the very moment that she'd walked into the office was a bonus. She loved her job and, despite her need for calm, peace, and solitude between cases, she loved being busy. There was nothing in her life that caused her grief or heartbreak, but when she was on a case, life seemed infinitely more thrilling.

Once at her apartment, she raced inside and grabbed her toiletries, extra warm jacket, and pre-packed overnight bag. All she knew about the case was that they were going to investigate the disappearance of a man who would now be in his late sixties. 'Would' now be. The wording had stuck with Ashley and confused her a little. She hadn't asked her supervisor for clarification about anything in the folder. With a six-hour drive ahead of them, she knew Tim would do his usual brilliant interpreting of whatever was in the file and relaying of that to Ashley as she drove.

That was one of the things she loved about having him as her partner on the job. They were in sync. No matter what kind of case they were working on, they did work together well. She was well aware that Tim's light-hearted nature evened out her more serious one. His attention to detail evened out her occasional over-excitement to get to the end. Then there was his ability to draw in women and men towards him. Ashley never tired of seeing that, or watching the way that Tim used that to his advantage to get whatever information he needed.

Jumping back in her car and securing her seatbelt, she smiled. She'd had her few days of calm. Now she was on with another case. That was always something to be appreciative and happy about.

CHAPTER 4

As always, Tim was ready and standing at the edge of the road outside his apartment building when Ashley arrived. They had so many well-tuned routines that had developed over time. One was the way he could jump into her car almost without her stopping it. He sometimes wondered if she liked that particular game a little *too* much. He was happy to see that she at least stopped the car completely to let him in this time.

"All set?" Ashley asked him as he threw his overnight bag in the back seat, then climbed into the passenger seat.

"Yep," Tim replied, buckling up and getting comfortable for the journey.

"You got the file?" Ashley asked. She didn't need to, and she knew it. Still, it did no harm to double-check.

She watched as he pulled the pages from inside his jacket pocket. The sight made her roll her eyes once again. The pages had seemed so pristine less than an hour earlier when they'd first been handed over. How her partner could get paper into such a state as quickly as he did always surprised her. It also amused her, so she'd given up scolding him for it many cases earlier.

Once sure they were ready, Ashley pulled out and psyched herself up for the long drive. It wasn't unusual for them to drive to their destinations, but even she had to admit, six hours was pushing the limits a little. Three or four hours might be normal. Six hours? Not so much. Over that duration, she might even have to hand over control for a while and actually let Tim drive.

Glancing over at Tim, she saw him reading the contents of the file. There was no hurry to hear or learn what they were. Letting him just read and process, she used the time to calm her mind, clearing it so that when Tim began to share details with her, she would be ready to receive and really hear them.

After a lengthy wait, Tim finally spoke.

"So, the person we are going to try and find is Mr. Jordan Simpson," he said. "The age he would be right now is sixty-seven…"

"What's with the 'would be'?" Ashley asked. "There's something there I don't understand."

"Patience, Power. Patience!" Tim said, grinning. "I'm going to tell you everything that's in here, so shush."

Ashley chuckled but nodded and waited.

"Mr. Simpson was last seen about a decade ago," Tim continued. "The person looking for him is his granddaughter - Kate Simpson. All that's on the file, that she's been able to say, is that family members have told her he was a war vet and after his wife died, he went to live on the streets in Compton."

When he stopped talking, Ashley processed the small amount of information he'd provided.

"Did anyone stay in touch with him? I mean, how do they know he lived on the streets?" she asked.

"That is part of what we have to find out from the granddaughter when we meet with her," Tim replied. "We've got Mr. Simpson's war records here. Looks like he was quite a hero in serving our country."

"War vets living on the streets is something that I don't understand," Ashley said as she shook her head. "Even if they want to do it, why do we let them?"

"You don't think they've earned the right to live however they want to? The ones who do want to live like that, I mean," Tim asked.

"Yeah, I guess," Ashley replied. "It's just so sad, but I know you are right. Some live like that because they have no choice, but others we've talked to over the years seemed to gain a sense of comfort from it. Even having heard some of those guys talk about it, I never quite got it," she said and paused. "But let's focus just on this one person. It's been over a decade since anyone saw him?"

Tim nodded. "Yep," he said. "File suggests someone saw him around ten years ago, living among a cluster of about fifteen homeless people on the streets. By the time someone next went to check on him, not only had he gone, but so had the entire cluster. There was nobody to ask anything else, it seemed."

"So that was it?" Ashley asked and saw Tim nod. "Well, where did the other homeless people go? The ones from the same cluster?"

"There's nothing about that in here," Tim said, shrugging. "I guess that's what we'll be asking."

Ashley let the small details sink in. They didn't always get a lot to go on when starting a case, but usually, there was much more that Tim could extract from a file. It seemed so little to begin with, but that only provided more of a challenge.

Hearing the silence that ensued with her and Tim both considering the case they were embarking on, Ashley relaxed back. It was going to be a long drive, but she knew Tim liked to get on with a case, just as she did.

As she steered the car onto the busy highway, she eased her foot down on the accelerator. She didn't mind driving, but she certainly liked it more when she could be on an open road and get some serious speed going.

Beside her, she saw Tim's head turn and face her just as Ashley made sure there were no other cars too close in front. When it seemed they were alone on the open road, her foot was planted. That Tim had already been prepared for it was something she found amusing enough to make her laugh out loud.

Tim looked at her but couldn't help but smile. She was a crazy driver when she could be, but a likable one.

CHAPTER 5

Five hours later, as they veered off the highway once again, Ashley slowed right down. It wasn't exactly a sprawling metropolis that they'd entered. From where they'd gained a view of the town of Compton, they could see it was big enough to possibly be considered a city, but only a small one. It was already close to 8pm. So far, they'd seen nobody even strolling along a footpath.

"I see now why there might not be an airport," she said as she pulled over and checked her GPS unit. "We have Kate's address, and we have the hotel address."

"Sarah said they are expecting us tonight," Tim said.

"Kate's place first then," Ashley said as she nodded and started moving the car again. "Is there nothing else in there that we need to know before we see her?"

"No," Tim replied. "Most of this file is about Mr. Simpson. More specifically, it seems to mostly be about his life in the military. There's not a lot about or from Kate, except that she wants to find out what happened to him."

"Hmm. Does it seem strange to you that we're investigating this?" Ashley asked. She knew it was a pointless question. They'd worked on a few cases that she was pretty sure the Bureau wouldn't normally take on.

"It does," Tim agreed, nodding. "Someone at the top likes giving us these ones, though."

Ashley grinned and nodded. She couldn't complain. She enjoyed the diverse range of cases she and Tim seemed to be assigned. Each one was just a little bit more unique than the last. That fed her analytical mind and her determination to not let anything - or anyone - beat her in figuring out what had happened.

As they pulled up to the small apartment complex the GPS had directed them to, Tim turned and looked at her.

"Let's do this," he said simply before opening the door and climbing out. It wasn't the best level of preparation that they'd had before meeting with anyone associated with a case. That was okay. Between the two of them, he and Ashley always got to the bottom of whatever they'd been assigned to figure out.

Walking up to the apartment door, both noticed a curtain move aside just enough so that someone could peer out. Before Ashley could knock, the door opened.

"Hi, I'm Kate," the young woman said as she held out her hand to each agent. "Please come in."

Ashley and Tim greeted her and walked into the small apartment, immediately finding themselves in a tiny living area.

"Please sit down," Kate continued, pointing to a small sofa.

"Thank you," Tim said as he watched her sit down in a seat opposite them.

"You are here to find my grandfather," Kate said, her words tailing up partially to indicate a slight question in her voice.

"Yes," Ashley replied. "Can you tell us about the situation with him? Whatever you can share would be helpful to us."

"I only have the little that I have managed to find out," Kate began. "My grandparents were in my life when I was little. I remember going to their house to visit. Granddad Jordy was never a very happy man, but he always put on a cheerful face for us…"

"Us?" Tim asked.

"Oh, my mother and me," Kate replied.

"Your mother is…"

"Yes," Kate replied to the unspoken question as she nodded. "Granddad Jordy was my mother's father," she said. "When my mother was alive, the two of them seemed to get on well, as far as I could see. We used to see Granddad Jordy and Grandma Missy most weekends." She paused for a long while. "When Grandma Missy became sick, the small amount of happiness that my grandfather seemed to have been able to summon before that just disappeared."

"How old were you then?" Ashley asked.

Kate shrugged her shoulders.

"I think I was about 13 or maybe 14," she replied. "Granddad Jordy stopped coming to see us, but my mom would drive us over to their house every weekend then." She paused as both agents saw her rub her eyes as if to stop a threatening tear. "One weekend, we went over there, and he was gone. Nothing looked like it had been disturbed. It looked like he'd just gone out, but we sat outside for hours. He didn't come back that whole day. My mom drove over there again the next day, and the day after that. He never returned. After a while, my mom stopped driving over."

"Your mom didn't contact the authorities and register him as a missing person?" Tim asked.

"No," Kate replied. "She seemed to think that he'd gone on holiday."

"And had he?" Ashley questioned.

Kate shook her head.

"No," she said. "One day, a man called our house and told my mom that he'd seen my grandfather living in some kind of makeshift cardboard box shelter over on 22nd Street. We went over there. At that time, there had been ... oh, more than a dozen, I'd guess ... homeless people living like that. They were all clumped together in the same spot." She paused. "We found him pretty quickly. My mom tried to convince him to come back to our home with us if he didn't want to be alone at his place. He didn't want to. Said he just wanted to be among his own people, whatever that meant."

Tim watched the young woman's face as she spoke. There was emotion there, but so far, Tim wasn't sure why they'd been assigned to investigate the man's disappearance.

"Anyway, we kept going back there now and then, but my mom started to distance herself. Kept saying there was no point in going to see him anymore because he didn't seem to want us there," Kate continued after a long pause. "When I was old enough to be able to go on my own, I went to find him. He was there a few times, but then I went to college and, well, when I next went, they were gone."

"They?" Ashley asked.

Kate nodded as she looked at Ashley.

"Homeless people," she said. "It wasn't just my grandfather who'd gone. They *all* had."

"Gone to a homeless shelter?" Tim asked quietly.

"No," Kate replied as she shook her head. "I went around all of the shelters in the city. Granddad Jordy wasn't in any of them. What was even weirder was that they weren't even full, those places. Most of them were almost empty."

"Hmm," Ashley said as she pondered what she was hearing. "Did the city set up some kind of new service, catering to the homeless?"

"Not that I ever found out," Kate said.

"Sorry, Miss Simpson…" Tim started to say before his words were cut short.

"Please call me Kate."

"Kate," Tim said, nodding. "Just how long ago are you talking about?" Tim asked, curious.

When Kate looked at him, her face revealed sadness.

"Almost ten years now," she replied. "I looked for him for months, and then let the years pass, just in case he came to find me. Finally, not having heard anything for the last decade, I decided to let someone know that I … I'm seriously worried, not only about him but also the others. I mean, where did they all go?"

Ashley turned and looked at Tim. There was far more to the request for finding Kate's grandfather than they'd realized.

"You're not just looking for your grandfather?" Ashley asked.

"I *am* wanting to find out what happened to him," Kate replied. "Since beginning to look for him, though, it seems like other homeless people have disappeared too," she said and paused. "I mean, aren't there other families who want to know what happened to *their* loved ones?"

Tim had been wondering the same thing.

"Do you know if anyone else has been trying to find any of the other homeless people who were in the same cluster as your grandfather back then?" he asked.

"I looked into it," Kate said as she nodded. "But nobody seems to have filed any missing persons reports in this area. Nobody knows who was *in* that cluster."

"And you've searched for clusters of homeless people elsewhere?" Ashley asked for clarification.

"Yes! I searched the city and surrounding area. Then I went out and visited three neighboring towns. The same thing was there," Kate replied.

"The same thing?" Tim asked and saw Kate focus on him.

"In the three nearby towns I visited, there were no homeless people," Kate said. "*None!*"

Even allowing for towns and cities stepping up and somehow incorporating new offers of assistance for those living on the streets, Ashley had to concede that it was odd that *no* homeless people were to be found anywhere.

"Very well," Ashley said finally. "Is there any other information you can tell us for now?"

She and Tim watched Kate as she reached down to

the coffee table between them and lifted a large wire-bound notebook.

"Once I began to notice that my grandfather wasn't the only person who wasn't around still, I started to write down my movements in trying to find him, and then trying to find any homeless people," she said as she passed the notebook to Ashley. "Everything I did to search for them is in there."

Ashley flicked through the pages.

"You have been very thorough in your documentation," she said before looking up at Kate. "Are you still hoping to find your grandfather alive?"

Kate shook her head a little before replying.

"I am prepared for the likelihood that he might not be, but if he vanished, there is still a chance. If he can be found, I have to at least try and find him. I know there's a chance that even if he is alive, maybe something has happened to his body or his mind. He may not know who I am. He might not even know who *he* is. But I need to, at least, know that I exhausted every possible avenue to find out what happened, not just to him but also to the others. I have no idea who they are, or if they have family looking for them, but something happened to everyone living on the streets, and I don't remember anything being reported on that."

Tim nodded. Silently, he agreed. In any small town or large city, there were usually at least a few people who chose to live rough each night. To not see any homeless people over four adjoining towns wasn't normal.

"Well, we will build on what you've already done and see if we can work this out," Ashley said as she stood. "Can we take this to read through?"

Kate stood and nodded eagerly.

"Yes, please!" she exclaimed. "I remember everywhere I went during that time. If there is something in there that can help you, please use it however you want to."

As Tim and Ashley reached the apartment doorway, Kate made her final plea to them.

"Please find Granddad Jordy," she said one more time. "But also, please find *all* of them."

Tim and Ashley nodded.

"We'll contact you again when we have something to report," Ashley said before they walked out into the dark.

Once settled into her car, Tim turned to face her.

"This case could be an interesting ride," he said as Ashley started the engine. "Do you think there *is* a case here?"

"Oh, yeah," Ashley answered with excitement in her voice as she moved the car in reverse to leave the carpark. "Whole clusters of homeless people going missing? There has to be something to that. I mean, maybe it will turn out to be a good Samaritan thing, like someone offering these people a place to live, but why wouldn't something like that be reported on?"

"Well, we don't know that it wasn't yet," Tim said. "Kate said she didn't *see* any report like that. That doesn't mean it wasn't reported on. Don't forget that she was full-on looking into the disappearance of her *grandfather* ten years ago. Wondering about other homeless people seems to be something that happened much later."

"That's true," Ashley replied, glancing at the GPS on the dashboard. "Well, our motel should be right about here," she said just as the full length of the two-story structure came into view. "Let's call it a night and start looking into this first thing."

Tim nodded before climbing out as the car halted.

"What about the notebook?" he asked, grabbing his overnight bag. "Do you want it, or you want me to read through it?"

Ashley grinned at him as she grabbed her bag and

locked the car.

"Are you itching to read through it?" she asked.

While they entered the motel office, Tim didn't reply. Once sorted with their keys, they walked to their adjoining rooms.

"Okay, I'll take it," he finally said, making Ashley laugh. He was a good agent. He was a good partner. He was also highly predictable.

She took her time to pass the notebook to him, enjoying seeing the eagerness in his eyes.

"Just remember to sleep tonight," she teased him. Usually, the teasing went in the other direction. She did enjoy it when she could turn it around.

Tim grinned as he accepted the notebook and put his key into the slot in the door.

"I promise," he said. "What time do you want to start in the morning?"

"Meet up at six-thirty for breakfast?" Ashley asked and saw him nod. "Alright. Sleep well."

Tim smiled then entered his room, closing and securing the door behind him. Setting his overnight bag on the bed, he placed the notebook on the small round table in the corner of the room and made his way to the bathroom. He was going to read that entire book as quickly as he could to find out as much as he could. First, though, a long hot shower was needed to relax him and get him into the right headspace.

Next door, Ashley dumped her bag, dumped her clothing, and then climbed into the large bed. It wasn't the most comfortable she'd ever been in, but it would suffice. For a long while, she let her mind mull over what she'd learned about the case so far. She still wasn't sure it was going to turn into something that needed involvement from law enforcement, but her curiosity was certainly heightened. Wherever it was going to take them, she suspected it was going to be an enjoyable and intriguing route they were embarking on.

That thought present in the forefront of her mind, it wasn't long before Special Agent Ashley Power fell into a deep slumber, her mind and body eagerly preparing for a long day to come.

CHAPTER 6

As if like clockwork on a mutual scale, Ashley wasn't surprised when she opened her motel door the next morning and saw Tim doing the same thing at just that same moment.

"Good morning," Tim said as he locked his door and waited for her to do the same.

"Hey, how was your reading last night?" Ashley asked when she approached him.

"That notebook has been written with amazing care," Tim replied as they started walking toward the car. "She's certainly done some serious investigating and a really good job of writing it all down."

"Yeah? Is there anything that will be of use to us?"

Tim nodded. "Lots. She's been pretty thorough, but I think we just need to focus on figuring things out and referring to that when we need to."

"Okay," Ashley said as they climbed into her car. "Did you learn anything that we should remember and focus on first thing?"

"You mean after breakfast?" Tim asked, making Ashley chuckle.

"Yes, Special Agent Timothy Moore," she replied, starting the engine. "Let's go and get you fed first, then we'll get into the case."

Tim loved how she always placed emphasis on *his* appetite, as though she rarely ate. He'd seen her consume meals many times, and she was hardly one for pecking at food. She could shovel it away at the same rate he could - but he was too much of a gentleman to point *that* out at that moment.

Once settled at a small dining table with coffee and food in front of them, Tim began to speak.

"So, ten years ago, Ms. Simpson began seriously trying to find her grandfather," he said. "Back then, she tried to speak to people in the general neighborhoods around where she knew he'd been living on the street."

"And nothing came of that?" Ashley asked.

"No," Tim replied. "According to her notes, nobody could remember who was in that cluster, and they didn't know what had happened to it. People didn't even particularly remember that there had been homeless people living there."

"Oh? Could Kate have been mistaken in the location she'd thought her grandfather was in?"

"I don't think so," Tim replied. "I think that's the first thing we need to ascertain, but it really does seem like there was a homeless presence that did somehow disappear."

"But nobody else reported anyone from their family missing, right?" Ashley asked.

"As far as Kate has indicated, that is true," Tim replied.

"Okay, let's start at the local police precinct," Ashley said, gulping down the last mouthful of her second cup of coffee and standing up. "Ready?"

"Eager?" Tim asked, quietly laughing at her. "Sit down, Power. I'm still eating, and it's not even seven yet. I think we have enough time for me to finish this off."

Ashley was about to bite and demand action on his part. That was until she saw his amusement. It helped her to relax. As she sat down once again, she smiled at him. It was always the same with the two of them. She could get ahead of herself. He was good for keeping her still when she needed to just stop and breathe.

"Okay," she said quietly, indicating to the waitress to bring her another cup of coffee.

CHAPTER 7

After walking into the local police station and introducing themselves, Ashley and Tim were shown into a small office.

"I understand you are here about the inquiries that Kate Simpson has made over the years concerning her grandfather," Mike Batch said as they all sat down.

"Yes," Ashley began to say.

"This isn't something I would have expected the Bureau to investigate," Mike said quickly, a defensive tone noticeable in his voice.

"What can you tell us about the disappearance of Mr. Simpson?" Tim asked.

Mike cleared his throat before replying.

"Disappearance is a word we haven't tended to use for Mr. Simpson," he said. "He was a retired war vet. He made a choice to live on the streets, and sometimes they move on to other locations when they live like that."

As Ashley studied the officer's face, she found herself having to fight a natural desire to dislike him immensely. It was rare that she took an instant dislike to anyone, but there was no denying it trying to push through.

Sensing Ashley's mood, Tim stepped in to resume questioning. She was usually mellow in her moods. When she looked like she was gearing up to not be, Tim knew it was good to take over.

"What can you tell us about the homeless situation here?" he asked the officer.

Mike shrugged his shoulders.

"What is there to know? We haven't had any

homeless people lingering on the streets for years."

"But there *was* a homeless presence here a decade ago?" Tim pressed and saw the officer nod in response.

"There was," Mike said. "Where Ms. Simpson said she'd seen her grandfather when she was a kid - 22nd Street - there was a small group of people who'd set up a small camp of large cardboard boxes and other stuff for shelter. They had their own little community going on."

"And?" Tim asked. "What happened?"

Mike let out a long, deep breath.

"We don't know," he finally replied. "To be honest, nobody really noticed they were there once they'd settled in. That group had been there for years. I think that people noticed them initially. Over time, they just blended into the pavement."

"Blended into the pavement?" Ashley asked, finally unable to remain quiet. "People? People who were down on their luck and trying their own way to find some sort of normality in their lives? *Blended into the pavement?*"

Although she hadn't spoken loudly, the dissatisfaction in Ashley's tone captured the attention of Tim and the officer.

"What do *you* think happened, at best guess?" Tim asked the officer, eager to keep things civil, at least till they got the information they wanted.

"To be honest? I don't know," the officer said, again shaking his head. "Whoever was in that group, nobody ever asked us about. Nobody seemed to interact with them. Nobody even seemed to notice them."

"But *somebody* must have noticed … when they'd disappeared, I mean," Tim said.

"No. It wasn't until Ms. Simpson came in and began asking about her grandfather that any of us even gave those people a thought. When she came to us, I went and visited the small shops in the area, but nobody could give any definite dates of when the people were there, or when they weren't."

Tim was equally intrigued and saddened by what he was hearing.

"Then you don't know if they disappeared one at a time..." he started to ask. The officer shaking his head answered the unfinished question. "They could have all gone at the same time?"

"They could have," Mike replied. "Like I say, nobody in the entire area noticed anything at the time. If all those people left at the same time, or the numbers dwindled one at a time until none were left, nobody knows."

"Well, someone does," Ashley said. "You just said that those people were living in large cardboard boxes for shelter. They'd set up their own little community. Even if they walked away, one by one, they must have been either carrying things with them or they must have left stuff behind, in which case, someone else took it away. Correct?"

The officer nodded. He'd dealt with plenty of agents from the Bureau before. The young woman in front of him was straight to the point, no doubt about that. He admired and disliked her all at the same time.

"One would expect so, yes," he replied. "When Ms. Simpson came in to see us, we did investigate, like I said. People in the area just don't remember seeing or hearing anything."

"Is there still a homeless presence around here? Perhaps somewhere else that they've gone to?" Tim asked.

"Not that we know about," Mike replied. "We searched street to street here, and then did the same for the neighboring towns."

"What about the land in-between? Is there any chance that they moved away from the population but are out in the bush or something?"

"I don't know about now, but back then, it wasn't a possibility," Mike said. "We sent out dogs when Ms. Simpson began asking her specific questions. They didn't find anyone out there."

All three sat in silence for some time, quietly contemplating.

"Do you know who the other people in that cluster were?" Tim asked. When the officer shook his head, Tim continued. "Nobody came forward, worried that someone in their family was missing?" Once more, the officer shook his head. "How can that be? How can only one person in a group of fifteen or so have anyone who cares enough to want to know where they are and that they're okay?"

Mike shrugged his shoulders, his face grim.

"It's just how it goes," he said. "It's not ideal, and it's not a pleasant thing to think about, but some people just don't have anyone."

"They can't have *no-one*," Ashley said. "Someone gave birth to them. At least some of them must have had a brother or a sister. Some of them might have even been mothers or fathers." She waited for some response. When none came, she continued. "Even someone who lives a reclusive life ... they have to have someone out there somewhere who, even if they don't know them now, they *knew* them at some point."

"I agree, but with this particular group, nobody else came forward," Mike said. "Only Kate Simpson. She is the only one who came forward in this city, and when I talked to the other police departments, she was the only one who had gone in there to ask questions too."

Tim sat up and rubbed his eyes. He and Ashley didn't know what was going to appear in their findings of the investigation but already it was affecting him, even without having found anything.

When they worked on cases that made Tim question the possibility of living life alone, he was reminded that his way of life - having several women as play friends, rather than one as a full-time partner - might not be something he wanted for the long haul. Maybe there was something to be said for having someone to come home to - someone who would actually notice if, one day, he disappeared.

"I'm sorry, Agents, but there really isn't anything else I can offer you in the way of information about this," Mike said.

Tim watched the officer's face as he spoke. He couldn't help but wonder if the officer had truly shown any interest in the mystery of the missing homeless community when it had been first brought to his attention. Even assuming Mike Batch had moved on to other cases - as would naturally be expected - did he honestly have no idea what had happened to those people? Did he even care? Maybe he did. Maybe he didn't. Tim knew he could ask the questions, but he equally suspected that either they wouldn't be answered, or if they were, they might not be answered honestly.

"Alright," Ashley said as she stood and held out her hand to Mike. "Well, thank you for your time."

As Tim stood to also shake the officer's hand, he felt a distinct level of dissatisfaction.

"One more question," he said. "Your city. Do you think that the people here are glad they no longer have to see people living on the streets?"

"You're asking if people are glad that those less fortunate are gone," Mike said as a statement even though it could have been perceived as a question.

"I am," Tim replied.

Mike stood and moved around his desk.

"To be completely honest, I don't think the majority of the population ever even noticed they were there to begin with."

Tim nodded and said nothing more as he and Ashley left the office. Once outside, he took a moment to breathe in the fresh air and appreciate the sun beaming down on him.

"You okay?" Ashley asked. Usually, Tim was pretty

happy go lucky. When he wasn't, she knew that something serious was going on in his mind.

"Yeah," Tim replied, frowning at her. "I just … I can't comprehend what it's like for anyone who just isn't … I don't know … *important* to anyone," he said, pausing a moment. "How do we, as a race, just forget someone exists?"

"Well, in this case, not everyone has," Ashley replied, watching his face. "Kate Simpson has stepped up. You heard her, and you've seen her notebook. She might have begun this journey only searching for her grandfather, but she has been able to very clearly see that other people are missing too. They aren't even her relations, but she's intent on finding out what happened to them."

"Yeah. There is that," Tim agreed quietly. He smiled at her, but it wasn't a happy smile. "Some cases make me assess my own life."

It was a moment when Ashley knew she could tease him about his 'Romeo' ways. She chose not to. He might have been a player when it came to women, but she had no doubt that inside, he was a good and caring man.

"It's not a bad thing for any of us to take a moment to reflect now and then, and remember how lucky we are," Ashley said quietly.

They stood together in the sunshine for several minutes before deciding to move.

"Where to next then?" Tim finally asked, looking at her. "It doesn't seem to me that we've really learned anything new yet."

"Well, it's still early. I think that we need to go to these neighboring towns. Let's go and chat to the police departments there and have a general look around. Kate said people were missing from the four towns. Maybe that's not all, and maybe things have changed since she was actively looking into it," Ashley said.

"Yep, let's do that," Tim agreed.

Moving out of the sunshine and into the car, he still

felt thoughtful about his own life. It took some doing, but he forced the contemplation from his mind. They were on a case. Once that was complete, he could take some time to figure his own life out. That was what Ashley did every time a case was over. She had developed a well-known habit of disappearing for a few days each time. Maybe there was something of value in doing that. She'd once explained to him that for her, those few days of solitude were like a routine of cleansing. Immediately after a case was over with, she always felt like she needed to 'reset' before beginning the next one.

As the car began to move and Tim thought about that cleansing routine of his partner, he decided that perhaps it was time he try it himself. Nothing to lose, after all.

"Let's keep our eyes open to the areas between the towns, too," Ashley said, pulling Tim from his personal thoughts. "I know Mike said that they hadn't seen any homeless clusters for years, but who's to say if they have set up again now."

"How many people do you think we're really going to end up searching for?" Tim wondered out loud. Sensing Ashley turning to look at him, he realized he hadn't just asked the question silently inside of his head. "As far as we know, there were maybe fifteen people in that cluster that Jordan Simpson was a part of, but that's only one cluster. From what Kate's said, it sounds like she visited other towns, and they'd lost their homeless populations too, but there's been no mention of how many homeless *were* in those towns."

"You're right," Ashley said, nodding. "That's at least one question we have to ask these other police departments about. With all due respect to Mike Batch and his career in law enforcement, I'd like to think that the police in these other towns have been far more attentive than he seems to have been."

"Agreed," Tim replied.

CHAPTER 8

On meeting the police chief of the second town, Riverside, Ashley felt far more at ease than she had with Mike Batch. At least this chief of police - Tom Reach - sounded actually interested in their quest to find out what had happened to people.

"Please take a seat," the chief said as he pointed to two chairs on the other side of his desk. "I have the file right here," he went on to say as he reached down and appeared to retrieve it from a drawer in his desk. When he placed the file on the desk, he looked at both of the agents in front of him. "I remember Ms. Simpson well. When she came in to see us, I'd been digging around as well, but not on the level she was."

"What do you mean?" Tim asked.

"We used to have three distinct homeless groups here. One had set themselves up under the Pamson Bridge. Another was in the local gardens, tucked away behind some of the big old trees in there."

"And the third?" Ashley asked.

"The third was quite a community. It was growing steadily in size out near the old cheese factory. It was a distance away from everything, but I guess those folk didn't need much," Tom said. "Every few months, I'd head out and do a drive-by just to make sure they weren't getting up to anything serious out there, with the buildings vacated and all, but there was never any problem. It didn't even seem to occur to them to try and break in and set up inside the old buildings. They found a little patch that was sheltered out in the grounds, and they seemed content there."

Ashley watched his face as he spoke. He seemed genuinely concerned about something.

"And then they just vanished?" she asked, prompting him to look directly at her.

Tom shrugged his shoulders.

"We don't know," he replied. "There was an entire thriving community out there the last time I saw them. Jump forward about five weeks, and it was all gone - the people *and* everything they owned. It was as if they'd never been there at all."

"And the other two communities?" Tim asked.

"Same thing," Tom replied. "I didn't check up on the ones right in town as often. They kept to themselves, and they didn't cause any problems, so I trusted that if anything happened, I'd probably hear about it. I never did, though. It wasn't until the group out by the cheese factory had disappeared that I went and checked on the others and discovered that they were gone too."

Tim considered what he now knew about the two towns and their reduction in the homeless population. It was hardly feeling like a case at all, there being so little to go on.

"Do you know of any other people who were among the communities here?" he asked.

The chief shook his head.

"No," he said. "The only person who ever came forward and asked about someone was Kate Simpson. Through her, we know of one name that was in the crowd in Compton - her grandfather, Jordan. I think she came here in case he'd made his way to our town, but nothing is recorded about him having ever come here. In the three known groups that were here in Riverside, I don't know who any of them were. They were mistrusting of me whenever I approached them, which is understandable. In general, I chose to just respect their privacy."

"Nobody else was asked about, or listed as a missing person?" Ashley asked, even though she already knew the answer.

"No," the chief answered. "Nobody. If the rest of the people had family, nobody seemed to care enough to come forward and ever ask if we knew where they were. It's a sad state of affairs, for sure, but we had to move on from searching for those people."

"Was the cheese factory interior searched?" Tim asked.

"It was," replied the chief as he nodded. "When I realized the entire homeless population had disappeared, we sent out groups of officers - and volunteers at times - in the hope that we'd find something, but there was never anything found. No people, and no remnants of their meager possessions. I think I found that more difficult to understand than anything else."

"What?" Tim asked.

"That there was nothing left behind. I know they used to own little, but most of the community - especially out by the factory - they had set up cardboard shelters and old blankets. They had lots of stuff that most people would regard as garbage. It surprised me that they would take every shred of stuff that they'd accumulated, instead of taking what they could easily carry in a bag and walk off, leaving the rest behind."

Ashley and Tim remained quiet, both thinking about their next possible move.

"Day to day, this is somewhat of a cold case. There is only one missing person among this search, but when I noticed that so many people had left to go somewhere, I was eager to try and find them. I'd still like to know they are okay, wherever they decided to move on to," the chief said.

"Do you think they *did* just decide to move?" Ashley asked.

"That is the biggest unknown," Tom replied. "As I

said, it's hard to imagine that so many people could be tempted to all pack up and leave so … *cleanly*. But they did go *somewhere*."

"They didn't just go to a homeless shelter?" Tim asked. "Maybe someone from a homeless support service came along and sold their service to all of them at once."

"It's possible," Tom agreed. "I can confirm, though, that the two shelters here in Riverside didn't see them in the weeks following the disappearance of those people."

"How can they be sure, if nobody knows what anyone in the group looks like?" asked Ashley. "Could the group not have been under the noses of the shelter volunteers, and them not know it?"

The chief shook his head as he recalled what he'd learned when investigating the disappearances.

"When I visited both of the shelters, not only were there no people staying there at the time, but they said there hadn't been anyone through their doors for months," he said. "Craziest thing, they said, to suddenly go from having to turn people away each night because they'd met their full capacity, to then have just nobody at the front door needing them."

"Are the shelters still open now?" Tim asked.

"They are," replied the chief. "I don't know why. Every time I've called in to see how things are there, both shelters have reported having very few people come in to stay, or even grab a free meal."

"Do you have any guesses or beliefs about what has happened?" Ashley asked. "Your gut instinct?"

The chief looked grave.

"My gut instinct has always been that something happened to those people, and it wasn't good," he said. "It was something that was calculated and permanent. Otherwise, we would have seen at least some of those people come back here. Our homeless population sometimes lost a member here and there for a few days or so, but they always came back. Occasionally, when I would go and check on them, someone would ask about this person or that person. A few days later, that person would be back, happily settling in again."

"It would take some effort to round up and remove large groups of homeless people and their possessions," Ashley said, her mind processing everything.

"It would," the chief said. "Then there is the aspect of cleaning. For entire groups to move and not leave some kind of mess behind them - well, I don't anticipate it would be that easy."

"The areas were that empty of anything from the people?" Tim asked.

Tom looked at him and nodded.

"Honestly, when I went round and studied the three scenes where populations had been living, there was nothing to indicate anyone had ever *been* there. Whoever did *that* cleaning, did it very well."

"Ms. Simpson mentioned she'd visited two other towns too," Ashley said.

"Yes," Tom replied. "Besides here and Compton, she told me she was looking at the disappearance of homeless people from Guthrie and Gordon too. When she'd told me that, I made contact with the police departments there. Both confirmed she'd been in there, asking questions. They also confirmed that she seemed to be right in her investigation."

He paused and studied the faces of the two agents. It was rewarding to know that someone else was interested in finding out what had happened to the community members who had disappeared. He was also curious to see if they could find anything out on a case that provided so few clues or even information.

"Are you planning to visit Gordon and Guthrie?" he went on to ask.

"Yes, we still have time to do that today, at least for our preliminary check," Ashley replied. "I think it will be worth going, perhaps, one ring of towns further out as well."

"Good idea," the chief said as he nodded. "I don't know if Kate looked at towns further out, but I know that I didn't. And remember that this all went on a decade ago. I expect towns are much changed by now."

"A decade," Ashley said. "What ages do you remember the homeless people being?"

"Oh, there were a few young ones among them, that's for sure. Mostly, though, they seemed to be in their 40s and upwards, although living rough like that can age someone. They might have been younger than they seemed."

"And the maximum age, at a guess?" Tim asked.

"Purely at a guess, I'd say a few were in their sixties or seventies," the chief replied. "It's a shame that people go down that route, living so rough, but the ones we had here seemed to survive alright."

"Until they vanished," Ashley said quietly, prompting the chief to nod again as his face revealed the grimness of the situation.

"Until they vanished," he acknowledged.

On seeing the expression on the man before them, Tim spoke up.

"If some of them were in their seventies then, there's a good chance they are long gone now, a decade later."

"Dead, you mean?" the chief asked and saw Tim nod in response. "It's possible. There are endless possibilities about what could have happened to these people. The hardest thing is that we don't actually know who they were. Other than Jordan Simpson, nobody else was ever asked about, so we have no other names to go searching for. They could all be sitting in our national prison system right now, but how would we *know?*"

Ashley nodded at him. She agreed. The worst aspect of the case was not knowing who they were meant to even be searching for.

"Well, thank you, Tom," Ashley said as she stood and held out her hand to the chief. "We'll get going and pay a visit to these other two towns."

As the chief stood and shook each of their hands, he spoke.

"Find them," he said. It was a simple two-word statement that delivered a powerful punch behind it.

"We will certainly try," Ashley replied before she and Tim walked out. When outside, she turned to her partner.

"How's your gut feeling?" she asked.

"My gut isn't set on any particular direction right now," Tim replied, smiling at her. "I'm still getting my head around the fact that we've been asked to even find these people."

"Actually, I think we were only asked to find one," Ashley replied.

"True," said Tim. "But I'm guessing we are now searching for these entire homeless populations, right?"

Ashley smiled and nodded as she felt her adrenalin begin to flow at the prospect of embarking on a new kind of investigation.

"Hell, yes," she said. "You know I love a good challenge."

"You do indeed," Tim said, chuckling. "This one might prove far more challenging than any we've been on before, though."

As they approached the car, Ashley grinned at him again.

"Challenge accepted, Special Agent Timothy Moore!"

"Alright, but can we get food first?" Tim asked once they were both seated inside the car, fastening their seatbelts.

Ashley laughed as she started the engine. There was no need to speak. Her partner asking for food always provided yet another aspect of familiarity to her. It was like a comfort when he did anything that she'd come to know as being part of him. It was nice. Working the kinds of cases they did, sometimes her head felt like it was stretched in her effort to figure out what had happened. Working with Tim as her partner for so long, she realized she'd come to rely on him for providing some grounding to her when on cases.

Turning to him, she smiled. It wasn't a teasing smile. It wasn't a sarcastic smile. It purely was a smile of appreciation for all they'd been through together, and the value she placed on simply having him in her life.

CHAPTER 9

Sitting in the offices of the chief of police in each police department in Guthrie and Gordon, Ashley started to feel like she was hearing the same details as she'd heard in the previous two towns. Neither chief in Gordon or Guthrie seemed overly bothered by the disappearance of homeless people who had been living on the streets of their towns. If anything, they seemed almost as cold and uncaring as Mike Batch had.

"I'm sorry I can't help you any further with this," said the chief of police in Guthrie, Dan Houston. Since the moment Tim and Ashley had arrived in his office, he'd emitted an air of having been inconvenienced. It was unsettling for Ashley to see in a fellow law enforcement officer. "Too much time has passed. I doubt you'll find anything, or any trace of these people."

Ashley studied his face. She usually got on well with people, and chose to give people the benefit of the doubt. To realize that two of the four police officers she'd spoken with in one day seemed to get her back up a bit was surprising.

Sensing he would be of no use to the pursuit she and Tim were on, she nodded, eager to be away from him.

"Can you show us where the homeless population used to be in your town, Dan? If you can indicate on this map, that would be appreciated," Tim asked, pulling out a map he'd started to draw on after he'd walked out of each police station.

Dan Houston looked surprised, but then seemed to check himself. Taking the map from Tim, the chief rested it in front of him on his desk and proceeded to place two markings in red pen.

"This was the primary one," he said, pointing to the location on the map. "I would say that at the height of the community being formed there, I'd guess that around twenty-five people might have lived there. This other one was much smaller. It seemed to only ever have maybe nine or ten at any time, but they changed over a lot."

"Changed over?" Tim asked. "Like different people, do you mean?"

The chief nodded. "Yeah, I'd go do a drive-by of this one, and there might be ten people there. The next time I'd drive by, a few weeks later, it would still seem like there were maybe ten or so, but the faces were different," he said. "It was a long time ago, though. A lot has changed in our town since then."

"Guthrie is completely homeless-free now?" Ashley asked.

"For the most part," Dan replied. "Now and then, someone will pop up, asleep on the side of a road or on a park bench. They don't seem to hang around long, though. It's like they're there one night, and just gone the next."

Tim accepted the map back and sat down again.

"Are you saying that people are *still* disappearing?" he asked as he felt his heart begin to beat heavily. "That you do have people who appear to be homeless and then vanish?"

Dan Houston looked surprised by the question - surprised and annoyed.

"People sleep rough when they need to, and then someone steps up and offers them a bed for a night," he finally replied. "We do have homeless shelters here."

The defensiveness in his tone was evident to both Ashley and Tim.

"And we will go and visit them," Ashley said. "You

are right. It is possible that anyone who has slept on the streets here in Guthrie could have just as quickly gone and made use of the free beds at the homeless shelters."

"Not possible," the chief said. "*Probable*."

"Right," Ashley replied as she smiled and nodded. "Well, thank you. We will take these shelter addresses you've given us, and go talk to them."

When Tim and Ashley were well clear of the police station building, Ashley turned to face her partner.

"Is it just me, or do you also get the feeling that there is more that these police departments know about these disappearances than they're saying?" she asked.

"Actually, I'm glad you said that. I've been getting the same feeling," Tim replied as they approached the car. "It feels like they're avoiding really answering anything."

Climbing into the car and securing her seatbelt, Ashley looked at him.

"What could they possibly be hiding, though?" she asked. "These are police departments. What could they know, that they don't want to share with us so that we can resolve all these questions?"

"I don't know," Tim replied. "We could be wrong in this. It might not be that they're hiding anything. It might be that they feel guilty for having let so many people disappear, without having found out what happened to them."

"True," Ashley replied, nodding. "Yeah, you're right. Maybe it's not that they know more and aren't sharing it. Maybe it's that they feel they *should* know more." She paused. "Okay, well, we have these files and printouts from the four towns, and we have Kate's journal of her investigation. Shall we head back to Compton and put our heads together as we work through all of this? We can talk to the homeless shelters tomorrow."

"Yep," said Tim. "Can we pick up takeaways to take back to the motel, though? I'm starving."

CHAPTER 10

After pushing the small hotel room table against the long desk and drawer set up in Ashley's room, one by one the documents they'd assembled were laid out. It wasn't much. All police departments had provided a printout of the meager files they'd established regarding the disappearances of their homeless populations. There was little in each one, and a lot of it seemed focused on Kate Simpson's concerns.

"How do we move forward with this?" Ashley said quietly, largely talking to herself as her eyes flowed over the documents in front of her.

Tim studied her face. He'd been wondering the same thing. Even though it was a case they'd been assigned to, it felt like it was growing into something larger, but with even less information to help them along.

"We have this too," he said as he picked up and laid out the map he'd started referring to earlier in the day. Folding it around so that the four towns they'd visited were the primary focus, he stared down at it on the table. "We know that Jordan Simpson was last seen here," he said as he pointed to the mark he'd made over the town of Compton. "We also know that homeless populations disappeared from here, here, and here," he went on to say as he used his pen to make sure Riverside, Guthrie, and Gordon were clearly indicated and easy to spot.

"Right," Ashley said as she moved closer to look down at the map. "These towns are all in the same area, but they are quite a distance apart. I'd say they were too far apart for people to easily walk between, even if they left all of their stuff behind."

"Which they didn't," Tim responded. "We know from the police departments that when these clusters disappeared, there was nothing left behind, but you're right. Even if they were super fit, and they did have the ability to walk those distances, there's no way that entire groups would have been able to do that without being noticed. The only way to get from Riverside to Guthrie, for example, is along this main highway. If a group of people walked along there, a report would have been made about it."

"Yes, it's unlikely they moved from one of these towns to another," Ashley agreed. "If they had, numbers would have increased in the other towns instead of decreasing and then diminishing."

"Unless they moved around," Tim said. "I mean, if ten people from Compton went to Riverside, and then the same number went from Riverside to Guthrie, the numbers don't change then, do they."

"And Dan Houston did say that in one of their clusters, it seemed like the numbers never changed, but the faces did," Ashley agreed.

"It is possible that they moved between towns, but even if they did, how did nobody notice them moving around, and where did they ultimately go?" Tim asked. "If the entire *populations* dried up from each of these towns, where did all of these people *go*?"

Ashley considered the question.

"When we drove around today, it didn't seem that far between each of the towns. This group is pretty condensed when I look at them on the map like this," she said, using her finger to detail the diamond shape the four towns made. "If they went anywhere, it could have been to somewhere else within this region. Right in the middle here is what looks like another small township..."

"Yes, it is talked about in Kate's journal," Tim said as

he picked up the book of handwritten notes. "Kerr," he read out loud. "She says in here that she passed through, but it was like a ghost town with no population to be seen. Her notes indicate that she stopped and looked in a few windows, but it was just deserted."

When he read out his summary of Kate's writing, Ashley felt a shudder move through her.

"An entire *town* has lost its population?" she asked, prompting Tim to nod. "Well, there must be something written about *that*, surely! I mean, it's one thing if small groups of people are vanishing, but the entire town? And it's right in the middle of these four towns." Ashley paused to think. "I'm thinking this is one hell of a case we're on, Timmy Boy."

"We need to find out more about Kerr," Tim replied. "You're right. The location of it compared to the other places we've already visited makes it a place of interest. And this place, too," he said as he noticed another small place name within the diamond-shaped area he'd highlighted on the map. "Pioneer," he read out loud.

"Is that mentioned in Kate's journal too?" Ashley asked, her intrigue growing.

After trying to visualize all that he'd read, Tim shook his head.

"No, I don't recall reading or hearing anything about a place called Pioneer."

"Alright," Ashley said, thoughtful. "Tomorrow, we'll cover the entire area again, going to all homeless shelters that the police have directed us to. We'll also call in at these two townships and see if there are any signs that people have been there lately."

She looked at Tim and saw his demeanor.

"We'll figure this out, Tim," she said quietly, prompting him to look at her.

"It's been such a long time since Kate did these active investigations, Ash," he replied. "Even if people were alive back then and they'd moved somewhere else, they might not be alive now. We could be chasing ghosts."

"We could, but there's only one way to find out," Ashley said before pausing to look at her watch. "It's still early. Let's go through all of this and make sure we're both fully knowledgeable about everything to do with the homeless populations in these places."

"Okay," Tim replied.

They'd only been on the case for a day, and already he felt a sense of discontent. Usually, he felt invigorated throughout cases, even when they felt like they were going to be impossible to solve. He wasn't familiar with the feeling of uncertainty he currently felt. In the back of his mind, he wondered who he was searching for the people *for*. Kate Simpson wanted to know where her grandfather had gone to, but the others? It didn't seem like anybody had ever even asked about them, let alone missed them.

He grabbed a chair and sat beside Ashley as they both began reading each document thoroughly. The notes were sporadic, at best, but they were all they had to begin to search for the suspected dozens of people who seemed to have just vanished.

"Kate's notes about Kerr are interesting," he heard Ashley say. Glancing at her, he saw her working her way through the journal. "She has quite a way with words. The way she's described looking in windows and seeing nobody makes me think of a horror movie," she said before pulling out her phone. "What does Google tell us about Kerr, I wonder."

Tim watched as Ashley entered search criteria a number of ways. He also watched as she turned her head and looked at him.

"There's nothing about Kerr online," she said, her tone one of disbelief.

"Did you enter the state as well?" Tim asked, amused.

"Tim, I'm telling you, there's nothing about Kerr,"

Ashley pressed again, prompting Tim to pull his phone out too.

"That isn't possible," he said. "Even a town that has no population is still a town. And it's on the map," he continued, pointing at the paper laid out on the table.

Ashley picked up the map and turned it over until she could find a date on it.

"This is almost fifteen years old," she said.

"But, wait," Tim said before firing up Google Maps on his phone. Finding no luck in searching for the town by name, he found himself more than a little curious. "Maybe it's just changed its name. If I zoom in here to where we are now - Compton," he said, finding their current location on the screen. "And now," he continued, glancing at the paper map. "It's right … here."

Tim and Ashley both looked at the map on the screen. Where there was a town on the paper map, there was nothing at all indicated on the digital map.

"Huh," Tim said. "I guess towns that are no longer populated, aren't considered worthy of keeping a name on a map after all. It only makes me more eager to go there, though. What do you think?"

"Yeah!" Ashley said. "We have to drive around it, so we'll definitely stop in and see what's happening there."

"*Nothing's* happening there, apparently," Tim said.

"Hmm, maybe," Ashley replied. "But just because something isn't on the Internet, doesn't mean that it doesn't exist."

"Like homeless people from this area?" Tim asked, his sadness for the situation returning.

"We'll figure all of this out, Tim. Worry not," Ashley replied. "For now, I'm almost ready to grab some sleep and let my head rest, so take whatever you need to out of that lot," she said, pointing to the table of documents. "And get out of my room."

Tim smiled, gathered a few of the police reports, and made his way to the door.

"See you outside at six-thirty," Ashley said.
Quietly, Tim nodded, opened the door, and left.

CHAPTER 11

"Homeless shelters, here we come," Ashley said the next morning when the two of them were once again on the road. After three cappuccinos, and breakfast of a size that some would only consider suitable for a man who worked in hard laboring, she felt energized and ready to get on with the day ahead.

"Let's see what these guys have to tell us," Tim said, his mood thoughtful but serious.

Ashley heard his tone and glanced at him.

"What's on your mind?" she asked.

"I don't know, to be honest," Tim replied. "We've worked on missing persons cases before, but this is starting to feel ... I dunno ... kind of eerie, I guess."

"Yeah, it's definitely a first for me," Ashley said. "But we have worked on cases before where we didn't know who the victim was..."

"Vic*tim*, yes," Tim emphasized as he cut her words short. "In this, we have no idea how many people we are even looking for, let alone who they are."

"I know, but once we get on a roll with this, it will all fall into place," Ashley reassured him. "You know it will. It always does."

Tim smiled at her but didn't reply. Usually confident, he didn't like it when he experienced negativity within him. It was something that would pass, as it always did, but on the rare occasion when it struck, it felt like someone was above him, pushing down with a pile of bricks, nudging him ever closer to the ground...

"And here we are in Riverside," Ashley said,

breaking Tim out of his thoughts. "Homeless shelter number one should be just up here."

Once parked up, she turned to face Tim.

"Ready?" she asked. His quietness told her how thoughtful he was. When he nodded at her, she smiled. "Let's do this."

The frontage of the first homeless shelter was bare of any signage or decoration. Being a box-shaped structure with a plaster finish that had probably been white once upon a time, it was difficult to understand how it would even attract anyone inside.

As they approached the large wooden double doors, Ashley noticed a small printed plaque on the right side of the door frame. Following its instruction, she pushed the button below it and waited.

"Yes?" a male voice asked through a small speaker. After Ashley leaned down to state her name and the purpose of their visit, she heard the voice again. "Come in."

The door latch unlocking was evident, although somewhat surprising to both agents.

"That is a higher form of technology than what I'd expect from somewhere like this," Tim said quietly as they both gently pushed the door inwards.

Once inside, the door closed behind them, leaving them in a cold, dark space until the light overhead switched on.

"I'm John Jones," a man in his mid-forties said as he approached, his hand extended.

Ashley and Tim shook his hand, silently assessing the man's nervous manner.

"Thank you for allowing us to come in, Mr. Jones," Ashley said. "I understand this is not normal open hours for you."

"No, they never are now," John said as he scoffed, with a slight tone of disgust in his voice. As if he realized he'd sounded how he'd not wanted to, he looked at both agents and smiled. "Come through to my office where I have a heater on," he said, turning to walk away. "I don't bother heating this area now unless I expect someone to come through the door."

Once seated in the warm office, Tim began the questioning.

"You don't have many people coming here now?" he asked.

The man behind the desk gave a look that bordered on confusion.

"Nowadays, it's rare for me to see *anyone* needing our help," John replied, shaking his head. "When I set this place up twenty years ago, we never had enough food or enough beds. Now ... well, things are very different now. It's bittersweet, of course. Like anyone else, I'd rather people - *all* people - had a solid, dependable roof over their heads. It should make me happy that there's nobody that needs our assistance anymore..."

"But you're not?" Ashley asked, curious.

John looked at her for a long while before replying.

"If all of the people who were ever homeless in Riverside are now happy, warm, and safe in homes of their own, I am happy for them."

"You don't think they are?" Tim asked.

Both agents saw the man shake his head slowly.

"I don't."

"What do you think they've done then? Where did they go?" Ashley asked.

"I don't know, but the way this town has gone from having so many people in need, to having nobody in need ... it's not just unusual. It's completely *unheard* of," John replied.

"Four towns in this area report the same," Tim said.

"I know," John said, nodding. "Over the years, I've taken to driving around and visiting other nearby towns. I've scoured the bush areas along the highways and in-between the towns." He paused, remembering his attempts at locating people. "I don't know what happened to our homeless communities. For all I know, they are all very happy and safe, as I said. If they are, that's all good."

"And if they're not?" Ashley asked.

"Then I hope that you being here might help all of us resolve what has happened."

"How well did you get to know the people who used to stay here?" asked Tim. "Would you know them by name?"

"I never asked too many questions when people would come in, to be honest," John replied. "Some would offer their first names, but it was a very high turnover place. We have a hundred beds here," he said, making Tim blink. The town hardly seemed populated enough to have that many people without a home. "A decade ago, we were full pretty much every night. Because of that, it had to work on a first-in first-served basis. That meant that we wouldn't see the same faces every night."

"But you had some repeat people?" Ashley asked. "Some you did get to know?"

John nodded. "A few. Only first names, though. Nobody ever offered up their last name to me, and I never asked. All I've ever cared about is making sure people were safe and warm so they could get through another day."

"When did the numbers begin reducing, do you think?" asked Ashley.

"It was about nine years ago when I really sat down and considered that something had changed around here," John said. "We went from having to turn people away, to being full most nights but there not being a further queue outside our door. Then ... then it seemed to drop off completely. It was like one day we were needed, and then we weren't."

"They just stopped coming?" Tim asked.

"Pretty much," John replied as he nodded. "I've continued to come in here each afternoon, and be here overnight, just in case anyone needs a bed, but it's been a really long time now since anyone came."

"But the interim," Ashley said. "You said they *began* to stop needing you about eight or nine years ago. What about the interim between then and now?"

"Oh, when I said it dropped off about eight or nine years ago, I mean that was when people generally just stopped coming," John said. "As I said, one night, they were here. Then they weren't."

"So," Tim began to say. "Please help me understand this. You haven't had people staying here for eight years?" he asked and saw John nod.

"Mostly, yes, that is right."

"But why and how do you stay open?" Tim asked in disbelief. "Who funds this place, and why do they keep funding it if it's not needed?"

"I own this place, having bought it about twenty-two years ago," John replied, smiling sadly. "Back then, it was dilapidated, so it cost me next to nothing to buy. I did work to it and made a small apartment for myself out here in the back, and set it up to help others out."

"But the costs of running it and feeding people?" Ashley asked.

"When I had mouths to feed, I would submit a monthly report to the city council, and they would reimburse me for the food and a percentage of the electricity," John said. "Since the numbers dropped off, I haven't bothered. Now and then, someone will knock on the door and come in for a night, but they don't ever seem to come back for a second night now."

"Right. Can you tell us when the most recent stay or visit was, John?" Ashley asked.

"Yes, that was in April," John replied. "It was Easter Sunday, so I remember the date. A woman came in.

Mary was her name. Said she wanted a bed, but she didn't want questions, so I gave her some food, showed her to a bed, and then left her to it. Next morning, she was still here, so I invited her to have breakfast with me and told her to come back that night if she needed to."

"But she didn't, I take it," Tim said.

John shrugged his shoulders and took some time to remember the woman before he answered.

"I don't know if she needed a bed again the next night or not. She didn't come back here. That's all I know." He was thoughtful for a long time before speaking again. "I have wondered if there is some other homeless shelter somewhere that these people are going to, but I really don't know what's happened."

"No guesses?" Tim asked.

"None," John replied. "I should be elated if they're all okay, but something makes me feel like they aren't. But then, what could have happened to people like that? They had no money. From what I ever saw, none of them had anything on them of value. They wouldn't be of *use* to anyone."

"Did a young woman by the name of Kate Simpson come and see you?" Ashley asked.

"You're the first visitors I've had in a few months - quite literally," John said.

"No, it would have been years ago," Ashley said. "She was looking for her grandfather, who had last been seen in…"

"Compton?" John asked in response. When he saw Ashley nod in confirmation, he continued. "Yes. Now that you mention the grandfather, yes, she did come here. She showed me a photo of him, but he didn't look familiar to me. That was before my numbers dropped off completely, but it had already become quiet enough for me to remember faces. Is she looking for him again?"

"Yes, we are searching for him on her behalf," said Tim.

"But you're searching for all the others too?" John asked. "All the other people who have been homeless, I mean."

"We are looking into that as part of our investigation, yes," replied Tim. "Is there anything else that you can remember, that anyone said to you that might help in us looking for the homeless populations of the four towns in this area? Any names that you can remember, or details of anything that might be relevant would be a great help."

John looked regretful as he shook his head.

"I'm sorry, but I can't think of anything," he replied. "Wherever the people in need in this town went, they seemed to do it pretty much altogether, and over a fairly short time period." He paused and watched both agents' faces. "In some ways, it seemed like someone might have driven a bus through and plucked them all from the streets."

The visualization in Ashley's head was stark.

"Do you think that could have happened?" she asked.

"I think that would have been a very tidy way to scoop up multiple people in a very short time and move them to a new location," John said. "Do I think it *did* happen? I assume not. If it had, someone would have seen it happening. We don't get many buses through here, and we never did for as long as I can remember. When one does come through and stops here - tourist buses and the like passing through - they're pretty easy to spot."

"You don't remember any buses or other large transport vehicles in the town around that time?" Tim asked for clarification.

"No," John said, shaking his head again. "I mean, my usual hours of staying up were from about four in the afternoon till four in the morning, then I'd only nap before getting up again around six in the morning to serve breakfast. The people who stayed here were expected to vacate by nine so that I could quickly clean, fix up the beds, and then go get some sleep then, so I missed a lot of what happened during the daylight hours. But no, I don't remember anything coming through town that could transport high numbers like that."

"Alright, well, thank you for your help, John," Ashley said as she stood. "If you think of anything, can you please call?" she asked as she handed him her card.

John nodded and walked around the desk to lead them out towards the front door.

"I will," he said. When they reached the large wooden doors again, and he opened one manually, he shook each of their extended hands again. "I hope you do find out what happened to those people. I know it's been a long time, but although this is a good thing, not having people who need help, something just doesn't feel right about it. It never has."

"We fully intend to figure this out," Ashley said as she smiled at him and walked out. "Thank you. We'll be in touch if we have further questions for you."

Almost immediately after stepping down onto the top step, Ashley and Tim heard the large wooden door close. The deep thud of it seemed to contradict the friendly welcome they'd just experienced with John Jones.

Looking at Tim, Ashley saw the same surprise in his eyes.

"Yeah, that was a bit weird, but maybe that's just how he closes doors," Tim said. His thoughts were already moving on to the next homeless shelter they were going to visit. He suspected none of the homeless shelters would have anything different to tell him and Ashley.

In that, he was absolutely right.

CHAPTER 12

"Six shelters and absolutely nothing new for us to work from," Tim said as he and Ashley climbed into the car in Gordon later that day. Buckling up his seatbelt, he turned to face her. "Well, we know that Kate's findings weren't any kind of over-exaggeration. People who were living out on the streets have disappeared from all four of these towns, and the overall homeless population has completely dried up. For months now - years, in some cases - none of these shelters have seen anyone who needed a bed."

"Yeah, I think it's fair to assume that all homeless people from this general area did vanish around the same time, and maybe in one go," Ashley said.

"You like the possibility that a bus came along and scooped them all up, as John Jones suggested?" Tim asked.

"I think…" Ashley began to say, taking a moment to consider all that they'd been told throughout the morning. "I think that would be a good way to move a lot of people in one go, if someone wanted to do that. But what could possibly be their intention? These people were mostly older and not in great shape…"

"Not necessarily, Ash," Tim said, contradicting her. "One of the police chiefs indicated some of the people were older,, but still seemed fit. Maybe they did have some kind of purpose to someone."

Both agents mulled the idea over for some time before Ashley started the engine.

"Well, that is a possibility," she said. "I mean, if these

people were all taken - or even if they were just peacefully led away somewhere and they wanted to go - there had to be some enticement for them, or whoever wanted to take them away." She paused as she maneuvered the car out into the meager flow of traffic. "Let's go and visit these other two places that seemingly don't exist anymore. Maybe we'll find some clues there."

Tim nodded. Although they were only on the second day of their investigation into the disappearance of Jordan Simpson, it was unusual that they wouldn't have found out *something* in a case by that point.

To divert his concerns, he concentrated on the upcoming visit.

"I can't say I've ever been to a ghost town before," he said, grinning at Ashley. "Have you?"

Ashley chuckled softly. "We don't know what's there yet," she said. "It could be a thriving community that was just forgotten, for all we know."

"No," said Tim. "How could it be? If anyone lived there, they'd be making news by demanding it was put back on the map."

Ashley grinned at him. She liked seeing him back to his usual carefree self.

"We'll see for ourselves soon enough," she said, pushing down on the accelerator a little more. She didn't say it, but even she was intrigued at the idea of visiting a town that seemed to have literally dropped off a map. "It's good that you programmed the GPS coordinates into here from that printed map," she continued, looking at the unit on the dashboard. "Just goes to show that we have all come to put too much faith into Google!"

"Well, there might not be a town there after all," Tim said. "Maybe Google is right in not showing anything in that location."

"Maybe," Ashley replied as she checked no other vehicles were around. Once sure they were the only ones, her foot pressed down the accelerator even more.

CHAPTER 13

As they drove over a hill with bush on either side of them, ahead in the distance, Tim and Ashley both saw the small town of Kerr. Despite having hoped it was still there, seeing the small gathering of buildings startled Ashley enough to make her heart beat just that little bit faster.

Checking her rearview mirror and seeing no cars behind, she edged over to the side of the road.

"I'm guessing that's Kerr," Tim said as he looked at her. "It's definitely in the right spot."

"And not exactly hard to see, which is surprising," Ashley said. "I anticipated that if somewhere was to close down, it must be so remote that it's almost impossible to see it."

Tim nodded. "True, but we haven't seen another car since we got onto this road. It's not exactly a high volume area."

"Yeah," Ashley agreed. "Okay, well, let's go and see what's up with this place," she said, easing out onto the road again. "No matter what we're going to find, this is a first for me. My interest is definitely piqued."

Sitting in silence for the last half mile of road, both agents watched as the township ahead of them appeared to grow closer and larger. There was little to see, but it was certainly a town. The road they were on continued directly ahead, through two straight lines of buildings with wooden frontages. Instead of modern asphalt sidewalks, what they saw were rows and rows of wooden slats forming a styled frontage that looked like it had been formulated for a western movie set.

Ashley slowly drove along the road, looking to the left and the right, wondering if they would see any other human.

"I guess this is the main drag," she said quietly. "What a weird set up, with these houses scattered among what looks like should be shops or something."

"I concur! Pull over and let's look around on foot," Tim said, eager to get out and explore. He had no idea if the place had anything to do with the disappearance of any homeless people, most of all who they were supposed to be focusing on finding - Jordon Simpson. Regardless, something inside of him told him that the township was somehow tied to all that they were investigating.

Climbing out of the car, habit made Ashley lock the doors even though there was no sign of life.

"Where to start?" she mumbled.

Tim pointed back to the direction they'd just driven.

"The start," he said. "Let's wander back to that first building and start checking around, one building at a time. Maybe we'll find something to explain why this town closed down."

"And if it has anything to do with our case," Ashley agreed as they began walking.

Each building they passed as they walked along the wooden footpath, they glanced briefly inside the window of. Preliminary glances revealed nobody. Although that was expected, it caused some apprehension.

"There's something about this place that's giving me the creeps," Tim said just before they reached the first building to explore.

Although she felt the same, Ashley smiled.

"Watched too many horror flicks lately?" she teased, attempting to make light of what felt very wrong to her too.

"I don't know what it is, but something is making the

hair stand up on the back of my neck … literally," Tim said as he raised a hand and rubbed it over the base of his head. "I actually feel like we're being watched…" he continued as he stopped walking and turned around. He half expected to see someone out in the street, looking at them. There was nobody there. There was nobody *anywhere*.

Ashley walked up to the door of the first building. It had the look of an old-style shop. Placing both hands on the glass, she leaned in, attempting to see more clearly without the sunlight hampering her effort.

"Maybe we can just do this," Tim said as he tried the door handle and found the door to open without restriction.

Having opened it and let it swing far enough to allow him to look inside from where he stood, he remained still for a moment.

"Hello?" he called out. It wasn't a usual way that he would announce his presence upon entering anywhere while on the job. Lack of indication that anyone was around made him forget all sense of formality. "Anyone here?"

Hearing no reply, he tentatively stepped inside the space and looked around.

As Ashley walked past him until she stood in the center of the space, she glanced around. She maintained the belief that it had been a shop. Shelves still held items for sale.

"Needles and thread," she said as she walked along one wall and took note of what she could see. "Scissors, books, paint … and spaghetti. Seems to have been a general all-round general store of sorts, I guess."

Tim glanced along the facing wall.

"This side has packets," he said as he picked one up. "This bag has a best-before date of … seven years ago."

"Yeah, it does seem a long time since anyone was here," Ashley said as she lightly touched a shelf.

"Nobody's been dusting in here, that's for sure."

Both agents turned to face one another and then walked toward the counter. Strewn over it were pages of different colors and sizes.

"These are all dated ten years ago," Tim said, picking up one page after another.

"Does anything give a clue about what happened to whoever lived or worked here?" Ashley asked, picking up and looking through several pages.

Tim shook his head.

"No," he said. "Seems like someone was doing some accounting. These are sales printouts, and the till drawer is open with cash still inside. It almost looks like they were about to do an end of day tally."

After a few minutes of checking each page, Ashley looked toward the rear of the store.

"Let's check out back and upstairs," she said, already moving in that direction.

Leaving the front store area, the two of them walked through a long but tight hallway. Doors off it revealed two storage rooms, a small kitchen area, and a restroom. There was nothing disturbed in any of them. In the kitchen, they could see two cups on the bench, the labels of teabags hanging over the side of each as if poised for making two cups of tea at any moment. The layer of dust covering everything was the only clue that said those cups had been prepared long ago, and that tea would probably never be made.

Walking upstairs, Tim felt his apprehension grow stronger. Logic told him that there were no people around. If there were no people, nothing could happen to him or Ashley. Unfortunately, logic didn't always rule the way his body felt.

From the top of the wooden staircase, they examined each of the three bedrooms, the bathroom, and what looked like a living room.

"No sign of life then," Ashley said as she walked

forward past the compact sofa and peered out the window.

"And no sign of struggle or anything bad happening here," Tim added.

"True, but equally no sign of them having packed up and left," Ashley said as she nodded toward an old rack in the corner that still had clothing hanging over it as if to dry. "Everything looks like it's meant to be here. Cupboards are stocked. Wardrobes are full of clothing. If they left, they did so without taking their belongings."

"Yeah, that would be weird," Tim said. "Well, this is only the first building. Let's move on to the next one. We have another twenty or so to go."

~~~~~

One by one, they explored the buildings along the peaceful street. In each - regardless of whether it was a shop and home, or just a home - the result was the same. Rooms looked like they had been lived in and used as normal. There were signs of people having been in the rooms before they'd left. Food was on benches. Newspapers were spread out on sofas or tables as if they had been being read when the people left. Laundry was still in washing machines, looking like the full wash and rinse cycle had finished, but nobody had gotten around to pulling the items out to dry.

"If there were signs of people having rushed away, maybe I'd believe that some kind of natural disaster had happened," Tim said as they walked out of the last building. "It would be understandable if they heard ... I don't know ... if they heard that a tornado was coming or something. If that had happened, though, surely there would be some kind of indication that people had rushed around in a panic, grabbing things or *something*."

"I agree," said Ashley as she nodded. "This doesn't feel like people rushed away in a panic. And look," she said, pointing at different spots. "Cars are still here."

As the two of them moved toward a red Camaro that
~~~~~

was parked to the side of a building, Tim pulled out his notebook.

"Well, at least we have some license numbers," he said as he wrote. "I'll get these all down and then see what we can find out about the owners when we're back at the motel later."

Ashley nodded and tried the Camaro's door. It was unlocked.

"They weren't big on security here in Kerr, were they," she said as she opened the door wide and crouched down to study the front interior. "I mean, all of the doors to the buildings were unlocked. Now this car is unlocked too."

Tim shrugged his shoulders as he peered in the back window of the car.

"I guess in a town this size, everyone knows everyone," he said. "Maybe that creates a different level of trust than what there is in cities."

"Maybe, but another place would have eventually had visitors who would loot somewhere like this. It's weird that it looks like everything literally is untouched," Ashley replied, checking under the front seats. "There's nothing to see here."

"Pop the trunk," Tim called out as he walked around to the back. As the boot flung open, he found himself prepared for anything. He'd seen more than a few bodies in the trunks of vehicles during his time with the Bureau. "Nothing here either," he said as he caught his breath, relaxed a bit, then closed the boot. As he did so, he saw Ashley glance into the distance behind the buildings and begin walking. Immediately, he fell into step beside her.

When they reached a cemetery, Ashley found herself drawn to a startling sight. A grave had been dug, obviously a very long time earlier. Beside it sat a shovel on a mound of dirt. As she peered into the hole, there lay a skeleton, half-covered with dirt.

"Didn't even get a proper burial," Tim said as he

looked down at the sight of bones from feet and legs.

"No, and the way that shovel is sitting makes it look like whoever was filling in this grave, left in a hurry," Ashley said, observing the scene.

"Or taken," Tim replied.

"Or taken," Ashley agreed as she looked at the bones. "You know what strikes me as odd in this?"

"You mean other than an entire town seeming to be stuck in time?" Tim asked, scoffing.

Ashley smiled and nodded.

"Yeah," she said. "But look. These bones - this body - seems to have been here for as long as the town seems to have been empty."

"About a decade," Tim said.

"Right," said Ashley. "But the bones are sitting perfectly, like they've never moved from the exact position they were in when the body was placed in there." She paused and looked around. "There's bush and woods all around here. Wouldn't something have come and at least tried to take these bones, or if not take the bones, feed off the body?"

"You are right in that it doesn't look like anything at all has disturbed this person," Tim said. "But what about the other aspect of this grave?" he asked, prompting Ashley to look at him. "No coffin? Is it a grave for a legitimate burial, or was someone trying to hide something?"

"Murder victim, you think?" Ashley asked.

"I think we need to get one of the forensics teams down here to determine that," Tim responded. "But if this grave has been like this for a decade, how come nobody has ever reported it? How come nobody has ever reported this *town* being like this?"

"Maybe nobody's been here since. Everything *is* untouched," Ashley started to say before realizing that couldn't be true.

"No," Tim said, shaking his head. "Kerr was

mentioned in Kate Simpson's journal. She passed through here. She stopped and looked in the windows."

Ashley could hear exasperation in Tim's voice. It was surprising.

"She might have *only* looked in the windows, Tim," she said. "Did she mention this graveyard at all?"

"No," Tim replied. "Okay, yeah, maybe she only walked down the main street and didn't come around here to the back."

Ashley walked up to him, nodding.

"Maybe that *is* what happened with Kate when she found this place, and maybe nobody else has ever been here," she said. "The town isn't on any modern map, and most people now do use their phones for maps, rather than paper ones. The road we traveled down to get here seems to have been erased from the digital version of the maps as well. It is feasible that this place has just been sitting here for all of these years, without anyone coming here."

"And the idea that no animal - not even one - came here from any of these bush and woods areas when they smelt a body decomposing?"

"That *is* odd, definitely," Ashley agreed. "Let's organize a team to come here in case there's anything to find. The way this body is lying, peacefully positioned, it needs someone from forensics to determine how they died..."

"And who they are," Tim added.

"Well, that," Ashley said as she looked further around. "That could be something we might be able to find out while we're here. There must be some kind of record of their dead."

"Yeah?" Tim asked. "Look around, Ash. There are graves, but they only have crosses on them. No headstones. No crypts. Nothing that indicates who is in or under any of these gravesites. Not only that, but we've been through all of the buildings. We didn't find any details of occupants who ever lived here, let alone who died here."

"Call it in," Ashley said, nodding. "Call it in and see what Sarah wants us to do. If we can, let's still get over to that other town - Pioneer - today."

Calls and decisions made in consultation with their supervisor back at headquarters, Tim turned to Ashley.

"We're not required to stay here," he said. "Sarah's going to send someone."

"They won't get here for…" she began to say.

"I guess they've been here for a decade…" Tim finished, nodding towards the half-covered grave.

"True," Ashley replied. It didn't feel right, leaving a skeleton as it was, but orders were orders.

As the two of them climbed back into the car, Tim turned to face her.

"You don't think…" he began to say before stopping to consider what was playing on his mind.

"What?" asked Ashley.

"The gravesites. They had no headstones, so there's no way to know who's in them," Tim replied, prompting Ashley to nod. "Could those people be our missing homeless population of four neighboring towns?"

Ashley was horrified at the thought, but slowly nodded.

"It is a possibility, I guess, but the dates don't quite add up."

"How so?" Tim asked.

"Well, I'm no forensic scientist, so I guess we'll know better when the scene is investigated, but the town looks like it hasn't been populated for a decade," Ashley said.

"Right."

"The grave also looks like it might be from a decade ago," Ashley continued.

"Yeah."

Ashley looked at Tim's face, her mind calculating.

"If those timeframes are accurate, even to within a

year or so, that means that the town was populated when the homeless were brought here…"

"Or came here…" Tim said.

Ashley nodded.

"Or came here," she agreed. "Even if that was the case, and those graves are of the population of missing homeless people from Compton, Riverside, Gordon, and Guthrie, where are the people who actually lived *here?*"

"Hmm," Tim responded as he put on his seatbelt. "I agree, it's all a bit weird. Let's go and see what's happening in Pioneer. Maybe all these people moved there," he said, all the while wondering if everything could possibly be as easy as that.

CHAPTER 14

Jordy Simpson screamed as pain shot through both of his legs. It was something he was well accustomed to, but equally, something that almost daily made him want to give up on life and just die.

His ability to tell time had long been lost and forgotten, but he sensed he must have been experiencing the daily horror for years. When he'd first arrived, he'd attempted to try and keep a tally of the times he'd seen sunshine. After he'd counted to 200, he'd given up. Seeing the numbers grow higher and higher had only made him feel increasingly despondent.

For the entire time that he'd been in the large old house, he'd honestly expected his body to one day just give up. One day he'd be alive. The next, he'd be dead. Sometimes he wondered if he *was* dead. No. He was still breathing, and he was definitely still able to feel pain. It surely wasn't living, but it surely wasn't the afterlife either.

In the distance, he could hear the others screaming. That was almost as unbearable as his own pain. Many, he'd never met. The shadows prevented him from getting to interact with whoever else might be in the big old place. He didn't know what the shadows were. He didn't know who else resided in the house. He only knew three things for certain.

One: he was alive, and he was feeling pain every day.

Two: usually kept awake by snoring most of the night, he'd just had his first decent sleep since arriving.

Three: George Jones had disappeared in the night.

CHAPTER 15

"It's so desolated, this entire area," Tim said as they drove along a dirt road that the old map showed ran between Kerr and Pioneer. "We haven't seen anyone even on any of the roads we've traveled today."

"Yeah, it doesn't seem a very popular area to live in, that's for sure," Ashley said, glancing at the GPS unit. "Nineteen minutes, and we'll be in Pioneer, this thing is saying."

"Nineteen minutes, and we'll know whether or not this is where the people of Kerr disappeared to," Tim muttered, mostly to himself.

He'd felt weird ever since walking through Kerr. Looking outside didn't make him feel any better. The previous vista of trees and bushes had been replaced by terrain more closely resembling a desert. There was only a scattering of plant life, widely spread out over what just looked like flat, dry dirt.

Turning to look at his partner, he could see she was in thoughtful mode. There was a look she had when her mind went into heavy analysis. Usually, when Ashley looked like she currently did, there was some kind of idea close behind that helped them to consider what else to look at in a case.

Sensing Tim looking at her, Ashley turned and smiled at him.

"What's up?" she asked, making him chuckle lightly.

"I was wondering what you were thinking," Tim replied. "You looked deep into something - maybe a theory?"

"No," Ashley replied, shaking her head. "I was thinking about the people, actually. We were asked to find one man - Jordan Simpson. That led us to following up on Kate Simpson's claims that he was one of only many homeless people who had disappeared across the four towns. Looking at those four towns on that old map, we've found another two towns, of which one, we know, people seem to have disappeared from around that same time."

"Right," Tim agreed as he nodded and waited for Ashley to continue.

"Well, I don't understand how that many people … how *that* many people could have vanished, and nobody has reported any of them missing," Ashley summed up.

"We don't know that they weren't reported missing, though," Tim reminded her. "I suggested to Sarah that she get the team to try and find out whatever they can about Kerr and its population. Part of that will be looking at missing persons cases from around this area. It is possible that an investigation was done with regard to at least *someone* in Kerr."

"True," Ashley said. "Let's wonder, though, just for a moment - if there's nothing in the database about Kerr or its occupants, those people could also be something to do with the homeless population disappearing, right?"

"It's possible," Tim conceded. "The towns are close enough to each other that if people have actually disappeared, especially around the same time, the occurrences could be related."

"Hmm," Ashley replied vaguely. "I'm keen to hear what the team finds out about Kerr. It doesn't seem possible that the population disappeared and nobody knows about it. Even if those people had been born there, they must have had other relations who wondered where they went. Sisters. Brothers. Parents. Cousins. *Somebody* must have known *someone* in Kerr."

Tim silently agreed but didn't reply. Returning his

gaze to the views outside, he felt confused about it all as well. He also felt his reflection of his own life return. Knowing a few people had disappeared without anyone noticing, had been a reminder enough of how few people in his own life might notice if something happened to him. With the numbers of people who potentially had vanished growing, and just as few people seeming to have cared, his self-reflection was further highlighting changes he needed to make.

"You're a good partner," he blurted out as he turned to face Ashley once more. He wasn't sure he'd consciously intended to say it, but he wouldn't regret doing so. When he saw her turn and look at him with surprise on her face, he took ownership of the words he'd said. "I mean it, Ash. I've worked with different partners over my time with the Bureau. I really appreciate how well we work together, and your strengths as an agent."

Ashley breathed in long and quietly. She was used to Tim expressing serious feelings of one sort or another, but that usually happened on the day that they finished a case and were about to part for a few days. For him to say anything so meaningful so early on in a case wasn't normal. The words didn't make her uncomfortable. They just weren't normal.

"Hey, what's up?" she asked him.

"Nothing," Tim replied. "I just want people who are important to me to *know* that they are important to me."

Ashley smiled sadly at him. She got where he was coming from. Whenever they'd worked on cases where a body had been found, but it didn't match with any missing person case, she'd felt a very distinctive level of sadness for the victim. She'd also been driven to question her own life and the people in it.

"You're important to me too, Tim," she said quietly. "We're going to figure out who all these people are. We're also going to figure out what happened to them."

Tim returned the sad smile. He hoped so.

CHAPTER 16

The final minutes of approach into the small town of Pioneer were minutes of no conversation between the agents. When the township came into view, neither felt surprised to see that it looked like a slightly larger version of Kerr. Again, the buildings and their frontages looked like they could have been a set for a movie. The biggest difference that Ashley and Tim could see as they got closer, was that Pioneer extended for several blocks in all directions.

"Sprawling metropolis," Tim joked quietly as the road they were on entered the first row of buildings.

Ashley grinned while she looked around, driving slowly to assess what the population might be, if there even was one.

"Can you see anyone?" she asked Tim as they drove along the same road they'd entered on.

Tim shook his head.

"Nope," he replied simply. The same eerie feeling he'd already felt that day was creeping up on him again. "And look," he said as he pointed to the edge of the road. "More cars that look like they've been here for a while."

Ashley grimaced. She'd hoped Pioneer would prove to be a normal town, accidentally left off the modern, digital maps by accident. She'd wanted there to be people, perhaps even some who knew some answers to the mystery of what had happened to its neighboring town, Kerr.

"Not looking too hopeful, is it," she mumbled before easing the car to a halt.

Tim looked at her but couldn't smile. He was used to murder cases. He was used to finding dead bodies and hearing details of the horrible things one human had done to another. He was used to so many things that weren't good in the world. The day he was currently having - and the feeling it was evoking in him - was completely new.

~~~~~

With Pioneer being three blocks by four, they established a grid layout to follow and began visiting buildings one at a time. Nothing seemed vastly different from the township they'd just come from. The buildings were slightly larger, and there were more of them, but the search result was the same.

"Do we even need to explore any more of these?" Tim asked when they were about halfway through the buildings. "All we're finding is more crockery that looks like the people were about to sit down and enjoy a meal, more laundry that looks like it was about to be hung out, and more piles of dust that look about a decade old."

"We keep going, Moore," Ashley said to him. She felt disheartened too, but she was determined to continue. "We do this thoroughly now, and then we won't need to return."

The idea of having to return to either Kerr or Pioneer did not appeal to Tim. Even considering it made him pick up pace.

"Alright, let's get this done," he said. He hated that he wasn't feeling invigorated by the case. Usually, he was energetic and eager to figure things out. Increasingly he felt like there wasn't anything *to* figure out. It felt more like they were filling in hours for no real reason.

In the second to last building they searched, Ashley spoke up.

"I think I have something here," she called out to Tim.

Thinking it might be anything related to the case,
~~~~~

Tim rushed to her.

"Look," Ashley said, pushing a large hard covered book to him.

When Tim looked at the open pages, he could see a ledger. Running his finger across the columns, he began reading out the words at the top of each.

"Date, Name, Born, Married to, Offspring, Died," he said before looking at Ashley. "A town register of births, deaths, and marriages?"

Ashley nodded. "Looks like it. I'll take photos of each page. At least we have some details of people who lived here. Maybe the database will give us a clue about where they went."

Tim scrolled back and forth through the pages, flicking to the front of the book and then to the latest entries.

"Started in 1979," he said. "Last entry was 2010. April 4th. That was the day that Shelly Thoms gave birth to twins, Robert and Edward."

"So all three are entered into there for that day?"

"No," Tim replied vaguely. "Weird. It shows that she gave birth, but whereas there are entries on these other pages that show a line for the mother giving birth, and another for the baby being born, this only shows her giving birth…"

Uncertain of what he meant, Ashley peered over to where he was looking. As she saw him flick from page to page, she better understood.

"Oh, yeah," she said. "They had a pretty set way of recording it. The mother gets an entry, and then the newborn gets an entry too."

"Right," Tim replied, nodding. "Except, in this case, the kids didn't get one."

"Maybe they were stillborn?" Ashley suggested.

Tim shook his head.

"I don't think so," he said. "If they had been, they still would have had their own entry, as a birth and a death, like this one back here," he said as he pointed to an entry several months earlier.

"The other possibility is…" Ashley started to say as she looked at Tim and saw him nod.

"Whoever was filling this in, stopped in the middle of the job," Tim said.

"They disappeared…"

"On April 4th, 2010," Tim summed up.

Ashley took a step back and just looked at Tim. Even if they had a possible date that the person who'd been filling in the ledger had disappeared, what did that mean? How did it help them with their investigation?

She found herself getting frustrated. It wasn't something she experienced often, but she definitely was. It seemed like they were getting all different kinds of information, but nothing seemed in any way to help them with *anything*.

Tim focused on her face. They were enough in tune with each other as work partners to have a pretty good understanding of how to read each other's moods. He could see that Ashley was beginning to get highly annoyed at everything to do with the current case. On a personal level, he wished he could help her by doing anything that would alleviate her annoyance. On a professional level, he was just as annoyed as she was.

"This is frustrating as hell," he said quietly.

He saw her face relax as she let out a long, deep sigh that was followed up by a weary smile. It was weary, but it was a smile. That was something, at least.

"I'm ready for a break," Ashley said at last. "Let's go search this final building next door, then do a walk around the outside of all of this. Maybe we'll find another graveyard, and it'll give us more clues."

Tim noted a hint of tired resolution in her voice but didn't respond with words. Instead, he nodded and quietly followed her out. They had photos of the pages of the ledger. Now that they had some actual names, along with dates of birth, maybe the Bureau database would provide something to move on to look at. Just maintaining that hope made him feel a little less stressed.

There was hope.

Not much, but some.

CHAPTER 17

Although a larger area than Kerr's, the outside of the township provided no more clues about anything at all. Cars were parked, unlocked, and intact. A park had overgrowth to a degree that said nobody had maintained grass or trees in quite a while. A children's playground stood empty, the only indication anyone had ever been there being a backpack that rested near a tall slide.

"Growth is slow in these towns, isn't it," Tim said as he noticed the blue and yellow color of the backpack under weeds near the slide. Reaching down to push the growth aside and retrieve it, he picked it up and opened up the main zip.

"How do you mean?" Ashley asked, watching him and curious about what the owner of the bag had been doing when they'd left it there.

"Well, if we are right in thinking that people left Pioneer and Kerr a decade ago, I'm no garden expert, but I would have expected the grass to be much longer than it is," Tim replied, reaching into the bag.

"I hadn't thought about that," Ashley replied as her eyes shifted to the ground. "It is a bit overgrown."

"A bit," Tim said, nodding. "Not a lot, though. On the other hand, it equally doesn't look like someone's maintained it. It looks more like the growth is just really slow."

After pulling out a handful of books from the backpack, he passed the bag to Ashley and began looking at each one.

"Handwriting, math, and art," he read from the labels.

"Emma Voy." He paused, flicking through pages. "What happened to you, Emma Voy?"

"Well, that looks like something that might belong to a girl aged … what? Seven or eight?"

Tim nodded. "Maybe."

"She wouldn't have been out at night with her school bag," Ashley said. "That might tell us the time of day that these people left…"

"Or were taken…" Tim added in, echoing comments they'd made previously.

"Or were taken. Either before or after school, but not during school hours," Ashley surmised.

"Assuming she went to school that day."

Ashley looked at him and grinned.

"Did you skip school when you were seven?"

Tim chuckled but shook his head.

"I see your point," he said. "One thing that's now got my attention, though, is that we haven't seen a school in this town. Or Kerr, for that matter." He paused for a long time, watching Ashley ponder his observation. "Where did the kids go to learn?" he finally asked out loud.

"Maybe they caught a bus to one of the neighboring towns," Ashley replied. "Even though it's bigger than Kerr, this place is still pretty small. It's possible that kids from these places with small populations, all were taken to one school that met the needs of several towns."

"It's a possibility," Tim said. "If that were the case, there should be some kind of report that's recorded those kids not showing up for school at some point. If one kid had a day off, that might be one thing, but if an entire town's worth of kids didn't go to school, surely someone would have asked questions or come to check on them."

"Maybe they did," Ashley said quietly. "Maybe they *did* come here … and maybe they got taken, along with everyone else."

After putting the school books back in their backpack, Tim spoke.

"That wouldn't work."

Ashley looked at him, silently asking for context.

"Well, let's say that I travel from here to school in another town each day," Tim began, prompting Ashley to nod. "One day, I don't go to school. It's noted that I'm off sick, but nothing gets done about it because the school knows I'm a good kid and there will be a good reason, like I'm sick, for example."

"Right…"

"If I weren't the only kid from an entire town that missed school that day, though, you're right - maybe someone called first, to see what was going on. After a few worried calls, someone might hop in their car and drive here to do a physical check that everyone's okay."

"Yep."

"But if *that* person came here right at the wrong moment, and was taken along with the residents of the town…"

"Why wouldn't someone question where *that* person had gone if they didn't return…" Ashley replied.

"Exactly."

"Well, either way, there must be some kind of report about something to do with either or both of these towns," Ashley said. "I just can't believe that nothing has been recorded."

"I think we need to get back to the motel, where we can use the laptops far more easily and do more thorough research," Tim said as they began to walk again. "I know we looked online to find Kerr and Pioneer, and we found nothing, but let's dig a little deeper. I'll get the team at the office to start doing a bit of digging too."

Ashley stopped walking and turned to face him.

"I feel like we're getting further and further away from what we were sent to do in this investigation - find Jordan Simpson."

"Further away?" Tim asked. "Or closer?"

CHAPTER 18

Later that evening, sitting in Ashley's motel room with laptops open and almost empty takeaway cartons between them, Tim and Ashley both analyzed all that they'd learned so far.

"The thing is," Ashley said after linking into the Bureau database and not finding what she was looking for. "We don't know anything for sure, do we? I mean, we assume the homeless people from four towns disappeared a decade ago. We assume that entire populations from two other small towns disappeared a decade ago. But we don't *know*."

"Ash, we *never* know anything when we first embark on a case," said Tim, smiling at her." That's why we're here - to figure it out."

"I know," Ashley replied, nodding. "But what if we're on a completely wrong path? What if Jordan Simpson just died a decade ago, and right now, his ashes are sitting in an unmarked box on a shelf in a crematorium or funeral home somewhere?"

"That's a possibility, but if it *is* what happened to him, we're still getting closer to finding that out," Tim said. "We could be on a path that leads nowhere. The people of Kerr and Pioneer might have just moved away to be closer to more people. If that turns out to be the case, then that's great; nobody is missing."

"Except Jordan Simpson."

"Except Jordan Simpson," Tim said, his voice calm. "But if all this turns out to be nothing, then we have at least learned what *didn't* happen to him."

"Yeah, I know," said Ashley. "And I do know we'll figure out whatever needs to be figured out."

"Of course we will," Tim replied, grinning at her. "We always do."

Ashley smiled at him, appreciating once more how good it was to be able to work with a partner she felt aligned with in work methods and dedication.

"Where's the map?" she asked, a thought popping into her head.

After Tim jumped up and then grabbed and unfolded the large sheet of paper over the spare bed in the room, Ashley moved to look over it.

"What are you thinking?" Tim asked her, liking seeing her move into analysis mode once more. It was far more rewarding to see that than to see her becoming despondent at not having anything definite solved in the case yet.

"Well," Ashley said as she sat on the bed beside the map and traced her fingers over the area they were in. "I'm just wondering if we're missing something altogether. All of this people-disappearing activity is around here," she said, pointing at the diamond they'd established previously. "Gordon, Guthrie, Riverside, and Compton are four towns that have recorded homeless populations vanishing. Within this diamond are Kerr and Pioneer - two towns that look like the entire population of each vanished."

Tim watched on, following where she was pointing on the map. Whatever was going on in her thoughts, he knew it was good to leave her in silence to figure it out.

Finally, Ashley looked up at him.

"We haven't yet worked our way outwards from this area," she said. "We don't know if the same issues have happened in other towns a little further out."

"True," Tim said as he sat down close to the other side of the map. Looking down, he moved his finger across the paper. "Kate's journal only shows her going to the four main towns we've already visited. She also briefly went to Kerr, but she didn't seem to know anything about Pioneer." He took some time to study the map. "If we treat this like the layers of an onion, there are these three towns on this map that we could go and visit - Shenglong, Oscar, and Richmond."

"Yes," Ashley said, nodding. "Too far for people to have walked to…"

"But close enough for them to be a possibility," Tim finished.

"Have you spoken to Kate since we left her?" Ashley asked out of curiosity. In response, she saw Tim shake his head. "Maybe you need to do that too, just to ask her about Kerr and double-check that she didn't visit any other towns."

"On it," Tim said as he stood. "I'll go call her now. Do you want to talk about this more tonight?"

Ashley shook her head as she felt fatigue set in.

"No, I'm feeling pretty drained," she replied. "Talk again in the morning?"

"Yep," Tim said as he made his way to the door. "See you nice and early," he finished, giving Ashley a smile that she knew would make any girl's heart beat faster.

"Sleep well, Tim," Ashley replied before closing and securing the door. Although they hadn't achieved much, it felt like they'd traveled far over only a few days. The growing number of uncertainties had further contributed to Ashley feeling exhausted. She'd hoped they would know something fairly quickly on the case. Instead of finding answers, what was growing instead was the number of questions they were discovering.

After a shower and readying herself for bed, she climbed under the covers and picked up her e-book reader. She had well-rehearsed routines. Sometimes her best time for thinking was after she slept, waking with a brand new consideration on her mind. Before sleep, reading was perfect for letting go of the day's thinking.

CHAPTER 19

Waking to her alarm, Ashley swiped her phone's screen to let the snooze kick in. Ten minutes. When she woke up, it was good to take just ten minutes to lie still and think about the day to come.

Although a part of her had hoped she would wake with something new to focus on, there was nothing there. Sleep hadn't provided her with any additional insight past exactly where they were in their investigation. That was mildly frustrating, but at least they had a plan for the day. They were widening their visits to towns nearby, and going to see if there was anything to learn in the towns to the north, east, and west of the diamond they'd already established on the map.

To herself, she scoffed. Maps. She'd come to rely on looking at maps online, but finding towns on old paper maps that were no longer recorded in the digital age made her question technology again. It had its uses - her job would be much different without it - but there seemed to be areas of history lost because of it.

Thinking about Kerr and Pioneer, she couldn't help but be drawn to wonder what had happened to those towns. It wasn't unheard of for populations to leave small towns as people desired to migrate towards cities. No, it wasn't that the towns were now empty and forgotten that disturbed Ashley most about them. It was the *way* that they seemed to have emptied. There was nothing orderly about the sense of abandonment each of the two towns showed. If it had been some kind of mass exodus of choice, wouldn't people have taken their belongings and then tidied or cleaned the building interiors in the hope that someone would come along and want to buy them? The small indicators, such as cups looking like they were being prepared for the boiling water to be added to make tea, and the washing machines with now-heavily-crinkled items inside of them, as if those laundered items would have been hung out to dry at any moment - it was those small things that made her sure that whatever had happened in Kerr and Pioneer, hadn't been a normal occurring event.

Although, of course, she preferred to be successful in working and solving cases, she wanted to be wrong about whatever had happened in the two small towns. She hoped that what they would ultimately find was that the residents had simply decided to leave. Nice and peaceful. Nice and easy. That would make things much more pleasant anyway.

The shrill of her alarm went off again, making her jump then grin. Every morning, she subjected herself to the same experience, but she never changed the timing of the alarm or the horrible sound of it. If nothing else, it worked.

Minutes later, as Ashley stood under the satisfying flow of hot water in the shower, her mind was active. No matter where their investigation was leading them, it did seem to be a fact that people were missing. Maybe some of them would prove to have just moved, but the odds that all of those people decided to move from one town to another location, all around the same time? Those odds seemed far lower. Then, factoring in that it seemed to be a blend of homeless people from four larger towns, and everyone from two smaller towns - if it was a coincidence, it was a remarkable one.

She took her time getting dressed and preparing herself for the day ahead. Finally, she was ready to embark on another day of investigation and exploration.

CHAPTER 20

"Good morning!" she heard Tim call out when she exited her motel room door. Looking around, she saw him standing against her car, smiling up at her.

"And a very good morning to you, Timmy Boy," Ashley replied, returning the smile. "How did you get on with your phone call last night?" she asked as she unlocked the car.

When both were settled into their seats, Tim turned to her.

"I did call Kate Simpson," he said, prompting Ashley to nod in expectation of more information. "I asked her to explain fully what she'd done and found in Kerr."

"And?"

"She didn't have anything more to say about that. She did confirm that she'd ended up driving there by accident, for the most part. When she'd found it, she'd pulled over, walked along the main street, and peered in a few windows. She said the vibe of the place put her off wanting to stay for long," Tim said.

"I understand that," Ashley replied, remembering the feelings she'd experienced there. "What about Pioneer?"

"I asked her about it, but she'd never heard of it," Tim replied. "From what she said, she only visited the four main towns, and then Kerr purely by accident. She didn't go any further out to the places we're going to today."

"Okay," Ashley said. "Well, I'm guessing you need to be fed before we do anything or go anywhere?"

Tim grinned at her.

"You know me so well."

~~~~~

Sitting in the diner, waiting for their big breakfasts to be brought to their table, Ashley and Tim decided to research the next towns to visit.

"Their names are quite different, aren't they," Tim said as he began using his phone to search for the towns. "Shenglong sounds Asian, Richmond reminds me of Canada, and Oscar reminds me of…"

"A grump who lives in a trashcan?" Ashley asked, teasing him.

"Hey! Don't knock Sesame Street," Tim said as he laughed softly. "I watched it as a kid, and I turned out just fine."

Ashley smiled, then resumed looking at her phone screen.

"No news of missing people in any of these places," she said finally.

"Yeah, but what does *that* mean?" Tim asked. "*None* of the places seem to have reported on anyone being missing. Even here and in Riverside, where people were noticed as having left, there was still no actual news released about it."

"You're right," Ashley said as the waitress placed meals in front of them. "We'll go and visit each of these three towns today, including the police department and homeless shelters of each. Hopefully, something will help us out a bit more. If nothing seems relevant there, maybe one of these places will be where the people of Kerr or Pioneer went to."

Even as she said the words, she knew she didn't believe them. Regardless, she reminded herself not to lose hope. They'd only been on their current case for a few days. It was too early yet to let her confidence fall.
~~~~~

CHAPTER 21

After being shown into an office by a detective in the Shenglong Police Department, Ashley took some time to look around the room. It was compact, but on the walls, she could see some familiar faces of people currently being searched for by law enforcement. For a moment, she thought it eerie that the worst criminals got their faces on so many walls around the country, but the average person who was overlooked day to day, and then went on to disappear, nobody knew the identity of, or what they looked like.

"Sorry to keep you waiting," she heard a strong female voice say, before turning to see the woman closing the office door. "I'm Detective Joan Malloy."

Tim and Ashley both introduced themselves and shook hands with the detective, then watched as she sat behind the desk.

"Now, how can I help the two of you? The officer who directed me here was concise in his words," Joan said, chuckling to herself.

When she looked straight at Ashley and Tim, both agents saw the seriousness that lay below the surface of the chuckling.

"We have been looking into the disappearance of a number of people in the general area around Compton, Guthrie, Gordon, and Riverside," Tim said.

"Oh?" the detective asked. "We share some cases with those police departments, but I haven't heard of any recent or new missing persons cases from any of them."

"We believe these people disappeared around ten

years ago," Ashley said. "It seems to be mostly homeless people."

Before her, Ashley saw the detective's eyes sharpen, and her demeanor change slightly.

"Our homeless population seems to only be growing," Joan said finally. "I wish it *was* a case of them moving on and finding somewhere safer and warmer to live. Don't get me wrong. I respect their choice, but I'd worry less about them if they chose a different one."

"So you *do* still have homeless people here then?" asked Tim.

"Of course," the detective said. "That's a problem that few places in the world can eliminate."

Ashley turned and looked at Tim.

"The four towns we mentioned haven't had any homeless residents for years," Ashley said the detective. "They all seem to have vanished."

"And you're wanting to find them?" Joan asked.

"We are, but we don't know anything about most of them," Tim said. "We've been asked to find a young woman's grandfather, who she knew was homeless in Compton. In trying to locate him, it's come to our attention that *lots* of homeless people went missing around the same time."

"I see. Serial killer?" Joan asked.

Ashley blinked. She hadn't wanted to consider that option, although she knew it was a distinct possibility.

"Maybe," she replied. "We're not yet ready to assume all of the missing people are dead. What we were really wanting to ask you about was whether you knew of a similar problem happening here in Shenglong. In these other towns, entire established communities of homeless residents were set up and then disappeared. Nothing like that has been happening here?"

The detective shook her head.

"No, not that I've been made aware of," she said, reminded that she hadn't checked on any of the clusters in a while. "In saying that, I haven't seen them in recent months."

Tim's head shot up at the words. It sounded like the admission in Riverside that a more recent person had been seen and appeared to be homeless, but the next day was gone and hadn't been seen again since.

"Now you have me thinking," Joan continued. "Do you guys want to come on an excursion to see the places our homeless have set up home?"

"Yes!" Ashley said with eagerness. "Who knows - maybe someone among them will know where some of the people we seek have gone."

Joan stood and grabbed her coat off the nearby rack.

"They also might be able to tell you if any among them are from those towns you mentioned."

Tim felt a little excited as he and Ashley stood and followed the detective out the doors of the office and then the building. Once outside, they continued to follow her until she indicated a large grey four-wheel drive parked in the police station carpark.

"Climb in," Joan said as she unlocked all doors and jumped into the driver seat. Once Ashley and Tim were settled inside, the engine started. "For as long as I've been a detective here in Shenglong, there have been two small clusters of homeless people that have remained pretty static," she said as she veered the vehicle out onto the road. "They don't cause any problems, and they tend to stay out of others' ways, so I haven't seen any reason to move them along."

"Do you think others would *like* them to move along?" Tim asked.

"Oh, no doubt," Joan replied. "It's the same in all towns and cities, isn't it. People say they want to help those in need but when they see someone sitting on the side of a footpath, do they help? Usually not. Instead, they look up at the sky or in the other direction, pretending to not see that person at all." She paused for a long while. "No, I think the general population would rather not see people homeless. For most of us, that's because we wish the homeless would have a better life, and we think that living in a home would make it better for them. Others, though, well, they think it would be good to not have homeless people because when they see them there, sitting on a footpath or sleeping on or under a park bench, it makes them feel uncomfortable. I think some people don't like that. It highlights to them just how little empathy they have for the less fortunate, and that reflects on who *they* are as people."

Ashley listened to the speech and silently agreed. Many people liked to say they wanted to help others. When the opportunity presented itself to do so, many of those people turned away and did nothing.

"Here's our first community here," Ashley heard Joan say, indicating a small area ahead of them. "Let's get out, and you can talk to these guys. Ask them whatever you want to know. I've always found these guys pretty approachable and chatty."

Tim and Ashley climbed out and began walking with the detective. Scattered around the small area of bush and trees were an array of shelters constructed of random items - a folded tarpaulin here, an old waterproof sleeping bag there, plus a range of cardboard boxes that looked like they might have once housed refrigerators or something else of a large nature.

As they approached, Ashley felt like all eyes were on them. She took her time with the details she could glean just from visual observation. She and Tim had found no luck in locating any homeless people in four busy towns. If anything were to happen to the people they were currently facing, she wanted to remember what they each looked like, even if she wasn't able to gather their names or anything else about them.

"Hi, Bob," she heard the detective call out.

When Ashley looked over, she saw Joan approach a

man who looked to be in his fifties, holding out her hand to him as though they were old friends.

"Joan!" exclaimed the man. "It is good to see you again. How's that man of yours treating you? You keeping him in order?"

Joan grinned and nodded.

"Always, Bob. Always," she replied before turning to face Ashley and Tim. "Bob, these two young people are wanting to talk to a few of you, in the hope of finding out what happened to someone who was living a bit rough. Would you be happy to speak to them?"

Although his face changed and became a little more serious, Bob nodded and moved forward to where Ashley and Tim stood.

After shaking hands, and the two agents introducing themselves, Bob seemed to relax a little.

"How can I help you folk?" he asked, glancing from one agent to the other.

"We have been looking for a gentleman who was last seen living on the streets in Compton," Tim said.

"Compton?" Bob asked. "That's quite a distance from here."

"Yes," Ashley said. "Do you know if anyone here has come from that area?"

"No, not that I know of," Bob replied. "These folks here, have all been here for as long as I have. But what's the name of the person you're after?"

"Jordan," replied Tim. "Jordan Simpson. Goes by Jordy to some."

"Never heard that name before," said Bob. "Is he in trouble?"

"No, not at all," Tim replied. "His granddaughter has asked us to find him."

"The others in Compton don't know where he went?"

"To be honest, Bob, we don't know where the others went either," said Ashley. "In Compton, the entire homeless population disappeared years ago. Have you heard of anything - or anyone - who might be offering people on the streets an alternative way to live?"

Bob chuckled lightly.

"An alternative way to live? No. If I had, I'd be taking advantage of that." He paused and looked intently at Ashley. "You're serious? People don't live on the streets anymore in that town?"

"They haven't been seen for a long time in Compton, or Guthrie, Gordon or Riverside," Ashley replied.

"Wait," Bob said, his face becoming serious. "No homeless in four towns?" he asked, prompting both agents to nod in response. "Did they all just disappear?"

"That's what we don't know. We only know the name of one person - Jordan Simpson," Ashley replied. "Whoever else was in the homeless communities of those towns, we don't have any way of searching for them because we don't know who they were."

"I had a granddaughter once ... and a grandson," Bob said quietly. "I don't know where they are now. I went back to their house one time, and it was all cleared out. My son didn't even come and tell me they were moving."

Tim heard the emotion in the older man's voice as he spoke.

"Did your son know you were here?" he asked.

"Yeah," Bob replied as he nodded. "To be fair, it wasn't his fault things were rough between us. I spent time at war. When I came back, I tried to make things work with his mother but ... oh ... I didn't handle anything well. Thought it best that I leave rather than cause them heartbreak or pain. Years later, I reached out and discovered his mother had died. I connected with my son again. At one point, he did ask me to go and stay with him and his wife, but I couldn't do that, not being how I am."

Ashley and Tim listened and said nothing in response. The emotion they heard and witnessed held them captive in their attention, eager to hear more.

"In many ways, this isn't an easy life, living like this," Bob said as he pointed around the small cluster. "In some ways, though, it's the easiest way to live at all. Here, we're all in the same situation. Many of the people living here in our group have served in the military and have demons inside their heads. It's good being among others who have seen and experienced similar things. It helps to have people to lean on in ways that family could never quite understand."

"Have you asked Joan, or anyone else, to find your son and your grandkids?" Ashley asked.

"No," Bob said as he shook his head. "If they wanted to know me, they know where to find me."

"Bob, that is how Jordan Simpson might have felt before he disappeared. He doesn't know it, but his granddaughter *is* looking for him," Tim said in almost a whisper. "Don't leave it too late. If you want to make contact with them, use us - law enforcement - to help you do that."

Both agents watched as Bob seemed to consider what Tim had just said. Then his demeanor changed.

"I'm sorry I can't help you in finding your homeless people," he said, abruptly turning away. "I hope you find what you're looking for."

A glance at Joan confirmed that as far as Bob was concerned, the conversation was over.

"Thank you," Tim called out to Bob before the agents began following Joan along the length of makeshift accommodations. Now and then, they stopped to ask if anyone there was from Compton, or knew of anyone from any of the six towns they had visited. Nobody knew anything. Nobody even seemed to have heard of Kerr or Pioneer. It was a frustrating discovery, but at least there was some consolation in knowing that Shenglong wasn't a town that had been affected by whatever had happened elsewhere.

When the three of them returned to Joan's vehicle and

settled inside, she turned to look at them.

"Sorry you didn't find out anything from these guys," she said before starting the engine. "Let's do a quick pass by the other cluster, and then I'll drop you back at the station."

In the ride, Ashley thought about all that she'd heard Bob say.

"He seems to want to know where his family is, but he won't ask you to help find them?" she asked.

"Yeah, he's mentioned them before, and I've offered to find them," Joan replied. "For me, it would probably be easy. I don't expect they're in a crime database, but the ages of his grandkids, at least, would make me think they might be on social media," she said. "I tried to get him to tell me his last name so I could go ahead and do that, but he's a stubborn old bugger. To be honest, I'm not even sure his name's Bob. One thing those people do seem to like is anonymity. He knows that I'll help him when he's ready. That's all any of us can do really - offer to help and then wait until they're ready to take us up on that offer."

Ashley nodded and looked out the windows of the vehicle. Shenglong seemed a little bigger than any of the other towns she'd visited in recent days. Bigger, but not necessarily any different in terms of style. Although Pioneer and Kerr both seemed to be from a different century, the other four had similar architecture to Shenglong, making Ashley think that all towns might have been established around the same time.

"Have you ever heard of two little towns in this region called Pioneer and Kerr, Joan?" she asked, not sure if Tim had already asked about that or not.

"No," Joan replied, looking and sounding curious. "Near here?" she asked for clarification. When she saw Ashley nod, she expressed her doubt. "I thought I knew all towns in this area. Where are they?"

"They are both located pretty much near the middle

of the diamond-shaped area that Guthrie, Gordon, Riverside, and Compton form on a map," Ashley replied.

"Never heard of them. I've been to each of those bigger towns you mentioned, but don't recall seeing any other little towns around there," Joan said. "Have the people there provided any clues to where the homeless population has gone?"

Ashley looked forward as she relayed the answer.

"There are no people left in those two towns," she said.

"Oh! Deserted?" Joan asked. "We do live in a world where people are moving around all the time. Maybe those folk wanted the bright lights and excitement of a city."

"Maybe," Ashley replied. "I hope so."

Joan looked at her but said nothing more on the subject. Looking forward, she suddenly slowed and stopped the vehicle.

"Well, I'll be..." she said, disbelief in her head.

Tim and Ashley looked at Joan and then out the front of the car. Whatever held her attention, it wasn't obvious to the agents.

"Is everything alright?" Tim finally asked.

Joan looked at each of them before pointing in front of them.

"*That* is where the second homeless population lives," she said. When Ashley and Tim looked forward to where Joan was pointing, they only saw an empty field. "That's where it *was*, at least."

Seeing her begin to climb out of the car, Tim and Ashley followed her. They watched on in silence as the detective walked forward into a field and began to look all around her.

"Where did they go?" she asked.

"You have the right..." Tim began to ask before being stopped with only one look from the detective.

"I know this is the spot. I've been coming here for

over a decade," Joan said. "I didn't come last month to check on them..." she continued before her words drifted off. "Where could they have gone? The only other cluster is the one we just came from. They weren't there."

"How many people were in this one?" Ashley asked. "Could they have wandered to somewhere new?"

"No," Joan replied, shaking her head in disbelief. "I mean, they *could* have, but this was a big cluster. I'd guess the numbers here, at any one time, could have been close to sixty. When they were here, they definitely weren't hard to see."

Although she began to wander in a larger circle, even looking out towards the bush that lay to the north of it, for Ashley and Tim, it was easy to see that the detective was momentarily stunned.

"Could the owner of this land have asked them to leave?" Ashley asked.

"No, this is a public space. For as long as I can remember, it was okay for people in need to make use of it by camping out here," replied Joan. "If anyone wanted them gone, I'm sure we would have heard about it at the station."

Tim looked around. Instead of it being years since people had disappeared, now they were hearing about people having vanished over only a couple of months. It was still a while ago, but recently enough to be able to wonder if whatever had happened in six towns a decade earlier was still going on.

"There's nothing here," he said out loud, remembering the points about the other homeless populations disappearing. "Did they own much stuff?"

Joan looked at him and nodded.

"Honestly, it was a chaotic mess to me, even though they seemed to think it was orderly," she replied. "It's weird that they had so much, and now there's nothing left here."

"And you're sure it was only a few months since you were last here?" Ashley asked.

"Yeah, I was here..." Joan began to say as she pulled out her phone. "I was here exactly seven weeks, two days ago. Usually, I visit every few weeks, but a case had me busy last month, so I didn't come out." After a long while, she faced both agents, disbelief still on her face. "Even though these guys have never needed my help, or anything else from me, I have made it a priority to get out here and check on them regularly. That's why I've kept a record of when I visited. I can't believe something has happened in the one period that I didn't make it out here." She paused for a long while, annoyance growing inside of her over something she knew she couldn't control. "I guess Shenglong now gets added to your search?" she asked.

Tim and Ashley nodded in reply.

"It can be if need be," Tim said. "But are you able to follow up with people in the area to see if anyone saw or heard these guys leave? We were going to visit any homeless shelters here today as well..."

"Let's go there now," Joan quickly replied as she turned and began walking towards the car. "There's only one shelter here. The few times I've been there, they've been serious about overcrowding and not enough funding."

Once inside the vehicle, she faced each of them.

"I'm hoping these guys are at the shelter," she said before starting the engine. "I know that the people who were here probably shouldn't mean anything to me, but ... well, the thought of people living rough isn't something I like. These ones made that choice, and I respect that, but I still wanted to make sure they were okay."

"It's not your fault if they've moved on," Ashley said gently, sensing the detective's current mood.

"I know," said Joan. "Let's see what the shelter has to

say. I'm hopeful these guys will have found their way there, one way or another."

Tim wondered if it could be as easy as that. He hoped so. Hell, he hoped that *all* of the people that he'd come to think had disappeared, were actually inside a warm and dry homeless shelter. Although that wasn't a pretty picture, it was a better thought than that something bad had happened to them all.

In the back of his mind were serial killers he'd investigated. He hoped they weren't going to find all of the missing people at once in something like the few mass graves he'd already seen in his career so far. How any human could treat others like that, he'd never understood.

Even with all the explanations he'd heard about killers, their psychological state, and what probably caused them to do what they did, he still didn't understand why it kept happening. Years would pass with single murders or abductions, and then one would happen that would give that first clue that one person was doing more than just one killing. They were on a rampage, and they were getting away with it.

Most of the time, Tim chose not to think about those people. In cases where people had disappeared, he didn't want to let himself think the worst - that they'd been killed. Recently, he and Ashley had investigated several cases of missing people who hadn't met their demise. Each of those had been found alive. He hoped for the same outcome in the current case.

"Here we are," he heard Joan say as the car was maneuvered into a parking space in front of a three-story building that looked like it might have been a factory in a past life.

When they all climbed out of the vehicle and walked to the door, it opened even before they could knock.

"Detective Malloy," a man in his mid-thirties said as he opened the door wider. "I was just going to go for a walk to the park. How can I help you?"

"John, this is Special Agent Power and Special Agent Moore," Joan said. "Can we come in and talk to you? It won't take long."

Ashley watched the man smile and wave his hand in a signal to enter. When the door closed behind them, he led them into a small front room that looked like the combination of an office and a reception area.

"Please sit down," John said as he moved behind his large wooden desk. "In what way can I help you?"

"These agents are here because some homeless people have gone missing from towns around here," Joan said.

"Oh, I don't think there's anyone here who has come from another town," John quickly said. The rapid answer surprised Tim.

"Do you talk to them enough to know where they've come from?"

John looked at Tim and smiled.

"The bigger question is do *they* talk to *me*," he said. "And yes, often they do. However, the reason I know none have come here from other towns is because *nobody* has come here for the past five weeks."

"Nobody at all?" Joan asked him. When he confirmed that was what he meant, she leaned forward. "The homeless set up out east..."

"The big one near Fables Farm?" John asked, prompting Joan to nod in reply.

"Yes," she said. "Have you been out there?"

John shook his head in surprise.

"Not for several months," he said. "I don't usually go to them. Normally, we're so full here that I don't want to promote anyone already settled in communities like that to come in to this place. The thought of suggesting it to them, but then having to turn them away because we're already full for the night ... well, it always seemed a bit cruel to even think about doing that."

"Have your numbers been dropping steadily in recent months?" Ashley asked, intrigued.

"No, not at all," replied John. "We were full each and every night for as long as I can remember, and then one day our full quota walked out one morning, and nobody came again. Not one soul."

"And that was about five weeks ago, you said?" Tim asked.

"Yes," John said as he reached into a drawer of his desk and pulled out what looked like a large diary. "I keep records of our numbers for accounting purposes, but generally, we're at full capacity every night."

"How many beds is that? Full capacity, I mean," Tim asked.

"Ninety-five beds is our maximum capacity," John replied. "It sounds like a lot, but it's always been pretty easy to fill them up in only a matter of hours from when the doors open in the afternoon until when we have to close them." He paused and looked through the pages in front of him. "April 12th was the last night that anyone stayed here," he said before raising his face and looking at the three people sitting before him again.

"Do you have any idea about what has happened, John?" Joan asked, concern heavily audible in her voice.

"No," John replied. "And you say that the homeless out by Fables Farm have gone?"

"Yes," Joan said, nodding. "I was last there about seven weeks ago. They were still out there then."

"And nobody mentioned they were moving on to somewhere else?" John asked.

"No," Joan replied. "When I last saw that group, the chatty ones were all as chatty as always. The others were as quiet as always. Nobody said anything about any *plans* to go anywhere."

"And the other group that we have here in town?" John asked her, his curiosity growing.

"All fine," Joan confirmed. "They all appeared to be

there, and they didn't know anything about the missing people these folk are looking for. No, they all seemed fine out there. No problems at all."

John focused on Ashley and Tim.

"But this is separate from what you are investigating, I take it?" he asked.

"Yes," Ashley replied. "We have come from Compton. We are primarily seeking an elderly man who was known to live among a homeless cluster there about ten years ago. Asking around about him, it has come to our attention that *all* of the homeless people from Compton disappeared. Nobody knows where they went, or why."

"Ten years ago?" John asked. When Ashley and Tim both nodded, he continued. "That is a long time ago. Much will have changed in this town and that one since then. Do you think these occurrences can somehow be related?"

"It's something we have to consider," said Ashley. "It's not only Compton, though. The same thing has happened in Guthrie, Gordon, and Riverside."

"Hmm," John mumbled, thoughtful.

Tim watched the man's face and hoped he would provide something useful for them. Only silence ensued.

"John, have you heard of two other towns that we visited - Kerr or Pioneer?" he asked.

"No," said John. "Are they outside of this area?"

"No," Tim replied. "They are right in the center of this area."

John smiled a little, almost as if he thought the agent before him had spoken in jest.

"I'm pretty sure we'd know if there were two towns near here…" he began to say before realizing the agents weren't smiling. It wasn't some kind of joke. "You're serious?"

"Yep," replied Tim.

"Do you think that's where these people could have

gone?" John asked.

"No," Ashley said. "Nobody has been there for a while. Right now, we have agents in both towns, seeing if they can find anything that can help us in our investigation, but no, it seems like nobody has been in either town for many years."

All sat quietly for a long while, each in their own thoughts.

"Do you think the group that's still here is safe?" John asked. It was a question that had already been playing on the minds of Joan, Ashley, and Tim.

"I don't know," Joan replied. "I never wanted to suggest them coming here before because I knew you had to turn people away, but…"

"Bring them here!" John exclaimed, standing abruptly. "Yes! We need to go and explain to them that they might not be safe. I haven't had anyone here for a long time. They will be safe here, and they can stay here day and night since there's nobody else needing to be here."

"Alright," Joan said as she stood. "You're sure?"

"Yes," said John. "I don't know what has been happening to all of these other homeless people, but it seems *something* is happening to them. If we can stop the same thing happening to this one group, we have to at least try."

"Okay, I'll organize transport and see if I can persuade them to come to you," Joan said.

"Oh, I'm coming too," said John. "I should have gone to see them before, when the general numbers dropped right off here. I didn't even think about it, truth be told. If I'd gone and offered beds to the ones out by Fables Farm…"

"No point in pondering that, John," said Joan. "That thinking is as unhelpful as me thinking I could have prevented those people leaving because I didn't go and check on them the last time I was due to. Right now, let's just see what we can do for the ones who *are* still here."

John nodded and grabbed his coat and keys. As all four exited the building, he turned to Joan.

"See you out there?"

"See you there," replied Joan before she, Tim, and Ashley climbed into her car.

"Well, that has added to the intrigue, hasn't it," she said as she started the engine. "You guys really don't have any idea what is going on with all these people vanishing?"

"I wish we did," Tim said. "The hardest thing about all this is that we don't even know who we're hoping to find. Other than one person - the grandfather who we were initially asked to find - we have no idea who these people are."

"And the numbers keep rising," said Ashley. "First, it was one person, then about fifteen. Since then, as we've moved from town to town to find out where the outer limit in the area is, the numbers just keep increasing. Each town has completely lost its homeless people."

"Except for us," Joan said as she looked at Ashley. "Our town has lost one cluster but not the other."

"Plus the numbers that were staying in the shelter," Tim said.

"Right," Joan said. "Yeah, John said he had more than ninety people a night in there, and I'm pretty sure the group that's missing, that I was keeping an eye on, was about sixty. That's a hundred and fifty people," she said, scoffing slightly. "A hundred and fifty people? Where could that many have possibly gone without someone noticing and calling it in?"

"That's pretty much the same question each town has asked when it's been brought to their attention that homeless clusters have disappeared," Ashley said. "In those cases, people don't seem to have noticed that the homeless were there, so equally didn't notice that they'd gone."

"They didn't notice the people were *there*?" Joan asked, incredulous. "The people fortunate enough to have housing, you mean?"

"Yeah," said Ashley. "It seems like people went about their days, not seeing - or choosing not to see - the less fortunate living on the streets. They appear to have blocked out the vision of it so much that when the people were no longer there, they didn't notice that they'd gone."

Joan shook her head in disbelief.

"What kind of world do we live in?" she asked. "I tell you, sometimes the things we see and hear about in law enforcement makes me wonder what kind of race we are. There's so much potential for everyone to be content with what they have, and to treat others with respect and kindness, but do we?" She paused for a long while as she parked in front of the police station. "The flip side is that we are doing good. If nobody else cares about these people, I'm glad that there are a few of us who do."

As Ashley and Tim stood outside the car, they turned to Joan.

"I am going to drive out to talk to the group that John's gone to see. Once we've convinced them to come into town and to the shelter, I'll organize transport for them to move," the detective said. "Are you two staying in town?"

"No, we have another two towns to visit today - Oscar and Richmond," Tim replied.

"Okay," Joan said, nodding. "Well, here is my card with my direct number on it," she continued. "Will you please call me later on tonight if you find anything in those towns that might be relevant to us here?"

"Of course," Tim said as he accepted the card and put it in his pocket. "Good luck with the move."

"It won't be easy, but I hope that between me and John, we can convince these people to go to the shelter," Joan said, smiling. "Maybe nothing is going to happen to them, but the beds are there, empty. They may as well make use of them."

Ashley reached out and shook the detective's hand.

"Thank you for your help today," she said, making Joan chuckle.

"I don't think I've answered anything you needed to know, Agent Power. I think, instead, I've presented you with more questions."

Ashley smiled and nodded.

"Maybe, but I'm sure we're getting closer," she said. "Thank you. We'll be in touch."

CHAPTER 22

When settled back into Ashley's car and out on the road again, Tim played over in his mind all that he'd learned in Shenglong. He'd gone there with the hope that everything would be normal, and it wouldn't have the same issue as the other towns did. He wasn't sure if he was glad or dismayed that one of the two homeless clusters *had* disappeared in the latest town.

"What are you thinking?" Ashley asked him, aware of his quietness.

"I'm thinking that this feels like a spiral that is never going to end," Tim said quietly as he looked at her. "Part of me wants to figure all this out, but the thought of exploring even more towns…"

"And them also having people who've disappeared?" Ashley asked.

"Yeah," said Tim. "There's something to be said for the whole 'ignorance is bliss' concept."

"There is, but if we wanted to live by that rule in life, we wouldn't be in law enforcement," Ashley replied.

"I know," said Tim. "The weirdest thing about the disappearance of people in Shenglong is that not *all* of their homeless population has gone."

"No, but all from one cluster have," Ashley said. "It's like … if someone *was* gathering these people up, they didn't know about the other group…"

"Or they didn't need them," Tim added. When he saw Ashley glance at him, he played out a scenario in his mind. "What if someone is doing this, and they have an actual *use* for these people? Here in Shenglong, they round up the homeless community who wander the streets of the town during the day but sleep in the shelter at night. After they've done that, they need some more, so they go and take all the residents of that one cluster, but then they have about a hundred and fifty people. Whether or not they know there's another cluster out there, they just don't need more than that hundred and fifty, so they stop there."

"But what could they possibly be using these people *for*?" Ashley pondered.

"I have no idea," Tim replied. "We don't know that *is* what's happening. Until we find some kind of concrete *proof* of something, we're just playing a guessing game, every single day."

"For now," Ashley replied. "But not forever. We're getting closer. I can feel it."

Tim smiled at her but didn't reply. He didn't know that they were getting any closer to anything. The upside of that was that he equally didn't know that they *weren't* getting closer to something. It was enough to provide not a lot of hope, but at least a little amount. In his career, he knew that a small amount of hope was infinitely better than no hope at all. That thought, he decided to cling onto.

"And this is Oscar," he heard Ashley say as they approached the beginning of a new town. "With the exception of Kerr and Pioneer, all these towns are beginning to look the same to me."

Tim silently agreed. Nothing was outstanding about any of the towns they'd visited so far. As far as prettiness went, none of them had it, but they did seem to have all that one could want for in a town one resided in.

"Can we eat before we go see the police?" he asked as his stomach rumbled.

Ashley chuckled. "Yep."

CHAPTER 23

Later on, sitting in the office of the chief of police in Oscar didn't provide any answers to Tim and Ashley. There was, unfortunately, no change in the homeless population of their town, the chief informed them.

"They're a rugged bunch, those ones," he said, his voice weary at the subject. "Don't get me wrong. They cause no bother here other than the odd person saying they wished the people living on the streets would go away. From my perspective, someone wishing that isn't reason enough for me to move these guys on. They're off the beaten path, out of the way of most people."

"But people *do* have an opinion on them?" Tim asked.

"Oh, yeah," the chief replied. "Every other month, someone comes in and complains, saying 'those people' are an eyesore or something like that."

"They're definitely seen then," Tim said, thoughtful.

The chief looked surprised by the comment.

"Of course," he said. "It would be difficult to *not* see them. What's this all about anyway?"

"There have been a number of disappearances of homeless people in towns around this area," Ashley said, watching the chief's face as she spoke.

"Disappearances?" the chief asked. "Or people just moving on?"

"We can't be absolutely certain, but it is looking like though entire populations of homeless people have vanished at the same time," Ashley replied. "The more towns we visit, the more people seem to have disappeared."

The chief looked at them as if she'd said something entirely illogical. Ashley understood the look. She couldn't argue with it. Everything they were discovering as they moved from town to town *was* illogical. At times, she was finding it difficult to maintain hope that eventually they would find something solid and everything would make sense.

"New homeless shelter open?" the chief asked. His question was met with the two agents shaking their heads. "Hmm. And no big township clean up of the areas that the homeless had been sleeping?"

Once again, Ashley and Tim shook their heads.

"Just how many towns are you talking about?" the chief asked.

"Four active towns have lost their entire homeless populations," replied Tim. "We've just come from Shenglong. It's lost one of their previous two homeless communities."

"And their homeless shelter has had nobody go to stay the night there in over a month," Ashley added.

"That might be norm…"

"That isn't normal," Ashley said over the top of the chief's sentence. "The man who runs it - John Spring - said that until the last night he had any visitor, his beds had been full every single night for as long as he could remember. It literally went from being at full capacity one night, to having not one person knock on the door since."

The chief pondered what he was hearing. There was an aspect of his town that he knew about but didn't know if he should mention. Weighing up the possibility in his mind, he spoke.

"You know, this town had a serial killer decades ago," he said, watching the faces of both agents to see if they would react to the news. "Bobby Gee. Killed thirty-nine people - that we know of anyway."

Tim leaned forward. He'd not wanted to associate disappearing people with a serial killer. Hearing the chief's words, he accepted it was something that he and Ashley might have to consider.

"What happened?" he asked.

"Young guy," began the chief. "We think he started killing when he was seventeen, but the first victims that we know about for sure, he killed when he was nineteen. Over only a two-year period, he murdered thirty-nine - maybe more."

"All in this town?" Tim asked.

"No, he traveled up and down the main road through here," the chief replied. "When he was caught and interviewed, he talked a lot, even though he would never say if there were more bodies out there. He said he purposely sometimes drove north and found victims, and then alternately drove south to find victims, all in the name of confusing law enforcement. Said he couldn't help but kill. It was inside of him, he told us. Seemed almost glad to be caught and locked up."

"So he's still away?"

"Yep, last I heard," the chief said as he typed into his computer. "Maybe we should double-check that, though." After a couple of minutes, he nodded. "Yeah, he's still there. There's no chance of parole. He'll never see the outside world again."

"What did he do with the bodies?" Tim asked, intrigue growing.

"Threw them on the side of the road like they were garbage," the chief said, shaking his head slowly. "Stabbed each one, then discarded them just like that."

"Why?" asked Ashley.

The chief shrugged his shoulders again.

"As I said, all he could say was that he was meant to. It was inside him, like something he just had to do, and he couldn't help it."

"Is there a chance there's a copycat out there, killing

people?"

"There haven't been any more bodies found around this area," the chief said as he shook his head. "If Bobby Gee had a copycat out there, we'd be finding the bodies alright. He never even covered them. Had a van that he'd pick the victims up in, kill them in, and then literally throw out on the side of the road. I'm sure if that was happening again, something would have caught somebody's attention. What timeframe are you talking about when you say people are disappearing?"

"Ten years," Ashley said. "Most of these appear to have disappeared ten years ago, but the ones from Shenglong disappeared in the past couple of months."

The chief pondered while he looked at her.

"And in between?" he asked. "Or you mean they've been disappearing over the ten years?"

"No," replied Ashley. "From what we've been able to ascertain so far, the majority of people who've vanished, did so around ten years ago, possibly all at the same time. There doesn't appear to have been any disappearances that we know of between then and this year when these new ones have happened."

"Hmm," the chief said, thoughtful. "Something that happens every ten years? Like a ten year ritual or something?"

Tim focused on the suggestion. He hadn't considered that aspect yet.

"Is there anything that you can think of like that, Chief?" he asked, curious.

"Not that I can think of, but history has certainly had its share of rituals that have been continued quietly in the background of different societies," the chief replied. "I can't think of anything in particular around here, but just because it hasn't come to our attention doesn't mean that something isn't happening."

"Do you know of any religious or extremist groups around here?" Ashley asked.

"Not that I know of. If there are, they haven't come to our attention," the chief said. "Tell me this, though. How have you come to be searching for all of these homeless people? That doesn't seem like a Bureau investigation."

Tim replied, feeling like he'd told the same story over and over again.

"We were searching for only one man, who happened to be known to be homeless," he said. "In trying to figure out what happened to him, town after town that we've visited has brought to our attention that they have lost their homeless populations."

"Well, that certainly hasn't happened here," the chief said, his tone indicating he was about to shut the meeting down. "As I say, people come in here fairly regularly to ask that we do something about the people living on the streets. If anything, there are too many here, and certainly none leaving!"

Ashley picked up on the cue the chief gave as he stood up and walked toward them. As she and Tim rose from their seats, the chief held out his hand.

"Sorry I can't help you with anything," he said, shaking each of their hands.

"Actually, you've helped us a lot," said Ashley. "Thank you for making the time to speak with us today."

The chief nodded but didn't say anything more, or move to see them out.

When the agents stood outside the station, Tim rubbed his eyes.

"How can it feel like we're getting so much information and so little information, all at the same time?" he asked his partner.

"I think we definitely are getting information, Tim," Ashley said, smiling. "We just have to decipher it."

As Tim grinned, he couldn't help but roll his eyes at her. In his mind, it was winding up to be possibly the oddest investigation they'd ever worked on together, not to mention one of the most frustrating.

CHAPTER 24

After visiting Richmond, the agents decided to call it a day. They'd learned a lot over their visits to the three towns. Whether anything they'd learned was actually relevant to the case they were supposed to be investigating was less known.

Driving south from Richmond, on their way back to Compton, Tim watched Ashley's face now and then. He knew when she was thinking a lot, analyzing and processing the information they'd gained. He generally left her to it when she looked like she was in processing mode. He also found he had a bit of liberty in watching her when she was like that, knowing she was usually so involved in her head that she noticed little else.

"You know it's creepy when you do that," she said, turning to look at him.

Surprised that she'd caught him out this time, Tim gave her a sheepish smile.

"What?" he asked with feigned innocence.

"What?" she replied, teasing him. "You know exactly what. Don't play coy with me."

Tim grinned but couldn't think of any reply.

"Where are you at in your thinking?" Ashley asked to change the subject.

"I don't know," replied Tim as he refocused his view to the outside. "I didn't want to consider the serial killer option…"

"But you do now?" Ashley queried.

"No, not really, but I guess it *is* something to think about," Tim said. "Obviously, it isn't the guy that the chief in Oscar was talking about. That guy's still secure in prison."

"And it doesn't sound like he has a copycat, with no bodies having been found," Ashley added.

"Right," said Tim as he nodded. "Yeah, it isn't the same kind of crime, if these people *have* been killed."

"Which we don't know they have," said Ashley.

"That's the frustrating part, isn't it," Tim said. "We don't know what has happened to these people. There are no bodies!"

"Yet."

"Yet," Tim agreed, nodding again. "But we're now up into the hundreds of people who have gone missing. Even if they were in a mass grave, how *big* would that have to be? It just doesn't seem feasible that so many people could be killed and disposed of in such a small area, without someone discovering at least one body."

Ashley pondered what he was saying and agreed. The overall area they'd been covering didn't hold many opportunities for masses of people to have been buried, although they *were* looking at an entire decade of time.

"The initial people who went missing did so ten years ago…" she began to say.

"That we assume," Tim said. "We don't even know if *that* is right."

Ashley could hear the frustration growing in her partner. It was a rare thing to see in Tim, but she understood fully why he was beginning to feel that way.

"Well, we know it's right as far as the four original towns go," she said. "Kate was there a decade ago and knows the homeless populations were no longer visible. She also remembers seeing her grandfather before that, and she's pretty sure it was not too long before then."

"Yeah, the ten-year mark does seem to be a fairly certain one," Tim conceded. "It fits with the stopping of people needing accommodation at that first homeless shelter too."

"It's also the timeframe of when it looks like people left Kerr and Pioneer."

"True," Tim agreed as he nodded. "The paperwork in both of those towns suggests it was 2010 when they were last populated. The guys looking through both of those towns at the moment are going to let us know if they find anything there that points to some kind of crime having happened, or if it looks more like people just left and moved away."

"Good," Ashley said. "I'm quite curious to see what they find out about either town, given that we couldn't find anything at all about them just on the Internet."

"You're the one who usually says we shouldn't rely on the Internet so much," Tim said, teasing her.

"And this case proves that!" replied Ashley. "So far, it hasn't helped us to find out anything about two separate towns, even though we were standing in them. It also hasn't produced any reports of people going missing, or homeless populations reducing in any towns. Really, it hasn't proved to be of any use to us at all so far in this case."

As they entered the motel carpark, Tim fought to think of anything more they could do to find anything else out. It was difficult to know even where to look, after talking to the towns close by.

Once settled in Ashley's room again, the agents looked over all the paper they'd accrued.

"Well, Richmond hasn't been touched, as far as we can tell," Ashley said, glancing at the map that was once again spread out over the cover of the spare bed in the room. "Neither has Oscar."

Tim sat on the bed, close to the other side of the map. Peering down at the map as well, he traced his finger over it.

"So these two are okay," he said as he pointed directly to the towns on the map. "This one - Shenglong - has one active homeless community, but the other one has vanished, as of the last couple of months." He paused and moved his finger over. "These places - Guthrie, Gordon, Compton, and Riverside - have lost their homeless communities. And these places - Kerr and Pioneer - have lost their entire populations."

Looking at where Tim's finger had moved, Ashley moved back a little and looked at the area on the map.

"Well, Shenglong is east, whereas Oscar and Richmond are north and west," she said, pointing them out. "What if someone was doing something in an orderly fashion, but instead of moving out this way to the west, they're moving out here, to the east?"

"But there's nothing out in that direction," Tim said. "Compton is almost on the coast."

"Almost, but not quite," Ashley said, glancing up at him. "We've explored all of this area out here," she continued, pointing at the map once more. "Maybe we need to check out this area."

Tim looked to where her finger was dancing across the paper. Beyond Compton was a small area of land that was represented on the old map as just green. To see if anything more could be learned about the area, he pulled out his phone.

"You checking out Google Maps again?" Ashley asked, amused since they'd had little success in locating other places on the digital maps.

"I at least want to see what it shows there," Tim said as he manipulated the screen until he could see the area they were discussing. When he found it, he held it down so Ashley could look at it too. "Doesn't look like it's changed in the fifteen years since this paper map was produced. It still looks like it's just a grassy area with no structures on it."

"Hmm. Google Maps didn't show anything where Kerr and Pioneer are, though. I don't even know how that can be, but it was showing nothing there, right?"

"Yeah, I don't have any idea how that could be

either," Tim agreed. "For whatever reason, those buildings were being hidden or *something*."

"Okay, well, do you want to check this area out tomorrow and see what we can find?" Ashley asked, tiredness once again falling over her.

"Yep," Tim replied. "It's not too far from here anyway. Nothing to lose by going and having a look."

The two of them sat in silence for a long while, each in their own thoughts.

"Have the guys looking at Kerr said anything about the identity of that body in the grave?" Ashley asked as she thought about the small town.

"No," Tim replied. "Sarah said it will take several weeks for them to be able to identify that body, or the others that were in the rest of those unmarked graves."

"It's so weird that none of the graves had names on them," Ashley replied before scoffing. "*Everything* about this investigation is weird, I guess. What exactly are we even looking at, Timmy Boy? Mass amounts of people not only disappearing, but seeming to vanish into thin air without anybody noticing? I feel a bit like Alice, getting further and further into that hole." She chuckled. "Curiouser and Curiouser," she added in a sing-song voice.

Tim rolled his eyes at her, then grinned.

"Well, I'm knackered, so I'm gonna go and get some shut-eye," he said. "Same time, same place, tomorrow?"

Ashley nodded and walked across the room with him.

"Yep. See you then," she said before closing and securing the door.

Turning back toward the spare bed, the table, and the drawers in her room, she felt tiredness fall over her too. When spread out like it was, so much paper looked like it would hold many clues. Unfortunately, it didn't.

CHAPTER 25

Sitting together in the small diner that had become a morning ritual to the two agents, both were quiet as they contemplated the day ahead.

"We still don't have anything definitive, do we," said Tim between sips of his strong cappuccino. He'd had an uneasy sleep, his mind surprisingly full of weird images and dreams that weren't normal for him. Although he never read anything into dreams, the ones from the night before did persist in his memory, like a salesperson trying to get his attention, no matter how much he tried to turn away.

Ashley watched his face as he spoke and then moved the large cup up to his mouth again. She understood his lack of energy and enthusiasm. It was easy to get disheartened about what they were actually trying to do when, no matter how much they learned, it just didn't provide them with anything concrete to work with.

"I know," she finally said, nodding. "But I think we might find something today. Don't ask me how I know that. I just feel it in my gut."

Tim smiled at her. He did trust her gut. On the cases they'd already solved together, Ashley had proven many times that when she got a feeling that something was about to happen that would help them out, it often did.

"Today might just be our lucky day then," Tim replied. He hoped it *was* going to happen. Anything would be a help to them. "I just hope we reach … whoever … in time."

Ashley reached out and touched his hand.

"Hang in there," she said. "I truly believe that all these pieces are going to come together. They *are* going to be related, and we're *going* to find Mr. Simpson."

"Maybe, but will he be alive when we do … or dead?" Tim asked.

"Come on," Ashley ordered. "Drink up. Let's get going and see if there's anything between here and the coast that will help us and give us a clue."

Tim gulped back the last of his coffee, threw down a tip, and then grabbed his coat. Before he and Ashley left the table, the waitress hurried forward towards them. Thinking she might have something to help them in their investigation, Tim stood still and watched her.

"For you," the young woman said, handing him a card. Thinking it might be something important, Tim turned it over. When he did, he couldn't help but grin. "Call me. I'll take you out for a drink."

He nodded and thanked the woman, taking a moment to make a show of putting her number in his coat pocket. He had no intention of calling the waitress. Getting distracted was the last thing he wanted. Still, it did brighten his day to be approached by a woman.

When he looked ahead to the door to the diner, he saw Ashley standing, grinning at him. The attention he sometimes got from women when they were working was nothing new. Ashley had teased him about that since the very first case they'd worked on together.

"Don't even think about giving me a hard time about that," Tim said, grinning at her as they walked outside.

Ashley chuckled but said nothing. He was a player towards women, but he did keep that kind of partying to times when they weren't working on something. She could only respect him for that. He was a handsome guy. Although she held no interest in him romantically, she couldn't deny seeing what other women found so attractive about him. She also couldn't forget that it had come in handy more than once in the investigations they'd worked on together.

Settling into the car, Tim pulled out the paper map, folded neatly so that only the area they were about to visit was visible.

"You're getting better at that paper-holding thing," Ashley teased him, knowing that he had quite a knack for getting anything made of paper into quite a state.

Tim smiled and rolled his eyes. Some days, he felt like he did that quite a bit, but it was in jest. Although they laughed together quite a bit, it never detracted from what they had to figure out. He'd always felt good whenever he was around Ashley. Regardless of her incredible beauty as a woman, she was an outstanding agent. Frequently, he found himself thankful that she was his partner on the job.

"Let's get out of here, smart ass," he said to her, making her laugh and nod.

"Yes, Sir," Ashley replied, continuing to smile before she became serious again. "Right! I don't know what we're looking for, but keep your eyes open. Maybe even look out to the side along this ditch that's running through there."

"Back to the serial killer theory?" Tim asked in surprise. "A copycat trying to do things like Bobby Gee?"

Ashley shrugged her shoulders.

"I don't know," she replied. "I mean, I don't get the feeling that those people are all dead - murdered and lying somewhere exposed or in graves - but until we find them alive, it's something we need to consider."

Tim nodded and turned his head to look out the side of the passenger window. Alternating his view to the ditch to the direct side of the road, with looking further out towards bush and trees, he fought to maintain hope. He didn't know any of the people who appeared to have gone missing. They weren't relatives or friends. He didn't even know anything about them. He knew no names, no ages, no anything. Regardless, he wanted to maintain hope that they were alive, and he and Ashley would find them. To think that so many people could have disappeared without anyone noticing, but then be murdered and dumped somewhere … well, it wasn't something he was prepared to accept yet.

Driving around the few blocks between where they'd sat for breakfast, and the beach that appeared to be growing visibly closer, neither agent saw anything that stood out. There were trees and grass and bushes. Now and then, they saw a park bench with a rubbish bin placed next to it. If there was anything to find there, it wasn't obvious.

"Where to now?" Ashley asked after she pulled over to the side of the road and glanced at him.

"Let's get out and walk around," said Tim. "This might not be the right place to find anything, but let's look anyway."

Ashley nodded and turned off the engine. After getting out of the car, she glanced around. They were in a large park, but there were no other people around.

"Start in that corner and work our way out?" she called out to Tim and saw him nod and begin walking toward her.

"Seems like a good place for someone without a home to sleep out," Tim said as he began using his eyes to work over an imaginary grid of the park.

"You think there might be some homeless here?" Ashley asked and saw him shrug. "Mike Batch was pretty sure there were no more people sleeping on the streets around this area anymore."

"Yeah, but if I were homeless, this isn't a bad spot to spend my days and nights, is it," Tim said.

As he spoke, he pointed out towards the ocean in the distance. From where they were, they couldn't see the shore, but the blue of the water out towards the horizon was invigorating even to just look at.

Slowly, they walked through a structured system of checking the area across the park. There was no more that they found in the exercise, apart from what they'd initially seen.

"Trees, bush, and seats," Tim said finally, as they drew nearer to a short cliff face. "Not even a piece of clothing or a bag to gain any clue from."

Ashley stood beside him and closed her eyes to the sunlight hitting her face. If nothing else, it felt good to be in fresh air, with no sounds around except the wind blowing through the large trees. It was soothing to her. It also served as a reminder that she needed to get out into nature far more often than she had for a long time.

"Well, I'm thinking this isn't the right place to be," Tim said as he turned and looked at her. Seeing her as she was, face upturned toward the sun and her eyes closed, he thought she looked the most serene he'd seen her in a long time. He didn't want to speak again. He didn't want to risk disturbing the moment she was in.

After a long while, Ashley opened her eyes and caught him looking at her. If she were to catch anyone else doing that, she'd think it far too creepy to be comfortable with, but she didn't mind Tim looking at her so intently. Over their time as work partners, they'd had a few moments where he'd begun to express some serious feelings toward her. She'd always dismissed the conversation. She didn't want them to go there. She valued him, she respected him, and she certainly didn't want to risk anything going wrong between them. He was more than a partner. He'd become her friend. That was something she'd always placed huge value on.

"Let's go down there," Tim said, breaking the moment as he pointed towards a track a few meters away from where they stood.

"Okay," Ashley agreed as they both turned and began walking. She dismissed her thoughts of moments earlier. They didn't matter. She and Tim were friends.

CHAPTER 26

Maneuvering the surprisingly steep track that had been etched into the side of the slope where land met sand, Ashley focused on just putting each step safely in front of the last. When her feet finally found the slope even out to more of a flat gradient on the sand, she moved her eyes upwards.

Ahead of them was a long stretch of the white sand they currently stood on. As Ashley turned and looked in the other direction, she was greeted with the same vista. Sand ahead. Sand behind. The beauty of the sight was enhanced by the smell of ocean air and the sound of small waves gently lapping at the edge of the beach.

She glanced at Tim. He'd stopped still and also appeared to be taking in the views in all directions.

"What do you think?" she asked him. When he turned to her and smiled, she felt relief. He'd seemed too serious minutes earlier. His demeanor had changed. Now he looked far more relaxed. That was always a good thing to see.

Tim grinned and moved his head towards the left.

"Let's walk," he said. "If we don't find anything around here, at least this should wake us up and energize us again."

Ashley fell in step beside him. As they walked, they were both silent. The beach seemed endless. She guessed they must have walked a good twenty minutes before she stopped walking and turned her attention out to the water. As she stood and maintained her focus there for a moment, she thought she saw something.

Without thinking, she began walking from where they were on the warm, dry sand, down towards where it was still damp from a recent outgoing tide.

At the water edge, Ashley lifted one hand to shield her eyes from the sunlight as she peered out over the water. Whatever she thought she'd seen, it was no longer visible.

"What is it?" she heard Tim ask from behind her.

Turning to face him, she shrugged her shoulders.

"I thought I saw something out there, but I must have been seeing things," Ashley replied as Tim approached and stood beside her.

"Like what?" Tim asked as he gazed out over the water.

"I don't know," Ashley said, resuming her stare at the blue of the ocean. "Something caught my attention, but I can't see anything out there now. It's kind of weird that we're standing here in brilliant sunshine but lower, at that level out that way, there's a weird fog."

"Yeah, I see it," Tim said, intrigued by it as well. "It looks a bit odd to me too, but then again, I'm no weather expert. Probably just some odd low lying cloud?"

"Maybe," replied Ashley. "Let's walk back along and to the other end of the beach."

"Okay," Tim said as the two of them began to move along the sand again. "To be honest, Ash, I think I've needed this. It feels really good to be out here."

Ashley smiled as she nodded at him. "It does."

Silence ensued as they walked to the point where they saw the track they'd entered the beach from. Walking past it, they continued for another fifteen minutes until they reached an edge.

"There's no getting past that at the moment," Tim said as he looked at the high wall of rocks they'd approached.

"Why would someone have put this here?" Ashley asked. "The white sand is so lovely, but then there's this!"

"It doesn't look manmade," Tim replied as he glanced up at the low lying cliff beside them. "Maybe something loosened that cliff face, and they fell from there."

Ashley looked briefly up over the high pile of rocks and then further still, up to the cliff face. Not seeing anything that even remotely interested her, she turned to look out over the ocean again.

"Wait," she said out loud, prompting Tim to look at her. "There *is* something out there." She turned and faced Tim. "Do you see it?"

Tim saw nothing at first glance. When he focused for a few minutes on the area she seemed to be pointing at, he finally saw something too.

"It looks like a light," he said as something bright flickered across his face. "But it's daylight…"

"No, not a light," said Ashley as she stepped closer to the water edge. "I think it's a mirror or something like that."

Both agents watched, mesmerized. The sharp brightness of whatever it was appeared and then disappeared. They stood together for a long while, watching the lack of pattern that the light flickers seemed to make.

"Is it a boat?" Tim asked. He was captivated by whatever it was. "It looks like it's out on the water, but it doesn't seem to be changing position."

"I don't know," Ashley replied. "Maybe it's something random like a bird has picked up some rubbish that just happens to be reflective."

"Yeah, but what's it sitting on, if that's the case? It's not moving at all."

Ashley looked around. They'd already stood in most parts of the beach and the park overhead.

"We need a different viewpoint," she said. "Do you think we can get over this rock pile, or maybe go along the top of this?"

Tim glanced upwards towards the cliff face again.

"I think we already walked along the top, up there," he said. "That must be part of the park that we covered."

"Yeah. Well, how fit are you feeling?" Ashley asked smiling at him before turning to assess the rock pile again.

Before they could step up to the first tier of rocks that were piled up, they heard a deep male voice call out to them.

"Please don't contemplate that, Special Agents Power and Moore."

Tim and Ashley turned and saw Mike Batch from the Compton Police Station approaching.

"It's not safe," Mike continued. "We'd much prefer everyone stay off this - including you two - for safety."

When he held out his hand, each of the agents shook it. Once again, Ashley found herself experiencing a very distinct dislike for the officer. Just like the day that she and Tim had sat in Mike's office, she had no real reason to not like him. It was purely a gut instinct that told her to do so.

"What brings you out this way today?" she dared to ask him. She knew it was none of her business why Mike Batch was on the beach. Regardless, something egged her on to ask the question.

"I got a call that a couple of people were getting a bit too close to this," Mike replied as he pointed to the rock pile. "Thought I best come down here and make sure you didn't do anything that could cause harm to you or anyone else."

"Thank you," Tim said.

"Perhaps I should ask what the two of *you* are doing out here? Just getting some air?" Mike asked.

"We are," replied Tim as he nodded. "We were just enjoying walking along here. It's a beautiful day."

Ashley listened and found herself surprised. Although she had a bad feeling about the police officer, she didn't think Tim did. She had expected him to ask the officer about the strange light. Instead, what she heard was mild small talk about the weather.

"Well, I won't stop you from doing that," Mike said. "But keep to the other end of the beach, please. This area isn't safe with all this rock falling going on right now."

"Of course," Tim replied as he nodded. "Thank you."

Tim and Ashley watched as the officer walked off, heading back to the path that led down to the beach from the park above.

"I don't know what it is about him..." Ashley began to say.

"Well, whatever it is, I feel it too," said Tim. "Now that he's gone, though," he continued as he looked up at the rock pile again.

"Tim, we can't," Ashley said, grinning. "At least, not in daylight if we've been told to keep away."

"Okay," Tim replied. "How about we go back up there, then, and get a little closer to the edge than we did before? Maybe now that we think something might be out there, we'll see it clearly from up there."

"Yep," replied Ashley as both turned and began to walk towards the sloping path up to the park. "It's kind of a weird coincidence that Mike Batch would turn up here right at the moment when we were about to go over that pile."

"If it *was* a coincidence," Tim replied. "The timing of it was definitely strange."

"You think he knows more about things than he's let on to us?"

"I don't know," Tim replied. "This seeing something flicker in the distance is just a curiosity, though. It's not likely to impact our investigation, whatever it is ... right?"

"I have no idea what *any* of this is tied into, Timmy Boy," Ashley replied, chuckling. "I think I said at the beginning that this could be a wild ride, and it certainly is turning out to be that!"

Once at the top of the path, Tim looked along the edge. With a scattering of shrubs, two garbage bins, and three bench seats, it was easy for him to gauge the point at which they'd walked up to earlier. He wasted no time striding to where the bench seats were situated.

As Ashley walked beside him, she kept turning her head to look out at the water. Whatever it was that she'd seen, it wasn't making itself seen again. It was easy to put it down to a seabird having picked up something that it shouldn't have. People were amazingly good at throwing stuff in the ocean that never should be anywhere near it. Who knew what kind of reflective plastic or metal could have been discarded for some unfortunate bird to pick up.

When Tim reached the seats, he moved forward from them until he could peer over the edge. He wasn't afraid of heights, but he suspected that if he were, he wouldn't have been quite so keen to stand so close to where the land dropped off.

"What do you see?" he heard Ashley ask from behind him.

Glancing back at her, he remembered her once sharing with him that she wasn't too good with looking down from a height. She'd said it was the one aspect of her nature that she wasn't proud of as an agent. On the ground, she'd do anything to apprehend someone if need be. Move the action upwards, and she didn't like how she felt or how she reacted. Despite Tim having reassured her that her fear of heights was hardly a reason for her to feel bad, after a while he'd given up trying to convince her of that. Now they had a healthy understanding that in situations like they were currently in, he'd move forward to do the observing, and she'd stay back to listen to what he said and do some analyzing.

Tim looked out from where he stood, taking time to focus on the water and the area where the fog resided.

"From here, that fog looks more like a ring," he called out to her. "Weird," he mumbled to himself before shifting his gaze to whatever he could see below.

Leaning forward, he moved himself to the left a little, until he could see the rock pile protruding out across the sand. It looked different from above, making him wary of getting too close to the edge if the rocks *had* fallen by themselves to form the wall they made.

"I can see the fallen rocks at this point," he called out to Ashley.

While the rocks were of interest a little, it was when he glanced along the coastline, where they couldn't see from down on the beach, that his interest piqued. Where the waterline pulled in a little way, causing a v-shaped miniature inlet, there were lines leading up sand. The indents in the wet sand looked more manmade than natural, perhaps like a dinghy had been dragged up the beach.

He walked along the top of the cliff face, maintaining focus on where the lines were and which way they led. When he'd walked twenty meters along the top of the land, he looked down and saw the lines disappear, as if underneath the edge.

"What's got your attention, Moore?" Ashley asked, almost catching up to him, but standing back as far as seemed safe. "Something worth mentioning?"

"I'm not sure," Tim replied. "It looks…" he began to say before moving further along the edge, which had turned a little, providing a different angle from which to view the beach. "It looks like there's a cave under there … a place where a boat has been dragged recently."

Ashley was surprised by the level of interest she could hear in Tim's voice. A boat and a cave on a beach? It wasn't something she'd expect to have caught his attention quite so completely.

She watched as he glanced along both directions of the cliff face and the beach. While he did so, she remained quiet, just seeing where he was going with whatever he was thinking.

As Tim surveyed the entire area from where he currently stood, he could see that the small inlet where it looked like a dinghy had been dragged up into, wasn't only cut off by rocks on one side. The rock pile had been duplicated by another one, making it almost impossible for the general public to pass by the inlet from either direction. Assuming it a slim likelihood that two rockfalls had happened that tidily formed walls on either side of where a boat was coming and going, Tim found himself eager to find out how he could get down there.

Looking around, he saw no path or any access way to provide him with an easy way to check out the small inlet area. Not seeing anything, he moved back to where Ashley stood.

"I don't think those rocks did fall by accident," he said to her, his mind still contemplating possibilities. "There's another one that mirrors it. Between them is a place where it looks like a boat can move in and out of a cave down there."

"Do you think it's something we should be looking at?" Ashley asked, not convinced it had anything to do with their search for people.

"I don't know," replied Tim as he looked at her face.

"You've got that 'dog with a bone' look going on," Ashley teased him in the hope that he'd relax a little.

"We both know your gut is usually right, even in the strangest situations we've been in," Tim said and saw her nod in response. "My gut is telling me we should check this out, whatever it is."

"Okay," Ashley said. "How do we get down there, if not over the rocks? Or do you mean to climb over them?"

"Actually, I'm wondering if we can hire a boat somewhere, and just cruise around the coastline instead," Tim replied. "If we do that, we could also cruise out there and see if there is anything there to look at," he continued, pointing out towards the area where they'd seen the shining light, and a low lying fog still hung.

"Okay, let's go see if we can find a boat rental place," Ashley suggested. "This *is* a coastal area. Surely there must be someone around who has a boat we can rent off them. We've only seen the one person in our time out here, making me think this isn't a tourist location, so there might not be a proper boat rental business, but for the right price…"

"For the right price, *someone* will oblige us, I'm sure," Tim finished. "Let's go and sit down on one of those benches, and look online to see if there's anything useful listed close by."

With searches of Internet browsers and map applications not providing any assistance, the two agents sat quietly and just looked out over the water for a long while. No matter where they looked, Tim's eyes kept moving back to the fog he could see.

"How does that not move or dissipate?" he asked out loud before turning to face Ashley. "Fog isn't static. It hangs around for a while, and then it gradually disappears as the air or land temperatures change."

Ashley looked at her watch.

"We've only been here for a couple of hours," she said. "I don't think it's that rare for fog or mist to hang around for that long. It *is* a strange weather kind of day. I can't decide if I'm even warm or not."

"True," Tim replied. "There *is* something odd about the feel of this entire area."

"Come on, Timmy Boy," Ashley said as she rapidly stood up. "Let's go find us a boat."

"Yeah, right after we get lunch. I'm starving," Tim replied in a purposeful attempt to ease the mood.

CHAPTER 27

Jordy again woke from a sound sleep. Trying to think about the day before, he couldn't remember anything except the same moment he was currently having - waking to the morning light. The rest of each day always evaded him when he tried to think about the hours following the first light.

He glanced over at the bed next to him. The first whole day that he'd not seen his room next-bed neighbor, George, had passed. Although Jordy had rejoiced in having gotten an entire night of sleep due to not having heard any of the unbearably loud snoring that George usually subjected him to, now he was just saddened.

In his time in the house, there had been plenty of people who had been regularly in that bed. They'd appear out of nowhere one morning when he woke, and stay a long while. Then, on another morning, they just wouldn't be in their bed, and Jordy would never see them again. Each time it happened, Jordy tried to remember and count how many people he'd seen come and go from that very bed beside his. He had no idea. That he couldn't remember them all was as sad as the fact that they'd left so quietly and unexpectedly.

He didn't know where they went when they just didn't appear again. Not that their disappearance was the most strange thing, of course. He just as equally didn't know where they *appeared* from. Sometimes he wanted to ask, but he couldn't. Something happened to people when they arrived at the house. Not that he ever remembered seeing anyone else, day to day. Only the beds in the room he shared ever revealed others in the structure, and that was only in the morning light.

No, he had no idea where they all came from, however many there had been during his time in the house. Even he couldn't remember. It wasn't from a lack of memory. He could remember everything about his life - everything from before, that was. Was he blessed to be able to remember the life he lived before? He could never make a definitive decision about that. All those memories of the people he'd loved and lost - they were reminders of life in normal times. He constantly swayed on the line of memories making him happy, to memories breaking his heart. Memories provided good times to smile about sometimes, but cry about having lost at other times.

Aside from the people he'd held close in his heart for most of his life, there were the fellow soldiers he'd served with. Thinking about them produced a similar range of emotions. There were good memories about people he'd formed close camaraderie with. Those good memories were challenged at times by remembering what had happened to those people. The sights and sounds of war never left his mind. He'd been lucky to have survived it all. He'd loved coming home after those tours of duty, when he'd known that Missy would be there, ready to greet him and pull her into her loving arms. He hadn't hesitated in leaving the military and trying to focus further on her and their offspring. He'd found some peace in that - living quietly and focusing on the people who mattered the most to him. Then that peace had been shattered.

Remembering Missy, the tears began again. Even with it being long past a decade since she'd been taken from him, the emotion was raw when he thought about her. So much joy, then so much pain. Maybe that was why he'd survived so long where he was. Yes, he was subjected to physical pain every single day. Those precise moments of days did stand out in the haze of lack of memory of anything else. Physical pain was something he'd long ago learned to handle. Physical pain was something he could remove focus from so that it was only in the background of his mind when it was happening. Physical pain had nothing on the pain of emotional scars and how he'd grieved when he'd lost his loving Missy.

Once again, lying in the morning light with his mind alert for the only part of any day that it was, he sighed. One day soon, his body would give out and shut down. One day soon, it would decide that enough was enough and it could take no more. One day.

He'd been saying that - 'one day' - for so long. Was it weeks that had passed? Months?

Jordy Simpson sighed yet again.

He had absolutely no idea that he'd been living exactly the same day, over and over again, for more than a decade.

CHAPTER 28

Back at their motel, Ashley and Tim both changed into more water-friendly clothing before meeting up again at Ashley's car. They'd had trouble trying to find any boat rental business. Not only that, but the people living closest to the coast had seemed remarkably unwilling to provide them with any assistance at all. Fortunately, after driving further down the coastline, they had found someone who didn't seem to regard the request with anywhere near as much open suspicion or annoyance.

"Ready for a sea adventure?" Tim asked as he secured his phone into the waterproof pocket of his jacket.

Ashley nodded and grinned. "Yep! You?"

"Absolutely!" Tim said, smiling back at her.

Starting the engine, Ashley turned to him.

"First time for us to be going on a boat together," she said. "You don't get seasick, do you?"

"Not yet," Tim said, laughing. "Although, to be honest, nothing would surprise me on this adventure."

It was a twenty-minute drive along the coast to the town where they'd located someone willing to help them. Climbing out of the car at their destination, the boat owner came forward with his hand extended.

"Tank's full, and she's ready to go," he said, glancing from one agent to the other. "Now, you are experienced in operating one of these, right? I know you said you are, but..."

"I grew up on the water, Mr. Clair," replied Ashley, smiling at him. "We'll look after her, don't you worry."

The man looked uncertain, but turned and began walking them to where the boat was tied up. Thankful it wasn't a dinghy, Tim wondered what lay ahead for them. The boat was a small motorboat. If they got in trouble, it wasn't likely to help them get out of it in a hurry.

"Climb in, and then I'll release the ropes," Mr. Clair said. Once Tim and Ashley were settled on board, he called out again. "Lifejackets are under those seats," he said and then waited for them to put the items on. Once assured they were going to follow the water safety rules he'd explained to them, he released the ropes. "Good luck. I'll be here when you get back. No more than two hours, you said?"

"No more than two hours, Mr. Clair," Ashley called back. "If we aren't back by then, please let Mike Batch at the Compton Police Station know."

They watched Mr. Clair nod and wave as they moved away from the small dock.

"I can't believe you get to drive *again*," Tim said as he watched Ashley skillfully maneuver the small vessel. "Even a boat? I'll accept this, but when the time comes when we have to fly our own plane, *I'm* in the driver seat!"

"Deal!" Ashley said to him, grinning. The feeling of fresh sea air on her face, and in her tied back hair, was invigorating. When she'd told the boat owner that she'd grown up on the water, she'd meant it. With parents who were both water lovers, she'd been taught at a very young age how to operate sailboats, motorboats, and larger yachts. It was a part of her life that she rarely revisited, but when she did, she was reminded of how incredibly free she always felt when she was on the water.

Tim felt good as they glided across the water. He didn't assume they were going to find anything that was related to finding missing people. Even so, he was glad he and Ashley had the freedom to investigate the small area he'd seen. No matter how far technology advanced, and how much they could research via the Internet and the various devices they were issued with, he never wanted to be just behind a desk. In his opinion, doing that took away all the joy he gained from getting out and exploring the old fashioned way. He loved adventure. It was something that reminded him of his childhood - getting out of the house, and exploring.

Lifting his head and glancing out toward the horizon, he saw the fog that had gained his attention earlier. It was persistent, alright. He supposed that meant nothing. As Ashley had pointed out, sometimes mists and fogs lingered for hours, or even days at a time if the temperature conditions were right for it.

Holding his gaze in that direction, he saw another instance of the same kind of light flickering that he and Ashley had noticed earlier in the day. He watched it happen once, twice, then a third time. In the moments that followed, he wondered if he'd been seeing things. He maintained a view of where it had been, hoping it would happen again so he could define the exact location it was coming from. Nothing more was seen. Whatever it had been, it had stopped.

"I can see the rock pile up ahead, Tim," he heard Ashley say to him as she slowed the boat right down.

Tim refocused and moved close to her.

"Can you get in close to the shore, so we can quietly move around there?"

Ashley nodded. She was silent as she guided the boat around the large pile of rocks that jutted out far enough into the water that even at low tide, it would be impossible for anyone to walk around them. As they moved around the large wall, the cave that Tim had thought he'd seen became more visible.

Ashley turned and looked at him. The level of concentration he maintained was evident on his face. While they often made decisions together, she remained quiet and let him guide their movements. He'd had a gut instinct with regards to the closed-off area of the beach and the cave within it. She was happy to see where that gut instinct led them.

Tim watched the vista change from just beach, shore, and cliffs, to the rock pile and then to the inlet. Looking up the small waterway that was filling slowly from the tide coming in, he was glad to see he'd been right in thinking there was a cave there - not only that, but he could see a dinghy well inside of it.

Seeing one sole post sticking up out of the sand close to the cave, Tim pointed at it.

"Can we tie up to that?"

Ashley nodded and moved the boat as close to the shore as she could. Grabbing the line that had been flung into the boat, she jumped out, ran up, and secured it with a well-practiced bowline. As Tim approached her, she felt a glare hit her eye. Looking out over the sea in the hope that she'd see it again, she wasn't surprised to not do so. Whatever it was, it wasn't consistent. It was, however, definitely *something*.

"Did you just see it again?" Tim asked, prompting her to nod. "Me too, when we were in the boat. I don't think we're seeing things, and I don't think it's a seabird that's picked up a random bit of rubbish out there."

"Well, let's look around here. When we leave, we'll cruise out there and check it out," Ashley replied, turning back to face the cave.

Tim nodded. "Okay."

As they approached the cave entrance, both agents looked around the rock formations that were visible on the exterior and interior.

"Wow, this is amazing," Ashley said quietly. "We really need to get into nature more often."

Tim smiled at her but continued his journey inwards, hopeful that something of interest awaited them.

CHAPTER 29

Although, from the outside, it looked large enough for someone to walk into, both agents had expected that the cave would be fairly small on the inside. Upon first entering the formation, that was what they thought the cave was like. It was well-shaped for humans to walk into, but they could see the back of it only a few meters in front of them. Thinking that was all there was, they turned when they reached the back wall. That was when something caught Tim's eye out to the left of them.

"What?" Ashley asked when she saw him deviate from their return to the outside.

"Light," Tim said cryptically as he moved toward what he could now see was a gap in the wall of the cave. Moving further towards it, he saw the gap widen.

Making sure Ashley was close behind him, he continued to walk toward the small glimmer of light. To his surprise, it led him to the edge of one wall, forcing him to peer around a corner just as if he were in a supermarket, moving around from one aisle to the next. As he turned the corner, he realized the cave they'd entered was one of two. The second one was much larger.

For a moment, he stopped and listened. There was light coming from further in, illuminating the larger space. As yet, he had no idea if it was natural light seeping from somewhere, or a manmade light, indicating someone might be inside. Hearing nothing from within, he continued his journey with Ashley close behind.

As they fully entered the middle of the large, open

space, both stopped to look around. Whatever it had been used for, it had definitely been *actively* used for. Around the edges, high up on what looked like natural rock ledges, were a diverse range of old wooden crates. Tipped on their sides, it was easy to see that they were currently empty, but their appearance suggested they hadn't been there for too long. They looked old and well used, but new to their current environment.

Tim and Ashley walked around for a while, taking in all that they could see while remaining mindful of the water level.

"The tide's coming in, Tim," Ashley said before they moved right through to the rear of the new cave. "We don't want to get caught."

"Okay," Tim said in response as he began walking quickly toward the furthest wall. "I'll just check back here, and then we'll go."

Ashley followed him, remaining a meter behind him until he seemed to disappear. Staring at a blank, black wall, it momentarily confused her until she saw his head pop back, indicating there was another wall to walk around.

When both agents were on the other side of that, they were surprised. Ahead of them was another large open space. This time, there was nothing natural or cave-like about it. What they had walked into looked more like a warehouse, complete with one lamp lit dimly.

"What *is* this place?" Ashley asked as she moved to stand beside Tim.

"I don't know, but look," said Tim as he pointed ahead of them. "There's a vehicle entrance and what looks like a road leading out of here."

"We never saw anything that looked like this from the outside," Ashley said.

"No, we didn't," Tim replied as he pulled out his phone. "But one thing my maps app is good for, is being able to record GPS coordinates."

Opening up the app, he was relieved to find that regardless of where they might be - inside a warehouse or a cave - the GPS seemed able to identify where they were. Quickly, he saved their current location and then turned to Ashley.

"Let's get out of here while the tide's going to let us," he said, seeing her nod in response before turning and walking back the way they'd come.

Once they'd retraced their steps and were out on the sand once more, it was a relief to see the boat still where they'd left it, securely attached to the post. After a few minutes of letting their eyes adjust again, Ashley turned to Tim.

"This tide is turning fast," she said, noticing how much higher into the cave the water was reaching, compared to where it had been only minutes earlier. "Let's go."

Back in the boat and moving away from the shore, Tim glanced at the cave structure again. Somewhere in there was a larger manmade structure. Pulling out his phone, he once again recorded their GPS location. In case the first one had been incorrectly noted from inside, he, at least, could visualize where that larger structure was in relation to the cave entrance. That would provide a double layer of assistance in finding the other side of it later on.

"I can't see that flickering anymore," Ashley said to him. "Can you?"

Tim moved beside her and looked out into the distance. Shaking his head, he wondered again if they'd each just been seeing things.

"No," he replied. "But that fog is still over there. Can we move a little closer to that, perhaps?"

"Yep," Ashley confirmed and immediately began directing the boat in that direction. "We need to keep an eye on the time too. The last thing we want is Mike Batch coming to tell us off again."

"Noted," Tim replied as he looked at his watch. "We've still got another hour yet before we need to have the boat back."

Well clear of the area where the rock piles and cave had been, Ashley increased the boat's speed, moving in a straight line toward where the layer of fog appeared to be. Looking back at shore, she gauged where they were at with regard to the location they needed to return the boat when they were finished.

"Is it my imagination, or is that fog cloud moving away from us?" she heard Tim ask.

"It does sometimes seem like things are never getting any closer out here on the sea," Ashley said, smiling. "We are getting closer, but it is further out than it had seemed when we saw it from the shore."

Watching where the fog appeared to be positioned, Ashley saw what she'd hoped to - the flickering of either a light, or something reflecting light.

"There!" she exclaimed, seizing Tim's attention. "See it?"

"Yep," Tim confirmed in wonder.

"We can't both be seeing things," Ashley said, her curiosity only growing stronger.

"No, I think that's real, whatever it is."

"Time till we need to be back on shore?" Ashley asked, aware that time on the water sometimes seemed longer or shorter than reality.

"Forty-five minutes," Tim replied, glancing at his watch again.

"Okay, set your alarm for fifteen minutes," said Ashley. "Fifteen more minutes of heading out this way, and then I'm going to turn us around and go straight back to return this baby."

Tim nodded and did what she'd instructed.

"Noted."

CHAPTER 30

Not expecting to reach the thick fog within the timeframe she'd set, Ashley was surprised to find them entering it a few minutes ahead of her anticipated turnaround time. She'd encountered fog up close many times when driving at heights, but what they were currently in felt different.

"It's so thick," she said out loud as they first passed underneath and into it. "I don't think I've seen anything like this before."

Tim agreed. If he'd found any of the towns they'd visited creepy, that was nothing to how he was feeling upon approach into the fog.

"I'm slowing right down so I can focus on making sure we're not going to hit anything," Ashley said. "Can you look out for the light, Tim?"

"Yep," he replied, distracted by the eeriness of their location.

Focusing on looking above and around them, he couldn't see the light again. If it was out in the thickness, it wasn't visible from their current viewpoint.

"Whoa!" he heard Ashley exclaim, prompting him to quickly shift his gaze from the fog above to her.

"What?" he questioned, concerned.

He saw her nod and point ahead of them. Just under the fog layer, they could see a shore. It wasn't a beach. There was no sand. All they could see were rocks, not unlike the ones that they'd experienced back at the coastline earlier.

"Land," Ashley said. "Tim, there's something here."

Tim saw it. He knew there was no point in dragging out his phone again and looking at the maps app on it. While he hadn't been looking for an island, he was pretty sure he would have noticed if one had shown up when he had looked at the immediate area on there.

With great care, Ashley edged in as close as she could while watching for rocks at a dangerous depth in the water below. Once she'd moved as far forward as she dared, she stopped and looked up. Through the gap in the fog, she found herself looking at a tall cliff face. When she sensed Tim move so close to her that their arms touched, she felt secure. There was something incredibly uncomfortable about where they were physically located. Having him so close provided reassurance that she wasn't alone in the experience.

"Now *that* is a surprise," Tim said quietly, peering upwards. "Even if we had the time..."

"Which we don't," Ashley said, cutting him off.

"Which we don't ... there's no way we could get up there," he finished, looking to the left and the right in the hope that there might be a gentler slope nearby. "I think we'd need to cruise right around this if we were wanting to find a way up there."

Ashley looked at his face. It wasn't difficult to see the level of excitement on it. It was good to see. After having watched him seem increasingly inanimate in his enthusiasm since beginning work on the case, seeing him express some boyish excitement at a new discovery was welcome.

Sensing her looking at him, Tim turned and returned the glance.

"We could come back tomorrow?" he asked as a suggestion before doing another GPS coordinate save.

Ashley nodded. "Yeah, let's do that. For now, though, we have to get this back to its owner. Hopefully, he won't have any problem with us hiring it again."

CHAPTER 31

After returning the boat and arranging to pick it up and take it out again early the following day, Tim and Ashley made their way back to the car. Once settled inside with the heater running to warm themselves up, Tim pulled out his phone.

"Let's see what all these coordinates show," he said as the screen leaped into life. "That island ... nothing. The inlet that we entered and left that cave on ... is showing as a normal section of the coastline." He paused for a long while, looking down at the screen and saying nothing. "That structure that looked like it was a warehouse ... *that*, I think, we can pass by on our way back to the motel."

Ashley nodded and started the engine.

"Direct me," she said before veering the car out of the park.

Fifteen minutes later, Tim spoke as he looked up from the map on his phone.

"Can you pull over up here, Ash?" he asked, prompting her to nod and do so. "Let's get out here and have a wander around."

Once out of the car, Tim alternated his glance from the screen, to the land they were walking on. Stumped by not finding anything obvious, he stopped walking and looked at Ashley.

"It should be right here," he said as he pointed to the ground at his feet. "Or close by, anyway."

Ashley looked around. A small hill nearby caught her eye. Instinctively, she began to walk toward it, then up and over it. When she reached the far side of it, she noticed the vehicle tracks looking like they entered the growth. They were faint, like they hadn't been made recently, but there was no denying they were a double track of some kind of vehicle.

"Here," she called out to Tim. When he reached where she was standing, she pointed to the ground. "Something's been here, although not for a long time by the looks of it."

"But…" Tim started to say as he followed the faint tracks forward. "There's nothing here."

Suspecting there was more to be seen than the obvious, he began moving his feet around in the plant cover over the ground. Eventually, the action of his feet was replaced by him kneeling and using his hands. After some time, he found what made more sense.

As his hand met metal, he carefully felt around, taking care not to disturb the area so much that it would be obvious they'd been there. His fingers moved around what appeared to be a large circular handle. When he was sure that's what it was, he pulled it gently. As soon as he did, the earth and plant cover shifted.

"It's a door," he said, surprise evident in his tone.

"Weird angle," replied Ashley as she watched his movements.

"Yeah, it seems to open up on this angle, like a storm bunker," Tim said, turning to look at her. "If we open it now, we'll disturb it. Someone'll know we've been here."

"Well, it's going to begin getting dark soon," Ashley said. "We can either dismiss this till daylight, or take advantage of the darkness."

Tim grinned. It was enough to show Ashley what she'd suspected. Of course he'd prefer to get straight onto it. He was on an adventure that he'd not experienced before.

"Okay," Ashley said. "Let's go get some food and then come back after sundown."

CHAPTER 32

Sitting in a small restaurant, eating their meals, Tim and Ashley talked about their day and their plan.

"It feels like we've veered completely away from what we were assigned to do, doesn't it?" Ashley said. "I haven't even thought about Jordan Simpson today."

"Yeah, we probably don't need to hang around here for long," Tim said. "I am intrigued by that warehouse behind the cave, though, and the island."

"You checked the online maps again?" Ashley asked and saw him nod. "No sign of that island at all?"

"Nope," Tim said. "There's nothing on this," he said, holding up his phone. "The paper map doesn't show anything there either."

"Well, maybe it's relatively new. I mean, islands can be created by volcanic activity underneath the water?"

Tim shrugged his shoulders.

"I have no idea," he said. "It's weird, though, that nobody seems to be mentioning the island or the fog. Mike Batch was there on the beach with us. He must have been able to see the fog, but it didn't seem to have his attention at all. Down the coast, the boat owner didn't ask what we were hoping to see, or suggest going to visit an island..."

"Maybe he isn't aware of it," Ashley replied. "He's a distance away from here. Even if he is a real boatie, it's possible his outings on the boat take him in the other direction, further down the coast instead of up this way."

Tim nodded but decided to keep an open mind on that point. Increasingly, it felt like people they interacted with knew far more than they let on through their conversation.

"Hopefully, Sarah will report back to us soon with something useful that the team looking at Kerr and Pioneer have found out," said Ashley. "When that one piece falls into place, Tim…"

"Yeah, I know," he replied. "For now, we have to decide what we're willing to do tonight. If that large door opens, all the growth over it will be disturbed. There's a chance someone will see us there."

"It's a dangerous thing to do," Ashley replied, nodding. "And it's like a secret part of that entire park area. Does that mean it's open to the public, or is it something we're going to need a warrant for?"

"It's location would indicate to me that it's part of public property," Tim said, scoffing. "How would you view it?" he asked, emanating an air of suggestion.

Ashley smiled but didn't answer the question. In their line of work, they knew what they were supposed to do - and *not* supposed to do. The line they sometimes stood on in decision-making, definitely became a hazy grey between the extremes of black and white.

"Anyway, maybe it will be nothing," Tim said quietly, his face serious again. "We've seen the warehouse from the inside. Will opening the doors from the outside tell us anything new?"

"We didn't stay very long inside there. It was only a few minutes that we had to look around before we had to leave because of the incoming tide," Ashley said. "There might be something of interest in there, or there might not be. Only one way to find out."

Sitting in silence as they finished their meals and second cups of coffee, both agents thought about where their investigation had led them so far, and where it might be taking them. Both knew there was a very high chance they were going off on a tangent that was completely unrelated to finding any missing people.

CHAPTER 33

Easing the car as far back into the park area as she could, Ashley turned off the engine and sat silent, listening and looking around to see if anyone was in the area. She'd judged they were approximately twenty meters away from where the earth mound was located. They hadn't seen anyone in the park during the day. There was no reason to suspect anyone would be there at night. Even so, as always, she wanted them to both be sure about what they were doing.

"Are you sure you want to do this, Ash? I can go in there alone…"

She looked at him with mock annoyance.

"Of course I'm coming in," she replied in a whisper. "Let's go."

Both of them opened and quietly closed their car door before beginning to walk over the vast area of grass. They were confident in the direction they were walking, but surprised when they saw that not only was there someone ahead of them, close to where the earth mound was located, but that person was opening the door.

Crouching down behind one of the bushes, Tim and Ashley watched on. From their angle, they couldn't see fully what was going on, but the sound of not one but two large metal doors opening and being folded back to reveal the opening was easily identifiable. Following that, they heard footsteps move across the grass and then become more pronounced as they appeared to continue inside the structure and contribute to a slight echo.

Remaining where they were for the moment, Ashley

and Tim continued to look and listen. Footsteps retreated out of the structure and back to the person's vehicle. There followed the sound of someone opening a vehicle door, shuffling around in doing something Tim and Ashley couldn't see, before closing the vehicle door softly and walking back into the structure. The process repeated three times before Tim couldn't stay still any longer.

Silently signaling to Ashley that he wanted them to move to a better angle so they could see what was happening, he waited until the person had moved inside the structure again. Tim then moved around the bush and crouched once more with Ashley close behind him.

Once settled in a position they could see the doors clearly from, they waited. A small amount of light emanated from within the structure, but the angle they were on didn't quite provide them with a view inside. With reluctance, Tim remained still, waiting to see what was going on.

Within a few minutes, the person they'd heard was more visible. It was a man dressed all in black, including a black woolen hat. He moved quickly but quietly to the back of what the agents could now see was a small van. Opening the door, he grabbed three large boxes, closed the van door, and then carried the goods inside. Ashley and Tim saw him do it again and again.

After he'd made ten or so trips back and forth, the man gently closed the large metal doors. Time was spent resurrecting the foliage to look as though it hadn't been disturbed. Finally, the man jumped into the van and quietly reversed from where he'd parked.

Tim and Ashley remained still for a long while, not wanting to move in case the man came back or another van turned up. When they were satisfied that it didn't seem like anyone was going to drive in again, they moved.

"Well, I guess nobody is going to notice if we disturb

all of this since that person already moved it and put it back," Tim said as he approached where he knew the doors were located. "Let's move this stuff."

After a couple of minutes, the large doors were clear to see. Initially surprised that there appeared to be no lock on the doors, Tim pulled one door open. From his viewpoint, once he turned on his phone torch, he could see a ramp winding down and around with only the slightest gradient. Without hesitation, he stepped inside the doorway and waited for Ashley to move beside him. When they were sure nobody else was inside, they eased the door almost closed.

Both agents took a long moment to look around, taking in whatever detail they could. The boxes were what captured Tim's attention. He wasted no more time assessing the wider area, instead choosing to move straight to them. He'd worked on drug trafficking cases in the past. If something like that was going on, it wouldn't be a waste of time investigating that, even if it had nothing to do with the case they'd been assigned.

"Looks like food," Ashley said as she gently prised open one large carton. "*Lots* of food."

Tim read the label of another.

"Medical supplies," he said as he opened the top. "Syringes, bandages … what could all this be for?"

Ashley moved away from the boxes. On one wall was waist-height shelving with a range of items inside of it. Above it was a large pin board with papers all over it. She used her torch to begin studying more closely the writing and documents.

"Tim?" she called out to get his attention. "Come and look at this."

When Tim walked over and saw the pages, he wasn't sure what she was pointing out.

"This," she finally said as her finger moved to one page in particular, and she began reading what was written on it. "April 12th, 2009. One hundred in. Twenty down. Compton," she read out.

Tim saw the details and continued with the next line.

"April 4th, 2010. Eighty in. Twenty down. Pioneer." He stopped reading and turned to Ashley. "This is it. This is what we've been looking for. Look here: March 23rd, 2008. One hundred and eight in. Twenty down. Kerr. April 8th, 2007. Seventy in. Twenty down. Guthrie."

"The list goes on, back not only ten years," Ashley said as her finger ran up the page. "This list alone goes back to the start of the millennium."

Tim flicked the page up and saw another one underneath.

"And twenty years before that," he said as he quickly scanned the page. "This isn't just confined to what we've found out so far. This is bigger ... *much* bigger." He paused as he touched his phone screen. "Keep your torch shining on the page, and I'll take photos of these and send them back to the team at headquarters. Maybe they can identify something about them that we can continue from."

After photographing pages from the pinboard on the wall, the two agents walked around further. In the distance, they could see the entrance they'd entered previously from the caves. Nothing on that side of the structure looked changed since they'd been there earlier. The only addition was the boxes of food that had just been dropped off.

"What is this for?" Ashley pondered out loud.

"I don't know, but if those numbers are what they look like, all of this might have something to do with our missing homeless populations after all," replied Tim.

"The food is for them? The homeless?" Ashley wondered. "That would be a good sign. It'd mean that they're still alive somewhere."

"We need to touch base with Sarah, but let's not do it here. Who knows if these guys are bringing another load here tonight. I'd rather not be here if they do," said Tim.

Ashley nodded. "Let's go then."

Outside, they took their time to cover the closed doors to make them look like they had when they'd arrived. No other vehicle came. No people were heard. It was peaceful as Ashley and Tim walked back to the car, climbed in, and slowly edged their way out of the park altogether.

On the drive back to the hotel, both remained silent. It wasn't until they had both gone into Ashley's room that they sensed something was wrong and spoke.

"Someone's been in here," Ashley said, glancing around.

"You mean, other than the cleaning maid? You sure?" asked Tim, prompting Ashley to nod.

"Yeah," she said, looking as she looked closer at the safe. "Someone's tried to open it. Those marks weren't on it when I secured our documents this morning."

Tim moved closer and looked at the small metal box inside the wardrobe.

"Better see if they were successful," Tim said before watching Ashley key in the code she'd set.

When she opened the safe door, Ashley half expected that all of their documents would have been missing. She was relieved to see that everything was there.

"Nothing's been taken," she said. "All of the police reports are here, and the maps and Kate's journal."

"What were they looking for then?" Tim asked.

"I don't know, but maybe you should go and check your room too," Ashley suggested, prompting Tim to stand and walk toward the door.

"Not without you," he said. "If someone's come into our rooms, they could do it again. Secure that, and stay with me while I check my room out."

Although it was instinctual for Ashley to reject any man subtly implying she was a woman and needed protection, she fought it. He was right. If someone had the desire and ability to get into their rooms, there was no arguing that such a person could either still be in one of the rooms, lying in wait, or intending to come back.

A check of Tim's room, his safe, and his belongings indicated his room had also been visited.

"Nothing's been taken here either," he said after checking.

"It might not be just us," Ashley said. "Someone might have gone through all the rooms here today, looking just for cash or something."

"True," replied Tim as he nodded. "Alright. I'd still feel better knowing you aren't alone tonight."

Ashley looked at him and smiled.

"How about we compromise? You walk me back to my room, see me inside, and wait outside until I've deadbolted the door and put the table in front of it. Then you come back here, deadbolt *your* door, put *that* table in front of it, and then text me to let me know you're as safe as I am."

"Okay," Tim agreed. It didn't fully put him at ease, but it was all he could do at that moment. The thought of anyone hurting his partner wasn't something he could bear the thought of, but in that, he knew he might be a bit overprotective when he didn't need to be. If anyone could take care of themselves, it was Special Agent Ashley Power.

After both of them had walked back to her room, Tim said goodnight and waited at the door until he heard what he needed to hear. As he walked back to his room, he became aware of feeling like he was being watched. Since embarking on their current investigation, he'd felt it far more often than he normally would. Regardless of how the hairs on the back of his neck were reacting to it, he concentrated on looking normal as he entered his room, locked and secured the door, and did a thorough check. He was very relieved as he messaged Ashley to tell her he was also secure in his room.

CHAPTER 34

"How did you sleep?" Ashley asked him the following morning when they met up by the car. "I, personally, had a really good sleep … eventually. I have to admit, though, I was a bit on edge after seeing someone had been in the room and tried to access the safe."

"Yeah, I stayed awake for ages too," Tim said as they climbed in. "Maybe it is like you said - someone just wanted quick cash or something. At least everything of value is in the safe. I thought about the idea of us bringing everything in the car, but we're going to be leaving it for so long while we're out in the boat, that we wouldn't be able to watch it in here either."

"True," Ashley agreed. "It'll be okay, though. There's not really anything that valuable inside the safes. It's only the pages provided to us by the different places. And we're armed. They'd be crazy to try and take us on, whoever *they* are."

"Big breakfast first then?" Tim asked, breaking the seriousness. "We're going on quite the adventure, visiting a remote island. We'll need all our strength."

"Not quite a remote island, but yes, let's anticipate being out on the water for a couple of hours, at least," Ashley said, smiling as she veered out of the carpark. "What do you want to do about the island? And the warehouse? It's possible those two things are related. You said you saw dinghy marks going up the shore towards the caves, which in turn lead to the warehouse."

"Yeah, I'm starting to think that all this isn't some weird coincidence at all. I really do believe that this is all tied in together - people disappearing; the warehouse where food was delivered and those pages of dates were found; the caves and boat; and the island."

He didn't need to say specifically what he'd come to believe. The look Ashley gave told him she understood what he was saying.

"If they're on that island, we need to think carefully before just you and I go onto it," Ashley said. "Do you think we should call for backup to help with this?"

Tim considered the possibility. There was still so much that they didn't know. Although pieces seemed to fit together, he conceded that they could be entirely on the wrong path to finding even just one of the missing persons.

"I think we should go out for a lovely cruise on the water on this sunny day," Tim said. "That's all it is ... a relaxing cruise before we wrap up our investigation."

Although he was talking only to her and nobody could hear anyway, Ashley understood he was preparing both of them for any questions that might flow their way.

Having seen someone delivering the goods to the hidden warehouse, there was a good chance that someone else was going to pick them up and take them somewhere. It could be crazy to assume so, but Tim thought it likely that the items were going to be taken over to the island. If that was to happen any day, he didn't want him and Ashley to be seen as asking any pointed questions about the hidden space under the park.

"Alright," said Ashley as she pulled into the diner carpark. "Let's eat and then go and enjoy some fresh sea air."

CHAPTER 35

Arriving at the small dock, Tim and Ashley were greeted by the boat owner. Although he extended his hand to them and spoke as though he were happy to still rent them his boat, they couldn't help but notice he seemed far more nervous than he had the day before. Neither agent questioned him about it, but both did notice it.

When they were putting on their lifejackets and about to take the boat out, they were greeted by a familiar voice.

"Special Agents Power and Moore," Mike Batch said as he approached them. "Where are you heading off to today?"

"Before we wrap up our investigation, we are going to enjoy some of your lovely coastline," Tim replied while Ashley remained quiet. "This kind gentleman is lending us his boat, and it is a perfect day for it, according to my captain here," he said, smiling towards Ashley.

"Be careful out there," Mike said to each of the agents. "Looks like a storm is coming in."

Neither agent replied, only nodding in response. It was an odd thing for him to have said. Ashley, having a boating background in her younger years, could see no hint of any storm approaching.

After speaking, the officer simply walked off.

"I don't see any storm coming," the boat owner said. "But do take heed of his warning. Be careful."

The words were cryptic and yet seemed to hold a very strong caution in them.

"We will," Ashley said as she smiled at him. "Thank you."

"There's enough gas in the tank for you to be able to be out, with the engine running, for a few hours," the owner said. "Best to not have her running for more than two out, though, then start heading back before she runs out."

"Right! Got it," said Ashley.

While she and Tim walked down to the boat and prepared to leave, she was aware that the owner was watching them. It was to be expected that he would, but the intensity of his stare was more than a little bit unnerving.

As fast as she could, Ashley readied the boat. Soon, they were on their way. To support their claim that it was a quiet sunny day cruise, she veered the boat to look like they were going to stay close to shore. She waited until they were well clear and out of sight before she turned the vessel and began moving them outwards rather than along the coast.

"That fog is still there," Tim said as he glanced to where he believed the island was. "It doesn't look like it's even moved, let alone dissipated."

Ashley looked to where he was nodding. She agreed. It was a strange cloud of fog that just sat in the one place for two days.

"Maybe it's normal for this part of the country," she said. "Nobody else has even mentioned it, so it can't be an isolated occurrence."

"True," Tim replied, nodding. "Then again, every time I speak to anyone at the moment, I feel like they know far more than they're mentioning."

"There was definitely a weird vibe going on back at the dock," said Ashley. "The timing of that happening and then Mike Batch turning up might not be a coincidence."

"I agree," said Tim. "I know he's law enforcement,

but every time we have an interaction with that guy, something seems off about him."

Ashley resumed focus on where she was maneuvering the boat to. She'd managed to move around the side of the fog, and then out to the ocean side of it. Admittedly, it was an approximation only. Truth be told, when they'd entered the foggy area, she had lost all sense of direction. Glancing back toward the rear of the boat, she expected to see the coast they'd left behind. Wherever it lay, it wasn't able to be seen at all.

Tim alternated between looking inwards towards where he anticipated the landmass would be, and looking at Ashley's face. He could read her concern. It wasn't enough for him to question, choosing to leave her to concentrate on what she was doing.

As he looked through the fog, he found himself increasingly anxious. It wasn't a feeling he was new to, but he was fortunate to rarely experience it. He considered himself a realist. In his opinion, there was no such thing as spirits or paranormal. As he felt his body respond to the sense of unknowing that came from being in the thick fog, he had to fight thoughts that conflicted with his beliefs. If ever he'd been to a place that might make him think there was something unearthly or paranormal happening, he was currently in it.

To break his discomfort, he focused on his partner again. Her face revealed a certain level of discomfort also.

Sensing him watching her, Ashley turned to face him.

"Are you alright?" she asked, glad to shift her focus to him, and away from the confusion that she was starting to feel in her sense of direction.

Tim nodded and delivered a half-smile. It was the best he could do, given the way his heartbeat was beginning to increase in tempo.

"Yeah, but I don't like this place," he said in complete honesty.

"Me neither," replied Ashley. "I keep thinking we should see the land any minute, but it feels like hours that we've been roaming around here ... doesn't it?"

"It does," Tim said before looking at his watch. "It's only been ... wait," he continued and then *really* looked at his watch. "My watch has stopped, but my phone..." he said as he pulled his mobile out of his pocket. "It's only been half an hour," he added, relieved that his phone was even still working.

For a fleeting moment, he'd thought about all the movies and TV shows he'd seen where an electromagnetic pulse had been emitted, shutting down everything electrical. That the thought of such a thing happening had even crossed his mind showed him just how stressed and anxious he was becoming.

"Huh," Ashley said, sure it felt like much longer. "Okay, well, we have to find *something* in this fog. An entire island didn't just disappear," she continued before pausing for a long while, turning the boat. "I'm putting us at 90 degrees to where we just were. In theory, we should now be heading straight towards that island."

Even as she spoke the words, she felt confusion wash over her again. There was no denying that the fog was having an effect on her. She hoped the island would appear before them. She *believed* there was a good chance that they would end up just out on the sea once they got away from the fog.

"Okay," Tim replied, breaking her out of her thoughts.

Both remained silent as the boat continued forward. It seemed a long shot that they would find the landmass they'd seen the day before. Both knew that was the case. The fog had seemed thick enough the day before. Now, it seemed almost impossible to see anything at all. If they'd gotten turned around, it would be understandable. Anyone could get lost in the thickness of it.

Then they saw rocks.

CHAPTER 36

Ashley felt relieved as a shore appeared in front of her. Looking at the rocks they could see, she knew she and Tim weren't in the same spot as they had been the day before. Regardless, it was obvious that the cliff face before them *was* just as steep as the slice of it they'd previously seen.

As soon as the vertical landmass appeared in front of the boat, Tim came and stood close to her once more. It was his way of allowing each of them to gather strength from the other. He liked her leaning on him now and then for support. He equally liked her being there for him.

Fighting to maintain a sound level of concentration, Ashley carefully and slowly turned the boat.

"Take note of this spot, Tim," she said, pointing at the rocks and cliff face. "If you start the stopwatch on your phone, we can work out how long it takes for us to cruise around the entire island."

"And that'll tell us … the size of it?" he asked.

"Only approximately," Ashley replied. "I'm going to try to keep us at a steady speed. Maybe that'll give us a clue."

"Okay," Tim said as he began his phone's stopwatch application running. Before they moved too far, he took a photo of one particular group of rocks that he also committed to memory.

Letting the boat pick up pace to a steady speed, Ashley kept the cliff face to her right as she moved them forward. It was her sole focus, knowing that Tim would be looking and taking note of anything significant.

Again, time seemed to slow down. It felt like an incredible length of time that she was seeing almost the same view. Wherever the actual shore was, it seemed to elude them. Regardless of how far forward the boat moved, the cliff remained just as high.

"That's it, Ash," she heard Tim say loudly. When she looked at him, she saw him pointing at a rock formation. "We've been around the entire island."

Ashley watched him as he swiped his phone screen.

"That can't be right," she said, even more confused. "We've been around the whole thing?"

"Yep," said Tim, bringing up on his phone screen the photo of rocks he'd taken earlier. "That is that," he said, pointing from the screen to the rocks in front of them.

"But we didn't see anything other than this cliff," Ashley said, her tone making her confusion evident to Tim. Seeing him nod, she continued. "Well, how long was that?"

"Twenty-two minutes," Tim replied. "Seemed like much longer to me…"

"Yeah!" Ashley exclaimed. "But, well, all that's here is cliff face, so I'm guessing there's nothing else to see."

Tim slowly shaking his head surprised her.

"Not so, Special Agent Power," he said, pointing behind them to the far right of the cliff face. "Look."

Following his instruction, Ashley looked up to the top of the cliff. It was mostly hidden by the angle of the cliff face but there was no doubting that high up, on top of the island, was a large house that looked like it had stood there for centuries. Not all of it could be seen, but the roofline indicated its size, while the large, double-hung sash windows indicated its age.

Ashley assumed it was a house that would likely have been long ago abandoned until she saw the thick smoke - not unlike the fog they'd been traveling in - flowing from both of the large brick chimneys.

CHAPTER 37

As both agents stood and looked up at the fog-like smoke flowing out of the chimney structures, what followed that held their attention was the reflecting light that was flickering now and then through one of the windows.

Standing a little taller in the hope that he'd see better, Tim noticed then that the windows of the home were boarded up. He hadn't noticed earlier, with the way that the fog reflected on the glass, but there was no doubt. It was odd that the wooden boards seemed to have been installed on the inside of the windows, but each of the windows he could see from their limited viewpoint was covered over. Despite that, there was still a flickering glare visible. It showed itself only periodically, like someone was purposely trying to do it while trying not to be *seen* doing it.

"That's where the flickering light or reflection is coming from, which is kind of weird since it feels so gloomy inside this mask of fog. I'm thinking it can't be a reflection of sunlight, like we'd thought," he said as he shifted his gaze from the chimneys to Ashley. "I can't see anything else up there from here. Just this weird fog that looks like it's coming from up there - manmade, maybe? Fog? I swear this investigation is getting weirder by the hour."

Ashley couldn't object to that statement. They'd started out looking for one person. It was beginning to feel as though they'd stepped into a fiction novel.

"We can't get up there by ourselves, and even if we

could, I think we need backup for investigating that," she said. "We don't know who or what is up there, or even if it has anything to do with *anything*."

"Okay. I'll log these coordinates, just in case they're handy later," he said, as he pulled out his phone then glanced at her. "We need to get the boat back, right?"

"Yep," said Ashley, relieved that they were going to be leaving. "Let's get the hell out of here."

Although she'd expected them to appear out of the fog, facing the shore, she wasn't surprised when the vista she was presented with upon exiting was actually the ocean. Something about the fog had seriously played with her sense of direction. It confused her. She'd sailed in mists and fogs before. Even without sight, she usually had some sense of direction.

"Thank God!" she heard Tim exclaim next to her. "Geez, that is one dreary and eerie place, in there. This, I like the look of much better," he continued as he opened his arms wide, indicating the sea ahead.

Ashley relaxed and smiled. He was right. It *was* good to leave the ominous feeling of the fog behind. Now she had to wonder whether it *was* a fog or something else. Whether man-produced or something natural, it certainly didn't seem to be going anywhere.

Finally getting her bearings again, she turned the boat to begin veering around the outside of the fog. After a long period of silence between her and Tim, both agents saw coastline that they could recognize.

Ashley wasted no time in following the route back to the coast and then along to where the boat owner resided. After docking and securing the boat, she saw the owner walk out towards them.

"Good cruise?" he asked, his face smiling even though his eyes revealed the same nervousness Ashley and Tim had observed earlier.

"It was really nice out there," she said, smiling to try and relax him. "Thank you so much for letting us use your boat over these two days. It really has been greatly appreciated. I do miss being out on the water. It's been good for clearing my head."

She watched the boat owner as he nodded.

"You won't be needing this again then?" he asked, his voice betraying what sounded like an urgency for them to leave and never come back.

"No," Ashley replied. "Thank you, but we'll be heading back home soon."

Once again, the boat owner nodded. He expressed no words, but Ashley thought his face began to look far more relaxed as soon as she reassured him she and Tim would be leaving.

After their goodbyes, the two agents began walking back to their car. It wasn't until they were inside, heater once again on, that they truly began to relax.

"Backup?" Ashley asked as she rubbed her hands together to warm up more.

"I wonder if we should hold off on that," replied Tim. "I'm thinking that tonight we should do a stakeout."

Ashley looked at him with curiosity.

"That warehouse is still set up with all that food, ready to go somewhere," Tim continued. "I think it's fair for us to assume someone is going to come and get it, either by vehicle or by boat."

"Yeah, but that could be a week from now, or a month..." Ashley started to say.

"True. Only one way to find out," Tim said, smiling.

"Alright. Let's go grab some food and eat it in the car at the park," Ashley said. "Maybe it's just a warehouse for a normal day to day company, and they'll transport it during the day anyway."

Although doubtful that was a possibility, Tim agreed and buckled his seatbelt. Maybe all they were doing would prove to be a waste of time. He hoped not. Despite them seeming to be on a tangent from their initial assignment of finding Jordan Simpson, the thought that there might be more people having disappeared still resided in his mind. If there was any way that he and Ashley could help locate those people, he wanted to do all he could to find them.

"Food requests?" Ashley asked him, surprised by his sudden silence.

Tim turned to her and smiled.

"Actually, what I'm craving is just an old fashioned sandwich," he said. "Wanna just go to a grocery store and buy some bread, cold meats and salad, and then make our own?"

"Are you feeling okay?" Ashley asked, resulting in Tim laughing out loud. "No, I mean it," Ashley further teased him. "Are you sure you're okay?"

"Yes!" Tim replied, his grin broad.

"Grocery store, here we come then," Ashley replied, laughing softly as she veered the car out onto the open road.

Tim stared out at the view as they drove. He'd felt odd since being in the fog near the island. He briefly wondered if it could be due to some form of oxygen deprivation or something, although that seemed a bit farfetched given that they'd still been out over the sea.

"What's going through your head, Moore?" he heard Ashley asked. "You're so quiet."

Tim looked at her, thoughtful.

"That fog or smoke … or whatever it is," he said and saw her nod in response. "It looks like fog, but it hasn't dissipated over the past twenty-four hours or so. We also saw what looks like the same stuff coming out of the chimneys of that huge house up on the cliff top." He paused as he diverted his gaze out the window once again. "What *is* it?"

"I don't know, but I'm sure someone on the team could figure that out," Ashley replied.

"We're calling for backup then?" Tim asked.

"I think if we seriously feel like that island has

anything to do with all of this, we should get up there and have a look," replied Ashley. "Those cliffs around every side of it are high, and they're steep. There's no way we can just walk up there. Our options are either get a helicopter in there, to come from the top, or we get rock climbing or abseiling gear…"

"Seriously?" Tim asked, surprised. "You don't like heights."

"I know," Ashley said. "That's why we should call Sarah and get a team down here to investigate."

Tim pondered their options.

"A helicopter might be easier to get up there with, but it's not going to be as easy to get up unnoticed that way."

"Yeah, it's not exactly subtle, especially for somewhere like that where it's going to be mostly silent, I expect," Ashley agreed. "There's no rushing around of traffic or people like there is in a city. A helicopter is going to be heard, and it's going to be obvious it's there for that exact location."

"Rock climbing it is then," Tim said. "Let's see if anything happens tonight, first. We might get some answers without having to even set foot on that island."

"Alright," Ashley said as she nodded in agreement.

Tim pulled out his phone and made a quick call to their supervisor, Sarah. After several minutes, he hung up the call and turned to look at Ashley.

"She said she'll request a team be ready to go tomorrow, just in case," he said, prompting Ashley to nod. "She wants me to call her later with an update about what we see, if anything."

"Okay," Ashley replied as she nodded. "It's hard to know if anything that's happening around here has anything to do with our search for missing people."

"It is," Tim agreed. "Either we're going to find out that it's all tied together…"

"Or we could literally be miles off target," Ashley finished.

CHAPTER 38

Grocery shopping out of the way, along with a quick change of clothing, Ashley and Tim later sat in the car. They'd chosen a quiet corner of the park to relax in. With the sun just beginning its descent, there were few people around. The odd person jogged past them. An elderly couple wandered along at a slow pace, seeming to be more engaged in each other than the younger couple that had passed previously.

Ashley watched the elderly couple meander past. They must have been in their seventies, but they held hands like they were in their youth and new to love. They didn't appear in any way distracted by the sun slowly going down. Even as they walked off into the distance, Ashley continued to watch them.

"Do you ever wonder what it must be like to live almost an entire life with one partner, Tim?" she asked quietly.

"If that's a proposal..." Tim started to tease her. Considering her tone, he stopped himself. "Sure," he said. "Despite my disinterest in getting married and settling down, I do believe in the power of true love. My grandparents were married from when they each turned twenty, until my grandmother died at the age of eighty-seven. Every time I saw them, they looked happy. I don't remember there ever being an argument between them. I mean, I'm sure they must have argued, but if they did, they seemed to get over it pretty quickly."

Ashley listened and felt a pang in her heart. She'd not wanted to get married either. With her job, she hardly felt like even dating was something she wanted to do. The last few dates she'd been on had ended up with the guy expecting sex, even though they'd known each other only a couple of hours. Not that she had anything against casual sex - she just didn't want it for herself. She was also a bit old-fashioned in that she wanted to actually know the person before they got that intimate.

"What's on your mind?" she heard Tim ask.

"Nothing really," Ashley replied. "Sometimes, it feels like this job takes up my whole life, but I love it. I don't want to do anything else."

"You know as well as I do that there are plenty of people in law enforcement jobs, who also have happy and fulfilling relationships," Tim said. "If it's something you really want, I have no doubt you *could* make it happen." He paused and watched her face. She was still looking off into the distance, in the same direction that the elderly couple had walked. "Ash … are you lonely?" he dared to ask.

In response to his question, he saw Ashley's head turn rapidly toward him. For a moment, she looked surprised at the question, before her face relaxed.

"Sometimes I think I am," she said quietly after she'd taken a moment to fully consider his question. "The alternative to not being alone, though - meeting random strangers for casual sex - it doesn't appeal to me."

"Those are hardly the only options for meeting people. You don't have to meet random strangers for casual sex, to begin getting to know someone," Tim said, finding her conversation somewhat intriguing. "There are other options out there…"

"Like what?" Ashley asked, cutting his words short.

"Like … well, I mean, we meet people all the time…" Tim said, stammering a little.

"Tim, I'm hardly going to ask either a suspect in a crime, or anyone associated with a victim, to go out on a date!" Ashley replied, giggling.

Tim saw her face grow animated. That made him feel happier. She was a beautiful woman. There had been plenty of times that he'd wished she would see him differently, but he'd accepted that would never happen. He was grateful they got on as well as they did. He considered her a friend. The conversation she'd opened up in the previous few minutes told him that she considered him a friend too. There was nothing sad about that.

"And you?" Ashley asked quietly. When she saw him look confused, she continued. "You date and shag lots of women..."

"Not *lots*, Ash," Tim replied. "Come on now, don't you go exaggerating on me."

Ashley chuckled. "Okay, not *lots* then, but certainly quite a few," she said. "When you're spending all this time with those women, do you never meet anyone with who you could see something serious?"

Tim took his time in considering the question before he shook his head. The truth was that *she* was the only woman he could see himself settling down for. That wasn't something he'd tell her in the present moment, or ever.

"No," he said quietly. "The women I go out with now and then, are women who like that. They aren't the kinds of women I could see myself dedicating the rest of my life to."

"Just flings, huh?" Ashley asked.

"Some," Tim said, nodding. "Some are one-time flings. Others, I've spent more time with. No matter the length of time, the mentality is the same. They want to have fun, and so do I. There's never anything more to it."

Ashley nodded but didn't reply. She simultaneously felt sad for her partner, knowing that he didn't want to experience anything greater with anyone, and envious of him for getting out there as often as he did to meet and spend time with people.

Taking a bite of her self-made ham and salad sandwich, for a moment, Ashley did feel oddly lonely. It was a feeling that occurred now and then. The feeling was caught short by Tim nudging her and pointing.

"Look," he said in almost a whisper.

When Ashley watched where he was pointing, she saw a small car approach the mound hiding the doors to the warehouse. She and Tim sat, continuing to bite into their sandwiches while gazing forward, watching while not seeming to be there for that purpose.

"We can't see what they're doing in there from this angle," she said.

"No, but to be honest, I'm more interested in whether they might go out that way," Tim replied as he pointed through the back window.

"Boat?" Ashley asked and saw him nod. "You think they might be going over to the island?"

"Maybe," said Tim. "Maybe not. There's only one way to find out. Let's give them ten minutes or so, then wander back to the cliff. Maybe we'll see something from there without alerting them to our presence."

"Alright," Ashley responded, diverting her sight back to the car, now partially hidden by the large mound. "We can get that car's plates," she added. "Get Sarah to run them through the system to see if she can get a match."

Tim wasted no time. Putting his food on the dashboard and pulling out his phone, he quietly opened the door, climbed out, and wandered forward.

As Ashley watched him, she conceded that he just looked like a guy who was on an evening stroll. It was an opportunity for her to look at him and think about the conversation they'd had minutes earlier. After a couple of cases they'd worked on, she'd heard something in his voice when he'd tried to have a serious conversation with her. Each time, she'd dismissed him. She didn't want to hear it. Now, she wondered why she was so afraid to hear whatever he'd wanted to say on those occasions.

Her thoughts were interrupted by him appearing in her sight again, walking back toward where they'd parked. She watched him open the door and climb in, giving her a smile.

"I'll send this off to the team now. Maybe they'll find something out about the owner that will make all this weird stuff fall into place," Tim said as he took action with sending the photo away.

"Could you see anything else from where you went?" Ashley asked, eager to clear her mind of any thoughts that weren't related to work.

"Only a little," Tim replied. "There's one guy in there. Looked like he was carrying boxes, one at a time, toward the back of the room."

"Toward the caves, then?" asked Ashley.

"Yeah, I think so," Tim replied. "He's got a few boxes to move, so we can wait here for a few more minutes yet," he continued, picking up his food. "Can't let this go to waste."

Ashley grinned but didn't reply. His appetite for food had become an ongoing thing for them to joke about, but in reality, she didn't think either of them actually cared about what - or how much - he ate. He kept incredibly fit through his running, and he had a physique that screamed fit and strong.

"What are we going to do if we see them in a boat?" she asked. "If we're up here and they're down there…"

"I think it's only the one guy, so it wouldn't be difficult to approach him, but if he's in a boat, yeah, that could be tricky," Tim said. "Let's see what we can see. Just getting an idea of what's going on around here would be useful. Then we can get a team down here if need be."

"Alright," replied Ashley as she wrapped up her food, then opened her door. "Let's do this."

CHAPTER 39

Walking quietly from their vehicle to the cliffside, Tim and Ashley looked along the edge and made their way to a point where they could peer specifically at the cave entrance. Once there, they stopped and crouched behind a bush, waiting to see if anything would happen that would justify the agents' presence and attention.

Silently, they waited and watched. After a long while, they saw the old dinghy pulled out from the cave area to the inlet. The man pulling it then retreated into the cave. Over a series of trips, he carried out boxes and placed them in the dinghy.

"He can't seriously be going to row to that island in that," Ashley whispered in disbelief. "It would take him forever, not to mention the safety aspect of it."

As she finished her sentence, a quiet hum alerted her to another boat approaching, just a little bit out from the inlet. Quietly, she and Tim watched as the rower moved the dinghy from the shore to the larger motorboat that had anchored. It was a lengthy process, rowing back and forth, delivering boxes to the motorboat.

For the duration, Tim and Ashley remained still. They heard exchanges of words each time the dinghy reached the larger boat, but there was nothing that they heard that would prove helpful to them as witnesses.

When the rower gave a large wave to the boat and called out his goodbye, the agents realized that the transportation process was at an end. Focusing on the motorboat, they saw it pull up its anchor, start its engine and then head straight out, sea-bound. It was a short time before it disappeared from sight and sound.

"Let's go," Ashley said, turning and standing up. "It's time for you and me to take a romantic stroll, lover," she added, holding out her hand.

Tim smiled as he took her hand in his, fully aware of what she was doing. It would take time for the rower to secure the dinghy, make his way through the two caves, and then close up the warehouse. With the care they'd already witnessed with regard to the warehouse doors being hidden, the agents needed to time things perfectly to see anything, while having a ready alibi about why they were in a park at night.

Enclosing her hand with his own, Tim felt comfortable. They'd done the same routine dozens of times. He'd never felt any kind of magical zing when holding any woman's hand. That was something for fairy tales, as far as he was concerned. Even so, there was something comfortable and nice about connecting with his partner physically, even for work, and even on such an innocent level.

The two of them began walking, saying nothing as they walked around the coast side of the large mound. Walking at a brisk pace, they were able to get on the other side of it so that they would be facing it as they turned around to return.

Neither said anything as they reached a far point and stayed there for several minutes, using their vantage location to look within the large, hidden structure. They could see the man slowly work his way over to the wall and inspect the paper that was attached there, as though checking he'd done everything on a checklist. He then quietly turned off the light, closed the large metal doors, and took his time securing them so that there were hidden once again.

Without moving, Tim and Ashley saw the car start and almost silently edge away from the area.

Once sure it was gone, Ashley let out a deep breath.

They were a distance away from the mound, so hadn't needed to remain still or silent. When the car left, Ashley realized she'd been holding her breath in fear of being seen.

"Okay, well, we have one guy who moved the food boxes and transported them to a larger boat," Tim said, glancing at Ashley.

"And one guy who's taken the food out to sea," Ashley added. "We don't know that he's taken it to that island, though. For all we know, he's someone who lives on a boat and just gets food delivered."

"Seriously, Ash?" Tim asked, grinning at her. "Food delivery to a boat on the water?"

Ashley shrugged her shoulders.

"Not likely, I grant you, but just because we saw what we saw, doesn't mean that stuff is bound for that island."

"I know," Tim said. "Let's go back to the car, and I'll call Sarah. She can make a call about whether it's worth sending a team out here to investigate or not."

As they walked back, in her thoughts, Ashley added their evening discovery to the pile of random things they'd seen, heard, and learned so far. In isolation, everything was odd, to say the least. Homeless people disappearing without a trace. Two entire towns of people having disappeared or left. An island that seemed to have a permanent manmade fog around it, but no way to get to the top of it except up almost vertical cliffs. And now, boxes of food being transported to who knows where via a motorboat.

"It's a lot, isn't it," she heard Tim say quietly as they climbed into the car. "Lots of things that could be completely independent of one another, or could be interrelated," he continued as he looked at her. "This is not turning out to be a case of one missing person!"

"If our assumptions are correct," Ashley said.

Tim nodded. "If our assumptions are correct."

CHAPTER 40

The phone call Tim made to Sarah went for much longer than he'd anticipated. In addition to what he'd told her about the warehouse and the boxes of food that had been removed by boat, Sarah had her own information to add into the mix.

"None of the people who were listed as being in Kerr or Pioneer during the 2010 census on April 1st, 2010, we've been able to find anywhere else," Sarah said over the phone. "Unless they are *all* now using fake names or dates of birth, every one of those people is nowhere to be found - not in this country, at least."

Tim found himself partially surprised, but partially not. It was beginning to feel like the case that he and Ashley were currently working on was never going to have any end to the surprises it provided.

"So, if you think these people really could be on the island that you mentioned..." Sarah continued.

"It's something that we can't guarantee in any way," Tim said. "There's nothing absolute about any of this. It's more of a gut feeling that, somehow, this island has something to do with the disappearance of all these people around this entire area."

"It could be that they just moved there," Sarah said, her voice giving away the doubt of the possibility.

"It could be," Tim replied, unable to argue with her logic. "On that island could be people who moved from those two towns, or the homeless people we've not located yet..."

There was silence at the end of the phone line for a

long while.

"You think it's worth checking out, though?" Sarah asked. "You and your partner both have this same gut feeling?"

Tim naturally turned and smiled at Ashley, even though she had no idea what was being said on the phone.

"We do," Tim said positively.

"Alright," replied Sarah. "I'll dispatch a team to meet you in Compton tomorrow morning. In addition to that, I'll get a boat big enough for the team to be at the ready, to take you all over to the island. You're gonna need rock climbing gear, too, I take it?"

"Yeah, there doesn't seem to be any other way to get up to the top..." Tim said as he considered all those boxes of food he and Ashley had seen put into the motorboat earlier.

"Okay, leave it with me," Sarah said. "I'm going to get a helicopter ready too, just in case. I know you said you think it best not to make noise, but I need to know that if anything is seriously wrong on that island, I can get the team out in a hurry if need be, without making you guys have to climb down a cliff."

Tim thanked her, and they said their goodbyes. When he hung up the phone, he could see Ashley's eagerness to hear what had been said.

"You know, you could have just put that on speaker," she teased him. "But now you can relay the entire call to me."

Tim couldn't help but grin before he became serious.

"A team is going to meet us at the motel in the morning," he said. "After that, a large boat will collect us all from a little up the coast to take us over."

Ashley nodded, absorbing the information.

"What else did she say?" she asked.

"Actually, what stood out to me in that conversation was that the investigation into the people of Kerr and

Pioneer were all there at the time of the 2010 Census," Tim replied, thoughtful. When he saw Ashley look at him with a question on her face, he explained why the detail was so interesting to him. "That Census was held on April 1st."

Ashley let the date sink in, then spoke.

"And it was Easter Sunday - April 4th - that it looked like the people disappeared?" she asked and saw Tim nod. "They were all there on the Thursday and then disappeared four days later?"

"Looks like it," Tim replied.

"That's pretty perfect timing," Ashley said. "I mean, if nobody visits those towns, except once a decade to do a Census…"

Tim processed the discovery in his mind. It was either a remarkable coincidence that two entire towns had vanished after their details had been officially recorded, or it was no coincidence at all.

"By the way, we're going up the cliff face, Ash," Tim said quietly. "The guys they're sending are professionals in this kind of stuff. Sarah was pretty sure they'd get you up without any issue. You might just need to close your eyes."

With a slight chuckle, Ashley replied.

"I can do this, Moore," she reassured him with more positivity than she felt at the prospect. "Just you watch me."

Tim agreed that she would be able to do it. That wasn't politeness or niceness on his part. He knew that when she put her mind to anything, she could do it. Her fear of heights had always surprised him. He didn't say it, but inside, he was glad she was going to force herself to face her fear in that.

"Let's get out of here," Ashley continued as she started the engine. "I want to have a long, hot bath, and then let my mind rest."

As Tim did up his seatbelt, his mind turned to the

following morning. Usually, he and Ashley ascertained something almost absolute before they requested backup to help them out. While he knew that there wouldn't be any reprimand if he and Ashley were off target and there was nothing to find, he still hoped that the island was going to provide them with some kind of answers.

The thought of wasting an entire team's time wasn't one he liked. It was only in his head, he knew. There was all possibility that the hunches he and Ashley had been having, didn't have anything at all to do with anything the Bureau needed to be involved with. It was a possibility, and if that turned out to be the case, the two of them would have to go back to the beginning and take a different route in their investigation.

If that was the case, that was fine. He didn't *like* the option, but he would accept it. Sometimes that was what was needed to solve a case - go back to the beginning and start all over again.

"All good?" Ashley asked as they drove out of the park area. "You're really quiet."

Tim smiled at her and nodded.

"Yeah, I'm all good," he replied. "I just hope that tomorrow *is* going to lead to something."

"Investigating and not finding something is *still* finding something, Tim," Ashley said quietly. "If that island produces nothing, that is one question solved."

"But it won't resolve not knowing about the *people*," Tim replied.

"We can't think about what won't happen tomorrow," Ashley replied. "That would be getting ahead of ourselves. You know that we need to focus on one aspect. Let's only think about the island, until the island shows us that it isn't part of this wild ride."

Tim smiled again but said nothing more. He knew she was right. Usually, it was him giving that speech, rather than her.

Turning to let his eyes take in the darkness now

surrounding them, he forced himself to think of more pleasurable things. He didn't usually let his mind wander too much when on a case, but something about their current investigation kept making him feel like his mind was being played with.

"We *are* going to figure this all out, Tim," he heard Ashley say softly. He hoped she was right. The number of people who seemed to have disappeared was up in the hundreds. If it had been only one person they hadn't been able to find, that would be bad enough. Not finding anyone from hundreds? The thought was almost unbearable.

Sarah had confirmed that none of the people who'd lived in Kerr or Pioneer a decade earlier had been able to be found by the team back at head office. The two towns hadn't been large so didn't have huge populations. That didn't matter. There were people in them ten years ago, and now there were none. That many people couldn't just vanish from the planet.

They just couldn't.

CHAPTER 41

"Special Agent Power," Ashley heard a deep voice say from behind her when she and Tim had moved to the motel car park the next morning. Vans had started arriving fifteen minutes earlier. Slowly, she'd watched one person from each van climb out of the driver seat and join with the other drivers in a small huddle.

Turning around, Ashley saw Chris Barnett grinning at her. For a moment, she found herself transported back in time by five years. They'd dated for a while before mutually deciding to give up on that. Now she couldn't even remember why she'd thought it a good idea to walk away. As she saw him and that smile he delivered, she was also reminded of how attracted to him she'd been.

"Chris," she said, turning off her thoughts and holding out her hand to him.

As she shook his hand, she sensed Tim approach and stand much closer to her than he usually did. It was an odd moment, but fortunately, only a very fleeting one.

"Special Agent Moore," Chris added, seeing Tim move beside Ashley.

After the two men shook hands, the tone was changed to business.

"I'm leading this team once we get to the island," Chris said to both of them. "Can you fill me in on what you've seen so far?"

"We've been around the island, in a small boat," Ashley replied. "It's … it's a weird place, Chris."

"Weird, how?"

"It has this thick fog around it, which has been

hanging around since we got here," Ashley continued. "When we finally got through that and saw the mass of land, we noticed that it might be manmade."

"The island?" Chris asked, curious.

"No, the fog," said Ashley. "It looked like it was coming from chimneys we could see."

"Okay," Chris said. "And the cliffs?"

"All around," Tim replied. "We went around the entire island, and there's no gradual decline in the land to the sea level. It's straight down at all points - or pretty much anyway."

Chris processed the information and nodded.

"Alright, let's get to the boat, first of all," he said. "We got one big enough for all of us. Onboard, we have gear for cliff climbing, but if people are up there, how do you think they *got* there?"

Ashley shrugged her shoulders.

"That's what we need to find out - if there *are* any people up there."

Chris nodded again and called out to the van drivers.

"Let's go!"

Ashley and Tim watched all of the vans start and quietly leave the large car park area before the two agents got into Ashley's car and followed. They were heading up the coast, in the opposite direction to where they'd already explored.

"Here goes nothing," Tim said in almost a whisper. He hadn't meant to say it out loud. Ashley turning and facing him told him he'd spoken louder than he possibly should have.

"Come on now, Timmy Boy," Ashley said, hearing the uncertainty in his voice. "We're heading out on an adventure, and you *love* adventure."

Tim grinned and hoped the adventure ahead was going to be worthwhile. If it wasn't, it was a long road back to the very beginning in the search for Jordan Simpson.

CHAPTER 42

Once all were aboard the motor launch, Ashley stood aside and watched the team sort and ready their rock climbing gear. It wasn't something she'd ever done in her life - not for work, and certainly not for pleasure. While she still felt nervous about venturing so high up a cliff face, the stronger feeling was that of anticipation.

She hoped they were going to find something. Although she argued with herself that there might not be anyone up there, she maintained hope because of the smoke they'd seen emanating out of the chimneys on the large home. She couldn't see any way for that to happen unless someone was on that island, feeding whatever form of fireplace the chimneys were connected to.

"How have you been?" she heard Chris's voice say from behind her. When she turned around, she found her chest almost touching his. Despite their time as lovers having ended years earlier, it was enough to unnerve her a little. "It's been a while."

Taking a step backward, and holding her head high to meet his gaze, Ashley politely smiled.

"It has," she said, nodding. "And I've been good. Work keeps me busy."

"Still the main focus in your life?" Chris asked. "Or the *only* focus?"

While Ashley resented the tone he used as he asked the questions, she maintained her composure. When she'd seen him back at the motel, she'd briefly wondered why she'd walked away from him. Two simple questions coming out of his mouth reminded her there was a side to him that she didn't particularly like.

"It won't always be my life, but it certainly is for now," she replied as she saw Tim on the other side of the boat, watching her talk to Chris.

Without saying another word, she walked to where Tim stood, leaving Chris looking after her as she did so.

"I didn't want to interrupt," Tim said when she reached him. "You've never mentioned him, but I'm thinking there's something going on there?"

"Once upon a time, there was," Ashley said. "That was over long ago!"

"He's a handsome boy," Tim said, making Ashley laugh.

"Yep," she replied. "On the outside."

Tim let the subject drop, filing it away as something to tease his partner about at another time.

"I gave the captain the GPS coordinates, but do these guys know what they're heading into with regard to the fog?" Tim asked her.

"I gave them an indication, but it's something one can only imagine once you're in it, isn't it," Ashley said. "It won't be long, and we should see it."

Glancing around them, they could see that the captain had moved the boat straight out from the point of land where they'd boarded.

"He's going to head out and then around, I'm guessing," Tim said. "I'm glad. I really don't want to see Mike Batch again. Hopefully, he won't even see us."

"Tim, he's law enforcement…"

"I know," Tim replied, nodding. "And usually, I wouldn't suspect a fellow law enforcement officer of anything untoward, but there's something off about that guy."

Silently, Ashley agreed. She didn't want to believe that someone in the police department might be deliberately interfering with their investigation, but growing inside of her was the belief that Mike Batch might have been trying to do just that.

"I see what you mean about the fog," she heard Chris's voice call out.

When Ashley turned to face him, she saw him pointing. The island was in sight - or, at least, the thick fog surrounding it was. Straight away, she began to walk to where the captain stood.

"Have you seen anything like this before?" she asked him.

"I've seen fog," replied the captain. "This *is* remarkably thick, however. I don't think I've been in anything quite like this." He focused as he began moving the boat further inwards. "You came in here in a small boat?"

"Yes," said Ashley. "We entered here and eventually found the land, but it came up on us quickly. We were lucky we were moving as slowly as we were. Almost as soon as we could see beyond the fog, we were at the edge of the land with a vertical cliff face in front of us."

The captain nodded before slowing the vessel. He had a lifetime of experience sailing in all kinds of situations and all sorts of weather. He'd learned to never assume he knew more than the next guy. If someone said to slow down, he'd slow down.

"Special Agent Power," Ashley heard Chris call out. "Let's get you rigged up."

Ashley was surprised at the speed with which the team on the boat had readied themselves for upwards travel. As she moved close to where Chris and Tim stood, she felt uncertainty. She pushed it down and tucked it behind her preferred feeling of anticipation and excitement.

"Are you sure about this?" Tim asked her quietly as Chris fitted her with gear. "There are enough of us to go up there and investig..."

"Tim, I'm ready for this," Ashley reassured him. "If you think I'm letting you have all the fun, you don't know me at all."

Tim smiled and held up his hands in defeat, but didn't argue with her. He believed in her abilities, sometimes more than she did. Truth be told, he didn't like the thought of her *not* going up onto the top of the island to investigate with him. They'd come so far on their journey to find one man. There appeared to be an equal chance that they'd find nobody because they were on the completely wrong path, or they'd find somebody. The only problem with that option was that even if they *did* find someone, they still might not find who they were actually looking *for*.

Day to day, he had to keep reminding himself what their actual investigation was about. Jordan Simpson. He was one man who a young woman wanted to find. The initial search for him had led Tim and Ashley from a standard search to one that was certainly not standard. The search for one man was now a search for hundreds. It was easy to get caught up in the magnitude of where their investigation was leading, and now and then forget about that one man.

As the boat slowed right down, Ashley and Tim looked over the side. Over a period of minutes, the boat eventually began to feel like it was drifting forward, pulled by the tide, rather than moving with the propulsion of its motor. The fog felt just like it had the previous day. Even though both agents had already experienced it, the denseness of it once again surprised each of them.

Everyone remained quiet as the boat edged forward slowly. The only sound was that of the water lapping against the hull.

Almost without any gradual process, before them, they finally all saw the steep cliff face.

"Shit," Ashley heard one guy say quietly.

All looking upward, nobody else said a word.

CHAPTER 43

"You weren't exaggerating about the steepness," Chris said quietly to Tim and Ashley. "You're sure there's no other side of this island that's not that high?"

"From the view we had as we circled it yesterday, the clifftop seemed pretty level all the way around," Tim said. "There were no lower areas that I could see."

"Okay," said Chris. "Well, your call. We can get up there without a problem. Are we a go?" he asked, facing Ashley.

Ashley nodded and watched as Chris quietly instructed his team into action. They were as quiet as anyone could be. Specialized teams were something Ashley always enjoyed watching. She had an analytical mind that liked to have things in order, but the teams like the one Chris was guiding ... well, they were something to see when they were in action.

"Once the first lot of men are up the cliff face, I'll harness you to me and take you up," Chris said, addressing Ashley again.

She couldn't help but notice a slight smirk, but chose to ignore it. He might try and tease her or make her blush before they got underway, but she knew he was a professional. Whatever he did - however close they had to get - it would soon be all business with him. There would be nothing behind it of a personal nature.

"Tim, you can climb yourself, I understand?" Chris checked.

Tim nodded, excited at the prospect. He'd done abseiling when he was much younger. He didn't expect going up a rock face to be the same as that, but that didn't stop his adrenaline kicking in.

The agents stood still and watched the first of the team scale up the cliff face. When they disappeared over the upper edge, everyone in the boat waited, watching. Whatever was up there, the first team members would already have an idea about it. All anyone down below could hope, was that upon arriving at the top of the cliff, those team members hadn't met any danger.

A few minutes later, faces appeared as the few team members who'd gone up, signaled for others to follow. Their body positions of lying down while they made hand movements made Ashley think that something was happening up there. Either the team on top of the cliff had seen something they weren't sure about, or they'd seen some*one*. The unknowing made Ashley want to just get up there as quickly as she could.

"Tim," Chris said quietly. "Go with these guys, and we'll follow."

Tim glanced at Ashley, uncertain for a moment that he wanted to leave her. When he saw her smile at him and nod, he, in turn, nodded at Chris before turning and focusing on the instruction of two men he was to join on the journey upwards.

"Your partner is protective of you," Ashley heard Chris say as he leaned in close to her ear.

Turning to face him, she nodded. She could hear that bitchy tone of his voice again. It made her cringe inside. How she could have forgotten he was like that, she didn't know. The pretty face he possessed hid something not so pretty on the inside. She certainly remembered *that* now.

"To be honest, Chris," Ashley said quietly. "I'm pretty protective of him too."

Chris shook his head as he smirked, but said nothing in reply.

CHAPTER 44

As Chris harnessed her against him, Ashley focused on every word he quietly said, and pushed every other thought out of her mind. She hated heights, and she needed to not focus on how high they were about to scale.

"You're safe with me, Ashley," Chris said quietly. It was one of his nicer moments. That voice - the calming one of reassurance - was the one that had won her attention when they'd first met. "Okay?"

Ashley nodded and clung to him, but allowed no words to leave her mouth. Within moments, she felt the reassuring surface under her feet disappear. Although she wanted to only feel strong and in control, she could feel her heart pound heavily. Remaining in the exact position she'd been told to, she closed her eyes and began taking deep breaths. Even that wasn't easy. The fog wasn't thick right where they were, but there were still aspects of it in the air against the cliff face. It had a foreign smell. It wasn't an extremely bad smell, but it was strong enough to not escape notice.

After his few snide comments, she'd considered that Chris might use their closeness for the duration to incur some more. Ashley was relieved that he said nothing else. He was concentrating on the job at hand. She was glad. Work was difficult enough at times, without having to worry about personal dynamics with anyone at the same time.

Tuning out to all around her, Ashley was surprised when she felt her feet touch the ground again. When that happened, she finally opened her eyes again.

Standing perfectly still, she waited while Chris detached himself and removed all of their climbing gear. At that moment, Ashley saw Tim approach. He remained low, hiding behind man-high shrubs and bush.

"This fog is crazy thick up here. What can you see?" Ashley asked him.

Tim nodded and leaned in close to her.

"The house we saw is at the far end from here," he replied. "It's larger than I expected, more like an old convent or something rather than just a house. It's not the only building either. There are four smaller buildings as well, that I could see from this angle."

"Okay," Ashley said. "Where are the team?"

"Closer," Tim replied. "There's another tree line ten meters ahead. They're waiting there, ready to move in on instruction from us."

Ashley turned and looked at Chris. Although sometimes a cocky bastard, he was clearly waiting for her command as well.

"Let's go connect with them then," Ashley said, prompting the remaining team members to move forward to group with the first who'd arrived.

When they'd all merged into one long team, checks were done of weaponry and protective gear. While that went on, Tim and Ashley watched forward. By their calculations, it was still morning or, at the latest, early afternoon. Regardless of actual time, the top of the island was dark, as if a serious rainstorm was about to hit. All around them, the dark fog lingered, not moving at all. In the distance, they could see more of it flowing out of four large chimneys. The flow wasn't the same as what would appear out of a normal household chimney. There was no dissipation or gaps in the flow. It just kept coming out of those chimneys, thick and consistent.

"I don't understand how we could have seen anything reflecting through this," Tim said in a near whisper.

"There's no sunlight even getting in here."

Ashley agreed but had no answer. They'd assumed it was a light at first. Then they'd thought it was something reflective, redirecting sunlight. Now she wondered if the first thought had been the right one. It was impossible to know until they got closer and could see what exactly was happening in the large buildings.

For a long while, all crouched and just watched. Apart from the action of the chimneys, there was no movement. It was a silent place. The fog even seemed to protect the land from any sound, or from any of the fresh air that one might ordinarily expect to experience when standing on a tall island surrounded by sea.

The eeriness of the place made Tim nervous. It was as bad as what he'd felt in the small, abandoned towns of Pioneer and Kerr. There was nothing he could see that should inspire such uneasiness in him. Regardless, despite how confident he usually was in his job, he could feel a hint of fear beginning to manifest inside of him. That was something he didn't like.

"Do you hear that?" Chris asked in a whisper, prompting Ashley and Tim to both look at him.

"What?" Ashley asked. "I can't hear anything."

"Exactly," replied Chris. "Nothing. There's not even a bird singing in this place."

"I'm not sure sea birds sing," Tim said. "But you're right. I would expect gulls or some other kind of sea bird to be around, squawking, or at least nesting."

Tim and Ashley both thought about the silence of Kerr and Pioneer. It had been the same as far as the silence went. Now they were in the third place they'd visited in a while, where they noticed the silence. It was a harsh reminder of how easy it was to never notice something - even something so simple as sound - until it was no longer there.

Determined to not rush until they'd watched the buildings under surveillance, Ashley remained still.

Everyone was silent and unmoving, watching and listening. There was no evidence of people being around. From where the team sat, there was no sign of life at all. If they were going to go in, it was without knowledge of who they might meet when they did.

Anticipating a good hour had passed with nothing heard or seen, Ashley and Tim liaised with Chris and set in place a plan for approaching the buildings and checking the rest of the island. Ashley remained still while she watched Chris send off smaller teams of two or three, some to follow the clifftop around either way from where they were, and others to move forward towards the outlying buildings. That left Tim, Ashley, Chris and three others, to move forward towards the main building.

In her ear, she could hear a whispered finding now and then, coming from team members around the island top. Nothing seemed to be anything to take particular attention of as Ashley moved closer to the home.

"We've found the way up here," one of the side teams said. "Large pulley system, big enough for supplies and probably for people too."

Ashley turned and looked at Tim. That made it possible for the food they'd thought was coming to the island, to have been moved up to the top and into the home. It was a small discovery, but enough to give a little bit of hope that their suspicions might have been right - at least about the food. It was enough to drive Ashley on, eager to find out what the island was really about. Was it someone's private residence? If it was, the four chimneys running at the rate they were was overkill. It would have to belong to a very large family if they needed all four sections of the huge house heated.

Feeling a hand touch her arm, Ashley turned and saw Tim pointing. Following his guidance, she saw what he was pointing at. Across the top of them, they saw it again - the light.

CHAPTER 45

Chris saw the movement of Tim and Ashley and looked up to see what held their attention. It was a clear line that flowed right above their heads. Following it, he saw one end heading out into the fog. Looking back the other way, he saw it coming from what looked like a space above the main building.

"We can't have seen it from this angle," Ashley said to Tim. "We were down at the water, and then it looked like was coming out of a window on the sea side…"

"Maybe it's another one," Tim said. "A different one … or, at least, one coming from the opposite side of the house."

"Someone's home," Chris said quietly. When he saw Ashley and Tim glance at him, he spoke again. "That looks like a laser pointer to me, so it isn't a natural thing, plus it wasn't going a few minutes ago. My guess is that whoever lives here, is definitely *in* there."

Before Ashley or Tim could say anything, a voice came through the small comms in their ears.

"We've got an incinerator room here," the voice said. "It's … it's bodies…" There was silence for several seconds before it continued. "Six or seven. All look big enough to be adults. They're burning … now."

"Are they alive?" Chris dared to ask. "Can you save them?"

"No," said the voice. "They're well past saving. Do you want us to try and shut this down?"

"They could still be identifiable," Ashley said quietly as she glanced at her partner.

"As soon as we shut that down, whoever is in there could be alerted to our presence," Tim said, pointing at the house before them. "We don't yet know what - or who - we're up against."

"Leave it," Chris said quietly as he received the nod from Ashley.

"Got it," the voice at the other end of the comms confirmed. "Leaving the incinerator room now."

In her gut, Ashley felt sick. She knew it was rational to leave the bodies burning if they were that far gone already. If burning humans was something that regularly happened on the island, time might be of the essence in focusing more on trying to prevent it from happening to anyone else.

As she focused on the living, and any possibility the teams might have to save any, she felt calm flow over her. Sometimes in her job, there were decisions that were difficult to make, especially those that needed to be made within a small pocket of time. In such times, it was good to maintain hope that they could find others who *could* use their help.

"Ready to move?" Ashley heard Chris ask her. In response, she nodded and reset her mind.

Silently, Chris led the way forward. There was no sign of life as they passed rows of neatly clipped shrubbery. It wasn't a natural layout, or a natural level of untidiness that would be evident in an unkempt garden or grounds. The perfection of it provided more evidence that they were on an island that was inhabited, without any doubt.

Forward they moved until they reached a small brick wall that stood two meters high, approximately ten meters away from the large house.

Stopping in the protection it provided from anyone who might be inside, Chris peered around the side of it. Letting his eyes follow the line where the building met the ground, he turned back to Tim and Ashley with a look of surprise on his face.

"I only see one door," he said. "It's chained and padlocked."

"But…" Ashley started to say. "But there are people inside."

"Maybe, but they didn't go in that way," Chris said. "We need to move around the side and see if we can find a doorway there. I've got bolt cutters, but if I can see that chain this clearly from this distance, these aren't going to cut through that. We need to find another way. It's a big place. There's gotta be a few doors to get in and out of."

Tim and Ashley both nodded and prepared to follow Chris again.

CHAPTER 46

Jordy Simpson felt dazed. It was always the same, day in, day out. Each time he woke and saw a few rays of sunshine entering the room via the boarded-up window near his bed, he knew that was going to be short-lived. The sun didn't stay out. Wherever he was, if the sun did make an appearance, it felt like only an hour or two before Jordy's inside-only world became dark once more.

That was what he missed most of all - light. Why he was living in the dark and dreary existence, always waiting for the morning light, he had no idea. All he did know was that it seemed like weeks or even months that he'd been doing it, over and over. Weeks … months … or was it *years*? Maybe it was. All concept of time had been lost long ago. That was about the time that he'd given up wanting or wishing for anything.

He didn't understand where he was or why he was there. He just wanted to not be there anymore. Whether his body left with his mind intact, or whether his body and mind shut down, ending the misery, he didn't care. He just wanted it over with.

There had been plenty of mornings when he'd wanted to give up, but that inbuilt desire to live kept kicking in. Even with the existence that he had, he could not stop appreciating that he was alive, and he should be happy about that.

He'd hoped something would change. Since old George had gone away, leaving that bed near Jordy's empty, Jordy had begun to even miss the snoring.

CHAPTER 47

Emma Voy crept up to the window once again. Since she'd been taken from her home in Pioneer as a child, she'd been careful to never let anyone know about the tiny green laser pointer she'd hid in her shoe that afternoon. She'd been young, but she'd already gained the knowledge that the small torch-like item didn't have unending power. It had been a gift from her mother when Emma had turned seven. Her mother, in her attempts to try and work toward self-sustainability, had explained that the rectangular surface molded around the small light was a solar generator - not a big one at all, but still able to be charged by sunlight.

It was a small thing for her to have remembered as a child, but Emma kept the small light hidden in a safe place. When an opportunity presented itself, like it did today, she pulled it out, walked quietly to the rare uncovered window she'd located in the large home, and pressed the small button on the end of it. Only a few times now and then did she do it. She suspected it was a dangerous move, but it had long ago become a habit.

Whenever she looked outside through the small window, for the most part, all she saw was darkness - except for that glimmer of sunshine on the odd morning.

She hardly ever saw herself anymore, but when she'd last looked down at the skin on her arms, she'd noticed how white she was. Despite being so young, she knew she shouldn't be healthy without any supply of Vitamin D from sunlight. But she was.

CHAPTER 48

"There's no way in at ground level," Chris said to Tim, Ashley, and his team after he and three of his men had left them to investigate the entire perimeter of the large home. "Three doors, all sealed up with concrete, of all things. Looks like someone really didn't want anyone to get in there."

"Or get out," Tim said.

"What about through the external buildings?" Ashley asked, directing the question to the small teams that had gone into each of the four smaller structures.

"No, the incinerator rooms each had only one door, and that was the exterior one," one of the men said. "They don't seem to have any connection to the main house."

"Four incinerator rooms for four chimneys," Ashley said, shuddering. "Bodies burning in each?"

"Not all four. They're all burning, but just two of them looked like there were bodies inside. The other two incinerators looked like they were burning something else … something not organic."

"Hmm," replied Ashley. "That fog, or smoke, or whatever it is that's coming out of those things … it's coming from burning bodies?"

Chris shook his head.

"If it is, it's got something else with it," he said. "I've smelt burning flesh, and it doesn't smell like that."

Ashley nodded. With the fires burning so actively, there would be no chance of getting in there to look more closely. Putting the fires out didn't seem a good idea either, at least for the moment. Even if it was feasible to get in and shut the fires down, she knew the advanced crime scene investigation teams would provide the best analysis, rather than what her limited scientific knowledge could provide.

"Alright," she said, turning to face Chris. "Well, we have to get inside now. Whether or not this has anything to do with our formal investigation, we've seen human bodies being burned. That needs to be investigated, even if it's unrelated. We can't walk away if there's any chance of other people being alive in there, also planned for a visit to the incinerator."

Chris nodded and began studying the upper levels of the house from where they discretely stood.

"Four stories," he muttered, observing all that he could. "All windows look boarded up."

He stopped talking and summoned forward several of his men, leaving Ashley and Tim to watch on. While Ashley was eager to get inside, she knew it was worth it to leave the team to strategize about how best to get in.

After a long while, Chris announced it was time to move.

"There's an east-facing window with boards that look more flimsy than the rest of these," he said. "Plus, there's easier access to it via the roof of one of the outbuildings. From there, we'll be able to shin up the drainpipe and a short distance across the wall to get to it."

Ashley nodded. She felt nervous but excited all at the same time. They had no idea what was inside the building, if anything at all. Logic told them all that someone must be inside, but who was that person, and what were they doing burning human flesh?

Tim listened and absorbed the plan for entering the building. At the same time, he couldn't help but wonder how they'd ended up where they were when they'd been investigating the disappearance of one man. He also found himself wondering what could happen next.

CHAPTER 49

The climb up onto the outbuilding and then up the drainpipe was completed by one swift sideways jump along the wall. Once the first man had reached that point and found he could push the glass window up, he used his strength to push in one board, then another. It was something for the others to watch, but finally, they saw his body pass through the space he'd created. Once inside, he was absent for several minutes before he leaned back out and gave the hand signal that all was clear, and all could follow.

Ashley maintained her focus on every handhold she used, and every movement of her feet, until she was inside the window. Standing on the floor, she looked around the room. To the left and the right were boxes like the ones she and Tim had seen in the warehouse.

"This must be the point where they hoist their supplies into," Tim said. "That explains why the window boards were easy to move."

"Yeah, but if people are here who don't want to be, why don't they climb *out* that way?" asked Ashley.

"Because this door's locked, or jammed shut," she heard Chris say. When she looked at him, he was on the far side of the room, working with a couple of his men to assess the door and whatever was holding it closed. "Opens outwards from here. No lock or bolts on this side. The hinges must be on the other side too," he continued before turning to face her and Tim. "Ram it?"

Ashley shook her head. "Wait a minute, Chris," she said. "I want to look around this room fir…"

Before she could finish her sentence, a deep male voice was heard. Although not coming from someone they could see within the room, it reached Ashley as if the person who said the words was right beside her, speaking clearly into her left ear.

"Welcome," the voice said, a hint of unpleasantness in its tone. "You're new home by the sea awaits. Here, you will now stay."

Ashley looked around, along with all the men in the room. Although initially startled by the voice, she and Tim began to walk around. From the door end of the room they'd been standing in, they split up and explored the walls that took them back toward the window they'd entered through. When they neared the window, the voice spoke the same words again.

"Motion-activated play of a recording?" Ashley wondered out loud.

As Tim joined her side, he nodded.

"I think so too," he said. "There's nobody here. The question is, has us setting that off gained the attention of anyone on the other side of that door?"

"If it has, I'm sure we'll know about it soon enough," Ashley replied as she saw Chris move his men to either side of the doorway in preparation for whatever might be to come. "This seems to be the entry point then, for supplies and for people who come here," she said, beginning to wander around the center of the room. "Someone must have been here to receive all of this." She turned to the men who had seen the pulley and hoist system outside. "The hoist that you saw," she said. "Do you think it could have reached up this high? Was it near this end of the building?"

"It was just on the other side of the outbuilding we climbed up on," one of the men said. "It wasn't visible which way it swung, but it was high enough to have been able to reach here, yes."

Ashley nodded her thanks and faced Tim once more.

"I don't hear footsteps approaching," she said. "Do you?"

"No," replied Tim, moving closer to the door where the majority of men still stood waiting.

"Open it," Ashley said to Chris.

In three well-practiced moves together, the men were able to get the locked and secured door open. Once again, Ashley wondered why someone wouldn't find a way to get out that way if they'd been brought to the house against their will.

As the team passed through the doorway, she stood back for a moment, looking at the door frame. It had been secured on the interior side with six large, solid slide locks, all with huge padlocks that looked as old as the house. They looked like nothing should have been able to break them.

"The locks are still secure…" she said quietly to herself.

"That can't be said for the door frame," said Tim as he appeared beside her. Running his hand up and down the door frame that now showed damage, he continued. "Looks like wood-boring beetles have been chewing away at this for probably decades. This damage isn't visible on the outer surfaces, though. If someone did reach this door and want to leave, they might not have realized just how easy it would have been to pull the door inwards towards them if they had some help."

The two agents looked around. It was another large room that was almost identical to the one they'd just walked out of. Ceiling, walls, and floors were all uncovered timber. The room looked like it hadn't been touched for years, with the amount of dust that lay around. Internal from the previous room, there was little light, prompting Chris and his team to switch on the small lamps positioned on their heads.

Ashley followed suit, pulling out her phone and turning on the torch. Boxes scattered the center of the room. A quick look at the labels indicated substances she hadn't heard of.

"Tim, look at these," she said. When he approached her and looked at what she was pointing at, she spoke again. "Do you know what these are?"

"That looks like some kind of chemistry symbol," Tim said. "Not my strong suit. Do you want to open one of these up?"

Ashley was about to shake her head when she saw a large notice board on the far wall. Walking over to it with Tim close behind her, she shone her phone light onto pages that were pinned to it.

"Newspaper clippings," she said, glancing from one page to the next. "'Missing People' ... 'Township of Kerr' ... 'Easter Rituals'. There's a lot to read here."

Tim looked over the pages closest to where he stood. "'Cleansing Souls' ... 'The Nature of Cults' ... 'Sacrifice to Save Yourself', 'Island Paradise Lost'," he read out loud. "Island paradise? This article looks like it's about this place. Look," he said, prompting Ashley to follow what he was reading.

"That does look like this house," said Ashley before beginning to read. "'The prominent, private Home by the Sea, belonging to the Henderson family for nine generations, is reported to have been destroyed in a fire last night. Witnesses said that the home quickly dissolved into destruction, with nothing anyone could do. It is believed that eight members of the Henderson family were inside at the time. There were no survivors.'"

"Huh," Tim said. "Well, obviously, it *wasn't* destroyed. Everything we've seen so far looks original, not like it was rebuilt. What year is this article from?"

"Nineteen-eighty," said Ashley. "April 6th."

"Forty years ago this year," replied Tim as he raised his phone to investigate something. "No cell signal," he then muttered.

"What were you thinking?" Ashley asked.

"That article over there," said Tim, moving along to where he'd seen something minutes earlier. "'Easter Rituals'. I was going to check if there was any chance that April 6th, 1980, was on Easter."

"You think someone tried to destroy this house as a way to perform some kind of ritual?" Ashley asked.

Tim shrugged his shoulders.

"I have no idea, but that article is of interest," he said. "We can't check it out till we have some form of access to the world away from this island."

Walking further alongside the wall, Ashley took her time to take in the headlines of the news clippings lining it. She didn't read all articles, wanting to move on with investigating more rooms, but there was a common theme among the clippings.

"Whoever has cut these out has a morbid interest in this house, in the Henderson family, and in ritualistic behavior," she said to Tim. "Nothing here to directly indicate why they're burning bodies in those incinerators, though."

"Or whatever else it is that they're burning down there," Tim added. "The chemicals in those boxes back there?"

Ashley nodded. "Maybe," she said. "Crime scene guys will better be able to figure that out."

She and Tim walked around, looking further at whatever they could before she walked up to Chris. His stance was of a true soldier, standing almost at attention even though he could be relaxed at that moment. Around him, his team stood equally rigid, waiting, listening.

"Still, nobody has come," Chris said quietly, directing his words to Ashley. "If they know we came in, they aren't giving us any clues to let us know that."

Ashley looked at the door before them.

"Another locked one?" she asked and saw Chris nod.

"The same as the last. I'm guessing there could be

just as many locks on the other side of this as there were on that one," he said, pointing his thumb back at the door they'd pushed completely out of the frame to enter the room. "Moving forward?" he asked her.

"Yep," Ashley replied. She didn't need to say anything more. Instead, she and Tim stood back a little way and watched the men repeat their actions.

The door wasn't as easily displaced. It took more men to join in the effort, and more attempts. Finally, it flew forwards, slamming down on the floor of the next room.

"Whoa," Tim exclaimed as he glanced into the room they walked into. He found himself almost speechless at what he saw. While the floor of the room was as cluttered and messy as the previous two rooms, looking up told a different story.

Ashley stood still, overwhelmed as she found herself looking at nooses hanging from the beams of the ceiling. Lined up in four neat rows - one row per beam - were six nooses in each row. Twenty four nooses, she quickly calculated. The nooses were bad enough. She wished that was all she could see.

As the entire team stood still and looked upward, one thing was certain. Just as they hadn't been able to stop the burning of bodies in the incinerator, there was nothing they could do for the people who hung from the ceiling.

"They've been there for a long time," said Tim. "Some of them look almost mummified."

Ashley nodded in agreement.

"Doesn't make it any easier to see that," she said, subconsciously looking over to see Chris looking back at her. He had his rare moments of compassion. She'd seen them as much as she'd seen his non-compassionate side. She was glad to see the scene was affecting him too. It showed her that there was still some humanity inside of him.

"Some kind of welcome, this room," Ashley

continued. "So, what happens? People get brought in through that window back there, and, unless we've missed a secret passage or something, they must pass through here … and see that?"

"That could be the very reason that they never escape if that's the case," Chris said. "It's a pretty effective message *that* sends," he continued, pointing up at the ceiling.

"Jesus," Ashley muttered, turning to look at Tim. "What have we stumbled upon?"

"I don't know, but it's certainly getting interesting," Tim replied. "I think we've seen all there is to see in here. This place is huge. Time to move on?" he asked, not able to stop himself from glancing up one more time at the corpses that hung over ahead. "I'm not enjoying being here."

Ashley smiled at him. It was rare they 'enjoyed' anywhere that their job took them.

She turned to Chris and met his gaze of anticipation.

"Let's keep going," she said. "If whoever is responsible for all of this is *here*, we need to find them before they harm anyone else."

"Agreed," Tim said, diverting his eyes forward. He'd seen plenty of dead bodies in his career. As horrible as it was, that was just part of the job, and he'd long ago accepted that. Regardless, so many people hanging from a ceiling right over where he stood was an image that he suspected would stay with him for a very long time.

While waiting for Chris and his team to facilitate their movement through the next locked door, Ashley found her eyes drawn upwards again. Up there, hanging from the rafters, were twenty-four people. She knew that there were now hundreds missing from the region. Where did those twenty-four fit in?

Despite the incredible sadness she felt, when the next door was accessed, she moved forwards.

CHAPTER 50

As he entered the chamber he was forced to spend time in every day, Jordy Simpson wished yet again that today would be the day he died. As always, that was his conscious thought. Despite him thinking it would be the best thing to happen to him, his body continued to refuse to just give up and be done with the life of mostly darkness it was living.

Silently, he did as he'd been bid every day since he'd arrived. He had no idea when that had been, but he knew it was a long time ago. People had come and gone since he'd arrived, but for whatever reason, he continued to breathe and live. He continued to have to feel the agony that was subjected to him day after day. There was craziness in that. He was sixty-seven years old. Well, that was the age he was when he last had a birthday. He guessed he was still in his sixties, but there was no way to know for sure. Time was a concept that he'd lost a long time ago.

Sitting in the large chair, he waited for the grips to close around his forehead and his wrists. He didn't know how that worked. There was nobody he'd ever seen who activated the movement. There had been, the first few times he'd had to do it. Back then, he'd put up a fight. At some point, he'd given up trying to resist. They'd told him what the shadows would do to him if he didn't do what they needed him to. Knowing people disappeared without warning or explanation, he'd decided to give up trying to figure anything out and just go along with it all.

As expected, within seconds of sitting, cold metal

moved, seemingly all by itself. His wrists were anchored, as was his head. He remembered the panic he'd felt when he'd first been subjected to it. Now he just felt resigned. One day, those holds would settle on him, securing him, and his heart would give out, maybe just from pure weariness. He hoped so - kind of.

It was no surprise when, after the grips had him in their hold, he felt two needles enter his lower back. He had no idea what they did to him. When people had first forced him into the situation when he'd first arrived, they had never said anything. No questions were answered. No explanations were given. They held him, they subjected him to what now seemed an automated process that resulted in agony, and then they returned him to his bed to wait for the process to be repeated.

It was always the same. It seemed like it had been the same forever. Day after day, week after week, month after…

In the distance, he heard a thud. That was something he'd never heard before. For a moment, he was startled. The situation was new. Should he call out? Would it be better to bring attention to himself, to alert someone that he was there? Was there a chance that alerting someone to his presence could be the *worst* thing he could do?

He remained still, and he remained silent. The needles were doing whatever they did to him every single day. The cold metal grips held him still, just as they did every single day. He was helpless. There was no way he could move … yet. One thing he did know was that, in time, the needles would pull out of him, and then those metal grips would release him. That also was something that happened every single day. The question was when it *did* happen - when he was released - what would happen next?

Jordy Simpson's mind went blank, making him forget all thoughts. That was his body's way of dealing with the agony … each and every day.

CHAPTER 51

Continuing to move through large wooden doors that were each locked, Ashley and Tim took their time investigating room after room. With the exception of the corpses hanging from the ceiling in the third room, the first six seemed to be used for the similar purpose of storage. It wasn't until they reached the other side of the sixth room that they discovered something different.

"Now things could get interesting," Ashley said as they finally passed through a doorway and were greeted with a long hallway ahead of them. "I guess that's the end of back-to-back rooms."

Tim stopped where he was and looked along the passageway. There were at least ten doors down each side of it.

"It's like a hospital or a hotel," he said quietly. "None of these doors have windows in them," he added. "We're still going to have to go in blind."

One glimpse from Ashley told Chris to send his men out along the corridor, small groups of two lining up outside each of the first doors. She watched as each couple tried a door to see if it would open. One group after another indicated with hand signals that the room they were attempting to open up was locked.

Tim and Ashley followed as the teams kept moving along the long corridor, trying the remaining doors. When none were easily opened, they continued to the far end. One final door was there, positioned like a stairwell door in any building like a hotel or hospital.

On passing through the large solid door at the end of

the hallway, they were greeted with the beauty of a sweeping staircase. It filled Ashley's sight so suddenly and so fully that she was startled upon first seeing it. Behind them was an almost sterile corridor with the twenty or so doors off it. That hadn't fitted with the building exterior. The staircase, on the other hand, did.

Following the varnished wooden banister and balustrades along their formation, Ashley could see that she and the team had choices. They'd exited the corridor onto a mezzanine type section of the staircase. They could go up, or they could go down. Logic told her that there were two or three stories above them, and there was at least one below them, allowing for the assumption that a home built as far back as it appeared to have been, likely had a basement as well.

She looked at Tim. There were enough team members to be able to split up and go in the two different directions. Sometimes that was the best move. Other times, it was better to keep the team as a whole.

"Split," Tim said, their experience together as work partners telling him the dilemma she faced.

Turning to face Chris, Ashley nodded and watched as he directed his team off.

"Up or down?" Tim asked her. "We haven't seen any sign of life yet. If it's here, it could be anywhere."

"Down," Ashley replied, already beginning to step in that direction. "If they're up there, they'd have to come down to get out."

Tim wasn't sure of the logic, but followed her. When down one flight of stairs that led them to what should have been ground level, they were faced with what looked like would have originally been a large foyer. Now it had doors off it, all locked. Grandeur seemed to have been maintained, with a small chandelier hanging two meters in front of what could have been the original front door.

There was nothing to indicate the best door to begin

looking in. Still nobody appeared, and no sounds were heard. If it hadn't been for the incinerators going, Ashley would have assumed they were alone in the house. That could still be the case, but she wasn't yet ready to make that assumption. They'd only just begun to explore.

Chris led his men in what he thought would be a logical path. Behind them, Ashley and Tim followed. Through the first door they were able to open, they found themselves in another long corridor, almost identical to the one they'd come from a level higher.

Trying each door along the long hallway, none proved unlocked. They'd have to come back to all the locked ones. Instead of worrying about them in the present moment, the group made their way to the other end of the corridor. Through the doorway there, they found themselves in another large room with a door on the far side of it.

Ashley looked at Tim. It was her guess that they were in a similar six-room formation to what they'd passed through initially on the level above. As she watched Chris and members from his team approach and try the first door, she was surprised and pleased that it wasn't locked as the similar door above it had been.

Walking into the large room, again they were greeted with boxes, mounds of dust everywhere, and papers pinned to the walls.

"Not big on dusting, are they," Tim said as he walked forward to study more of the pages. "These articles are all from 2010. There's nothing more recent..."

His sentence stopping prompted Ashley to approach him.

"What?" she asked, curious about what he was looking at.

"This article," Tim said, pointing. "It's a newspaper article from The Guthrie News..." He read silently and then turned to her. "It's ... it's about the homeless population in Guthrie."

"Which we already know existed," Ashley said, still uncertain what was going on in her partner's head.

"Yes, but … bear with me," Tim said. "We think that the homeless populations in the four towns disappeared about ten years ago. What if … what if it was an article like this that alerted someone to *where* there were homeless people?"

"Someone needed these people for something?"

"Yeah," said Tim. "Well, what if they needed people who wouldn't be missed?"

Ashley felt sick at the thought. Missing populations inland. Bodies being hung and burnt on the island. The two things were possibly completely unrelated and yet…

"Let's keep moving," she said, a shudder going through her as she looked at Chris. His nod told her he was ready to move on whenever she was.

Before she could say anything more, she heard a voice inside her ear.

"More locked rooms on level three," the voice said.

"Copy," Chris said quietly in response before facing Ashley again. "Ready?"

Ashley looked at Tim and then nodded at Chris. Through three more rooms, they walked with each door unlocked and easy to open. Nothing indicated life had passed through any of the rooms in recent times. All of them looked like they'd been just left in a certain state a very long time ago. Dust had built up on every surface, including the floors.

When they reached the very last room, no second doorway was present. Thinking about the layout of the large house, as they'd seen it from outside, Ashley knew that on the other side of the final room must have been the outbuilding they'd climbed up on to reach the window above. Having not found any people on the current level - living or dead - for a moment, she felt disheartened. She'd been so sure they'd find something there. Instead, it looked as though those hopes had been pointless.

"There's nothing here," she said quietly before a voice came through the comms again.

"Moving up to level four," it said.

Once again, Chris gave his reply then turned to face Ashley. He was about to ask for their next move when they heard the voice speak again, this time in a much more hushed tone.

"We've got people," it said. "Corridor is same as levels two and three, but there must be at least eighty people up here, all in formation."

Chris focused on what his team member was saying.

"Can they see you?" Chris asked.

"Don't think they're seeing anything," his team member said. "They're walking by themselves, and there's nobody else around, but they look like they're zombies, moving on autopilot."

"Stay still and observe only," he said.

"Copy," the voice replied.

"What do you see? What are they doing?" Chris whispered.

"Doors just opened. All of them at once. The people are filing into them. They look like they're in a trance, or drugged up or something. They're not speaking or looking at one another. Just walked into the rooms," said the voice. A few seconds later, it began speaking again. "Doors all closed together. Corridor is empty again."

"Hold your position," Chris said. "We're coming up to your level."

"Copy," the voice said.

After a quick exchange of glances between Tim, Chris, and Ashley, they and their team began working back through the rooms they'd checked. Along the corridor, then up two flights of the glamorous sweeping staircase, they saw the other team waiting for them.

"Has anything else happened?" Chris asked.

"No, nothing more," replied his team member.

"They're all inside these rooms. We haven't heard anything, and I'm pretty sure they were completely unaware that we were right here."

"Okay," Chris said before turning to face Ashley. "Check out the remaining rooms?"

Ashley nodded. "Yeah," she said, her heart beginning to pound in anticipation. "If there are eighty people in these rooms, someone has to be here to feed them and … do … whatever they're doing to them."

Chris signaled to his men to move forwards, past the rooms they knew were housing living people. They knew that, in theory, there should be six large rooms on the other side of the corridor, possibly identical to the levels of such rooms they'd already explored.

As they left the main corridor behind, they walked through the door at the end. Immediately, all could see that they'd been incorrect in their expectation of seeing more of the large, dusty storage rooms. Instead, what lay ahead of them was what appeared to be a smaller hallway running the length of the left-hand side. Down the right-hand side, there were twelve doors, all closed.

Ashley and Tim walked forward, eager to know why - and in what ways - things were different on the level. Ashley tried the first door handle. The door wasn't locked. Tentatively, she opened the door as Chris and several of his men quickly flanked her.

All who saw into the room at that moment stopped still in surprise. It took some moments of just looking before Ashley could prompt herself to move forwards.

"What the fu…" Tim started to say when he focused on what was in front of him.

Chris quickly signaled for his team to break up into small groups and check the remaining eleven doors. A few minutes later, one of the men returned.

"The other eleven rooms are the same," he said to Chris. "Nobody in any of them."

"Jesus," Chris muttered. That was all he could say.

CHAPTER 52

Once Ashley had ascertained there were seven identical sets of machinery set up in the room, she took her time to walk around and study the detail of each. The most obvious part, of course, was that there was an adult-sized seat, not much different from the kinds she'd sat in when she'd visited dentists. It was also easy to see the strength of restraints each housed, presumably for forcing someone to keep their head, arms, and legs still.

"What has been going on here?" she wondered out loud.

"I don't know," said Tim. "But look at those," he continued as he pointed to holes in the part of the seat where someone's back would rest.

Once they'd studied the front, they moved around to the seat back. There, they found the source of what would pass through the holes.

"Syringes," Ashley said. "Attached to these tubes. That's not normal."

"Nothing about this is normal, Ash," Tim said before he followed the tubes and found their source. "This is what seems to be flowing in to one of those needles."

Ashley walked over to where he stood.

"What about the other line?" she asked.

Tim put on one of the rubber gloves he constantly had in his trouser pockets, then picked up the tube.

"Leads nowhere," he said, showing Ashley the end of it. "Maybe they ran out of whatever it was delivering."

"Maybe," said Ashley. "Or maybe it wasn't delivering something *to* whoever sits in the chair."

"Taking something *from* people?" Tim asked.

"Maybe."

"Seven of these in here, and twelve rooms," Chris said as he approached them. "That could be your eighty people that have just gone into the rooms at the other end of this floor."

"Could be," Ashley said. "I'm going to have a quick look through the rest."

After walking out, she entered, looked around, and then left each of the remaining rooms. They all looked identical, right down to the single tube from each chair mechanism that looked like it went nowhere. If they'd been used as recently as the team had seen the people entering rooms, someone must have been in the room since - perhaps even in the previous few minutes.

She remained wary as she entered the final room. Although it did look like the rest, something in the corner of the room caught her eye.

"What is it?" she heard Tim ask when he appeared beside her.

Ashley didn't answer as she walked right into the corner. It was then that she noticed a wall panel that looked out of place. The twelve rooms, in general, were sterile, like dental or medical rooms. The one panel that had caught her eye was just faded enough, with the surface slightly duller than all the others, to stand out.

Putting on a glove, she raised her hand and touched the wall. Nothing happened. She placed her hand flat against the surface and pushed a little. The amount of movement was little, but it was enough to nudge Ashley on to repeat the action, this time with more force.

As the entire flat surface of her hand pressed hard on the panel, there was a click. She moved back quickly as she watched the panel open back towards her. For a moment, she was reminded of an old record cabinet her mother and father had loved. She remembered as a kid, pressing that perfect spot on the corner of the glass door.

Press once, the door opened. Press again, the door closed. Open. Close. She'd loved that cabinet when she was little, purely because of the press action of the cabinet door. Now she stood before something similar, on a much larger scale.

She turned and looked for Chris. Through the six-inch gap that had opened, she could only see darkness. She wasn't too proud to silently signal to Chris for him and his team to lead the way into the dark.

Ahead of her, she saw the space light up, as if by a motion-activated light switch. As the team spread out, what appeared for Ashley and Tim to see was a desk with four computer screens lined up in a row. The space wasn't large, and neither were the screens. It looked like a tiny area intended for only one person to man.

She and Tim looked at the visions on the screens. There was one exterior view, focused on the pulley system. The other three views appeared to be of the interior of the main building they were in. After a few seconds, one of the views changed, then another, then another. In none of the views that showed, did they see any people.

In the corner of the room stood a tight-looped spiral staircase. One glance exchanged between Ashley and Chris, and he was off, leading some of his men up it.

At the top of the small set of stairs, Chris and his men waited as Ashley and Tim joined them. As Ashley looked along the small corridor they'd opened onto, she was surprised. From the ground, there had been no view of a further floor to the large building. It wasn't as wide and seemed like an add-on, like a modern penthouse area she'd seen on an old building before.

Curious about what might be on the other side of the door at the end of the small hallway, Ashley moved on.

CHAPTER 53

When the team opened and moved through the single door that sat at the other end of the small space, they found themselves in yet another corridor.

"It's like a rabbit warren," Tim muttered. It was only one building they'd been moving through. It was beginning to feel like they'd been at it for days.

Looking ahead, they could see five doorways down each of the right-hand and left-hand sides of the hallway. At the end, lay one more door. It was a smaller scale and more lavishly decorated, but not too different from the lower levels.

Noticing the décor, Ashley had to concede that, apart from the large staircase they'd been using to move from floor to floor, the current hallway was one area that seemed in keeping with what she'd expect from a house so old. The rest of the rooms and spaces they'd seen seemed to have been neglected for the most part, or transformed for modern use. She found it ironic that the area they were in appeared to have been added at a much later date than the building had been built, but it had been decorated with antiques, fittings, and wallpaper that screamed 'old'.

The men tried each of the doors lining the sides of the corridor. All were locked. When they reached the door at the end, they considered it might be too.

Ashley was glad when she saw Chris open the door without any problem. She was equally surprised when she heard a voice call out to them, saying only one word.

"Welcome."

CHAPTER 54

As Ashley, Tim, Chris, and his team all entered through the doorway, they found themselves in what looked like another world. Ashley guessed there were around thirty people scattered around the large space, sitting on lush antique seats. Some appeared to be playing cards around a small wooden table. Some were standing near a fireplace that had a low flame burning in it.

One of the three things that stood out most to Ashley was that the room and the people were all dressed in attire from the early 1900s. Another was that each of them wore a mask on their face. Some faces were fully covered, revealing only a small glimpse of their eyes through the mask cut-outs. Others were not unlike ones that Ashley had seen on a visit to Venice years earlier. The third thing that captured her attention was that not one of the people before her seemed at all bothered that an entire armed team of law enforcement had just entered the room.

Finding herself temporarily dazed by the scene before her, Ashley was broken from her daze when she saw a man approach her. Chris was quick to move closer, weapon up and at the ready. The man merely glanced at Chris and smiled.

"My dear boy, there will be no need for that here," he said before turning to face Ashley full-on. "Sir Thomas Henderson at your command, Madam," he said as he reached out with implied intent to take her hand in his and kiss it.

Ashley pulled her hand back.

"Henderson..." she said, thinking about the newspaper articles she'd read in one of the rooms they'd visited earlier.

"And you are?" Thomas asked, his voice revealing an air of superiority from an age long past.

"I am Special Agent Ashley Power," Ashley replied. "What is going on here, Mr. Henderson?"

The gentleman looked at her for a long moment, not replying straight away. The intensity of his gaze began to affect Ashley until she caught herself and regained her inner strength.

Finally, Thomas Henderson spoke.

"We are living as we have *always* lived, Ms. Power," he said. "This is our home, as it has been for hundreds of years."

"But it was reported as having burned...," Tim began to say. The look he received from Thomas silenced him.

"There was a fire here, it is true," Thomas said, nodding. "Let me just say ... that ... well, we have friends everywhere. We live quietly. We do not interact with anyone. We appreciate you coming all this way to check on us, but I assure you, we are all well, as you can see," he continued, using his hands to indicate all the other people in the room. "I shall alert you to our one rule, however, that being that when you come here, you can never leave. I am sure you understand. Our family is prestigious and private. We shall not allow anyone to report on us, and the only way we can absolutely enforce that is to keep you here."

Ashley walked up to him, only feeling stronger in herself by the threat he'd made.

"You are breaking the law..."

"As this is our home, I do not believe so!" Thomas exclaimed, his tone changing. "We live a very quiet existence, I assure you."

"And the bodies you're burning?"

For a moment, Thomas looked surprised. He regained

his composure remarkably quickly.

"Merely an efficient way to dispose of those who do not survive here," he said. "Death comes to all of us, Ms. Power - if not today, then perhaps tomorrow."

"And the people walking around as though they are not thinking for themselves?"

Thomas grinned. It wasn't a pleasant grin.

"Our friends," he said, his voice changing to almost cocky. "They help us. You see," he began, again indicating all the other people in the room. "There was a fire here, it is true, during which many of our great family perished, but many - as you see before you - suffered greatly from burns. We needed a way to help our bodies recover..."

"Such as a hospital? On the mainland?" Tim asked, his dislike for the guy in front of him growing.

"Of course not! We do not attend such places!" Thomas replied, sounding utterly outraged at the suggestion. "We stayed together, and we found a way to rebuild our bodies ... regenerate, if you will. The people who've come to be with us are remarkably healthy, I assure you. The human body is an incredible machine, but that is all it is - a machine. Feed it goodness, and it will process that into the perfect separation of prime health and waste. That is what our friends help us with."

"You say the word 'friends' ... but they didn't come here willingly, did they," Tim said.

"Didn't they?" Thomas asked, challenging Tim in his assumption.

"Well, *did* they?" Ashley asked. "Or did you take them?"

Thomas smiled at her again.

"My dear lady, *I* did not take *anyone*..."

"We think you did," Tim said, demanding the man in front of him to shift his focus away from Ashley. "We think you sought out people who wouldn't be missed and forced them to come here."

Thomas laughed a laugh that could only be described as mutually evil and insane.

"I have never left this island, Mr. Moore," he finally said, his tone sobering and almost beginning to sound threatening. "If you think you can convince anyone that I have, I am afraid that will be a waste of your time … and mine."

Ashley looked around the room. Everyone else continued with whatever pursuits they had been doing when the team had entered. They must have been able to hear the conversation taking place, yet looked as though they were completely oblivious to it. The exception was one young woman. Although she held in front of her a full hand of cards and appeared to be happily playing with the two other people at the small table, Ashley didn't miss that through her full-face mask, the young woman's eyes kept darting to the crowd that had just entered the room.

"These are all your family?" Ashley asked Thomas. When he nodded, she further questioned him. "*All* of these people? *All* have been born as Hendersons?"

A slight waver in Thomas's confidence made Ashley think that she might have asked a question he hadn't anticipated.

"Why would you think otherwise?" Thomas asked.

Ashley smiled at him.

"Why? Because two entire towns of people vanished ten years ago, including children," she said. "When I look around this room, I can see several young people who appear to be aged between 15 and … hmm … maybe 25. And I'm wondering whether your family - the mighty Hendersons - are guilty of incest," she said, enjoying seeing the look of horror on Thomas's face. "Or if, perhaps, you took entire families from those two townships and made the children your own."

"Why would you think such a thing, Ms. Power? What use could we have for anyone who is less than a

Henderson? To think such a thing..." Thomas began to say. Ashley cut his words short.

"You must need new blood, at least now and then," she replied. "To keep such a great family as the Hendersons alive over generations, unless you use incest, there is no other choice but to take someone and bring them into your fold." She looked around, particularly at the youngest in the room. "I wonder ... do they remember that you *stole* them? Do they remember the families they came from? Do they know what you did to their mothers and their fathers? Their brothers and their sisters?"

Ashley watched Thomas's face as she talked. The more words that came from her mouth, the more uncomfortable he seemed to grow. Slowly but surely, his confidence and cockiness were being chipped away. It was enough to drive Ashley on.

"Tell me, Mr. Henderson, when the rest of our Bureau teams get here, how many people will we find in this building?"

Thomas gave her a stare that looked almost murderous.

"Building? My dear lady, please do not refer to this as simply a *building*. This is the Home by the Sea. It is the generational seat of the great family of Henderson. We founded this area. Quite simply, it belongs to us - *all* of it belongs to us."

"And the people of the area too?" Tim asked. "Is that what you think? That all people around this entire region should bow down and be ... what? Your slaves?"

Thomas looked disgusted.

"We would never have *slaves*!" he exclaimed. "How dare you imply..."

"Isn't that what all these people are doing for you? Slavery?" Ashley asked as she saw Thomas become increasingly less able to maintain his gentlemanly composure. "You made them come here against their will, and you make them work by somehow using their bodies as 'machines', as you called them, so that you and your family can improve *your* health and regenerate from the burns you suffered." Ashley paused and looked closely into his eyes. "That actually *is* my interpretation of slavery - people being used and abused against their will, purely for whatever their owners decide they want in their lives."

Looking around the room, Tim wondered briefly how much any of the people in there even knew about life outside the island.

"Where are the people from Kerr and Pioneer?" he blurted out. When Thomas looked at him, he saw a slight level of concern that hadn't been present on the older man before. Even without looking around the room, Tim saw movement out the corner of his eye. At least one person - a young woman - had turned her head sharply at the mention of the two deserted towns. "Answer the question, Mr. Henderson. You took the entire population of two towns…"

"I assure you, I did not…"

Tim felt his patience begin to be tested.

"Someone did … *for* you," he said. "Now tell us, are the people of Kerr and Pioneer here, or have you already killed them?"

Thomas looked like he was going to object. Then he appeared to consider his options. After a long period of silence, he answered and nodded.

"I believe some of the people here are from those towns, yes," he said. "I do not know for sure where the people were collected from. We need numbers each March or April for East…" he began to say, then stopped himself.

The months said out loud reminded Tim of other articles he'd seen.

"Easter … what?" Tim asked. "Is that the time of your special 'regeneration' process?" He waited for

Thomas to answer. The lack of reply made Tim weary. "Or is that your time … for sacrifice?"

Ashley looked on as Thomas's body language changed completely. He'd seemed confident, cocky, and too sure of himself at the start of the questioning. With each round of questions, his body language changed to less confident. Progressively, he began to look increasingly tired.

Thomas nodded and then answered the question.

"Every day, our friends help us by giving us their special blood that has been processed in their systems using nutrients we feed to them after the blood taking process," he said. "Day to day it helps, but every year we seem to go forwards and then have times when it's more like we're going backward. Our bodies regenerate temporarily, but then, after each summer, they go *backward.* We found out about the Easter rituals long ago. They've been used each year for many years now."

"There are no reports of missing people on the mainland. How did you know who wouldn't be missed?" Ashley asked, beginning to *really* feel like she was inside a fictional story.

Thomas looked at her for a very long time before he spoke.

"Those who you see here," he said, waving his hand around the room. "They are Hendersons, but they aren't the *only* Hendersons. Out there are members of our family who have given up their prestige here to live among the lesser, and help with our great cause."

"Like … members of the police force, perhaps?" Tim asked, curious. "Mike Batch?"

Thomas looked surprised but then nodded.

"Mike Batch is my nephew. My sister - his mother - Mary, was one of the few who perished in the fire. Mike was always thankful for me treating him as my own son after that."

Ashley was surprised, and yet not so much. Now, at

least, the actions of the Compton police officer made sense. Mike Batch was a Henderson. He was part of *all* of what they'd been investigating.

It was a lot to take in. Ashley considered all they'd learned just in the previous few minutes. There was so much the family could be charged for - kidnapping, at the very least, but no doubt murder too, since they weren't denying the human sacrifices they'd made.

Chris approaching her broke her out of her thoughts about the magnitude of what they'd stumbled upon.

"I'll call it in?" he asked. "Get teams out here?"

Ashley nodded. If nothing else, it was a huge home, and it would take a suitably huge team of forensics professionals to work through it.

"How many people are here, Mr. Henderson?" she asked. Seeing him begin to indicate only the people within their view, she stopped him. "No, not your family. How many *other* people are here? The ones here against their will?" she asked.

Thomas looked utterly defeated as he looked down. To see someone go from such confidence to such deflation was interesting for Ashley to watch, even though she'd seen it happen many times throughout her career.

"At present, I believe there are approximately one hundred and fifty," Thomas finally said.

Tim found himself astounded at the admission. Throughout their search of the building, Tim had thought it unlikely they were going to find anybody they'd thought had gone missing. Hearing the number that Thomas had provided gave Tim hope. Even if not all of the people who'd gone missing, a hundred and fifty was far better than none.

"We need to see them," Tim said. "*All* of them."

He saw Thomas open his mouth as if to object.

"Now!" Tim said with more force.

Thomas nodded and turned to face one particular

person in the room. When that person came forward, he addressed him.

"Richard, release all of the doors when these officers tell you too," Thomas said, prompting the other man to nod.

"How many floors are they over?" Tim asked.

"Two," said Thomas. "Just the two below us."

Chris heard the details and immediately dispatched some of his men to head downstairs and prepare for addressing people when the doors opened.

"Choppers are on their way here," Chris said to Tim and Ashley. "Teams will be here within half an hour."

"Stay here and watch them," Ashley said before she and Tim walked away, following the teams towards the staircase.

"Let's hope that these are our missing homeless people," Ashley said to him.

"Let's hope that one *particular* missing person is amongst these people," Tim replied. "If it wasn't for Jordan Simpson's granddaughter, we wouldn't have found this place. I know all of these people are important, but I particularly want to be able to take good news back to Kate Simpson. She searched for her grandfather, and then other homeless, for years. She needs closure."

CHAPTER 55

Ashley and Tim stood back and watched as the doors of the corridor on level 3 were opened. They'd each considered they might see people rush out, happy to have some freedom. Instead, nothing happened.

After several minutes, Ashley began walking down the hallway. Peering into the first room, she saw four beds, lined up like in a dormitory. The room was dark, the gloominess coming from the blend of wooden slats over the windows, and the general darkness outside. It had seemed gloomy enough outside, with the thick fog blanketing the island. Inside the room, Ashley realized just how depressing it must have been for the people being forced to stay there.

She approached the first person she saw. They were awake and sitting on the edge of their bed, but they didn't seem responsive. When she spoke to them, they remained still. She couldn't see their face clearly in the darkness, but even in the shadows, she could see facial features unmoving and with no expression.

After a few attempts to talk and try to get them to respond, she moved on to the next person in the room, and then the next room. One by one, she and Tim tried to speak to the people they found. There was no difference in any of them.

At the end of the first corridor, they walked up the stairs to the next level. Everything was the same - lots of people, completely unresponsive. Some rooms had three or four people in them. Others had only one or two. Regardless of the number, there didn't appear to even be any contact or communication between the people who resided in the same room together. The word that the first team member had reported - zombie - seemed a suitable description of the state of the people they found.

Tim felt sad for the people they'd found. He had no idea who they were, and couldn't find that out if they weren't awake enough to answer questions. Answers could still come, even if they remained in the state they were in, but not till a forensics team was involved, and DNA, fingerprints, or dental records could help with identification.

When he entered the eighth room on the third floor, Tim finally found a reason for joy. Sitting on the bed closest to the boarded-up window, with no other person in the room with him, was a face that Tim was sure belonged to Jordan Simpson.

Tim rushed forward. If nothing else, at least this was a person who could be addressed personally, by name.

"Mr. Simpson?" Tim asked, fairly certain it was the right person. At first, the man seemed to be in the same unmoving state as all the rest. As Tim repeated the name, he saw the man's head animate slightly. "Mr. Jordan Simpson?" he asked again. The head turned further until it was facing him. "Are you Mr. Jordan Simpson?"

Jordy heard the questions, but it took time for them to sink in. When they did, he really noticed the young man sitting next to him.

"That was my name once," he said quietly. "Now I'm just a shadow, like all the rest."

Tim sat quietly. He hoped Jordan would keep talking. There was silence for several minutes before he did.

"Morning light," Jordy said as he faced the boarded-up window. "That's all we have to look forward to now. Morning light." He turned and looked at the young man again. "If you're here, you'll have to stay. There's no way out. You won't get away from here. Now, you'll too become a shadow of the person you once were. All we have here are memories of our lives - the times of delight, and the times of sorrow. We're nothing more now. Wait for the morning to come. Wait for death to come. That is what being a shadow is all about."

Listening to the man's rambling, Tim felt incredibly emotional. Given the circumstances, it would be fully understandable if the people in the large house had completely lost their sanity over their time there. Regardless, Tim was determined to maintain hope. In the previous few minutes, he'd seen Jordan Simpson change from completely unmoving, to moving and speaking. That was *absolutely* reason to maintain hope.

"Mr. Simpson, I'm Special Agent Tim Moore," he said, holding back tears that threatened. "We've come here to find you. Your granddaughter has been searching for you for a very long time."

Jordy heard the words but found it difficult to process them. He turned the words over and over in his mind.

"Granddaughter?" he asked. Always in the mornings, when he could see little amounts of sunlight, his mind felt sharp. It was never the same in the dark. Mornings were his time to shine. That was what Missy used to always say.

Missy. He didn't usually think about her during the times of darkness. She was always a hit in his thoughts in the morning light, though. Missy.

He smiled. He thought of Missy, and then he thought of his children ... and then his grandchildren.

"Which one?" he asked the young man beside him.

Tim looked at him, not sure what he was asking. In front of his eyes, he saw Jordan Simpson animate one more level.

"Which granddaughter?" Jordy asked, making Tim smile and chuckle in relief.

"Kate," Tim replied. "Kate Simpson."

Jordy grinned and nodded. "I remember little Katie."

CHAPTER 56

"Job well done," Ashley heard Chris say to her when they were on the boat back to the mainland. It had been an incredibly long day, culminating in hours of crossover as large teams had arrived from the Bureau to take over investigation of the scene.

Before she responded, Ashley took some time to think about the day. All of the members of the Henderson family that had been residing inside the large home, had been rounded up and flown to the mainland for more intensive questioning and charges. The victims who had been initially unresponsive had been assigned medical professionals who were staying on the island for the night and coming day to monitor the people while doing what they could to bring them out of their seemingly brainwashed state.

"It's been a long one, this one," Ashley finally said. "At any moment in this investigation, we could have been on a completely wrong path…"

"But you weren't," Chris said, smiling. "And you wouldn't be, because you're a good agent."

Ashley heard the compliment and smiled.

"Thanks," she said quietly.

There were days when she didn't feel like she was a good agent, but when she was part of a successful case closure, she forced herself to accept some credit.

"Are you staying in Compton for the night?" Chris asked, the simple question making Ashley cringe inside with anticipation of the question that might very well follow. "Maybe we could have a drink together?"

Although she didn't voice it out loud, inside of her head, Ashley heard a very loud, 'ugh!'. Rather than express that, she smiled again.

"Thanks, Chris, but Tim and I are going to have an early night," she said, purposely constructing her words in a particular order, so it sounded entirely different from its true meaning. "We have to get up early to drive back to HQ."

Chris looked surprised but nodded. When he turned and saw Tim walking over, he smiled sadly at Ashley and then walked away.

"He doesn't look happy," Tim said when he reached her.

Ashley shrugged her shoulders.

"I told him you and I are having an early night," she said, watching Tim's face.

Tim burst out laughing. He knew very well her ability to twist words into a particular order to give completely different meanings.

"As we are, Special Agent Ashley Power. As we are!" he said, grinning and nodding. "Actually, I *am* knackered, and we have that long drive back tomorrow. I still don't know why Sarah just didn't let us fly…"

"But you love my company in the car," Ashley said, teasing him. "*And* think of how many food places we can stop at on the way back!"

As Tim laughed again, he wrapped his arms around her and kissed her forehead. It was natural, and it was nice. That's all there was to that, and they both knew it.

"Has Kate been told about her grandfather?" Ashley asked as she pulled away.

Tim nodded. "Yep. Sarah called her and gave her the good news. Said she was over the moon, and asked Sarah to pass on her thanks to us."

"That's good," Ashley replied. "I'm so happy for her, and for all the other families who will learn about their loved ones."

"Loved ones, Ash? These other people haven't even been noticed as being missing, as far as we know," Tim said, sadness evident in his voice.

"Maybe," replied Ashley. "We don't know the situations. Sometimes there are good reasons why people lose touch with members of their families. However these stories go, when each of those people is identified, our team will find relatives and make sure their stories are told. There are so many victims in this. I can't believe that there's nobody out there for any of them. They each must have so many great stories to tell about their lives, if not about the past decade or so. Somebody will want to hear those stories, I'm sure."

Tim nodded again and smiled at her.

"I hope so," he said. As he turned his head, he saw land ahead. "It's good to be out of that fog and the darkness of that place."

"Yeah, if that wasn't a reason for someone to give up on life, I don't know what is," replied Ashley. "Living mostly in gloom, like it's almost constantly night? That can't be good for anyone's mental health."

"Hopefully the medical staff can start getting the victims back on the path to being well again," Tim said. As he saw the shore get closer, he noticed the presence of Bureau cars. "Looks like people are getting rounded up there too," he continued as he pointed to the land.

Ashley thought about all the people they'd questioned during their time searching for Jordan Simpson.

"Mike Batch should be among them," she said, prompting Tim to nod.

"Sarah said they've done full searches back at HQ for anyone and everyone who was ever registered as offspring to the Henderson family line," he said. "I told them we got the same bad feeling about Dan Houston in Guthrie too. Something was off about that guy too."

"You think they - the Hendersons - purposely planted cops in departments of towns they planned on sourcing people from?"

"I think that is a definite possibility," Tim replied. "If Mike Batch was planted for that reason in a town where mass amounts of people disappeared, I think it's worth investigating the law enforcement in the other towns that they disappeared from, too. It could well turn out to be nothing, and the others are all good, but no harm in looking closely at them."

"True," Ashley said. "There's the dock. I'm definitely ready for a long shower and much sleep."

"I concur," replied Tim, nodding. "I'm so tired and emotionally drained that I don't think I'm even hungry."

Ashley chuckled and appreciated once again how good he was to have as her work partner.

CHAPTER 57

"Breakfast, and then we're off," Ashley said to Tim the next morning. When they'd gotten back to the motel the night before, they'd both gone to their own rooms and almost immediately fallen asleep. The day before hadn't necessarily been physically challenging, but it had certainly played with the emotions of both agents.

"I'm ready," Tim said to her, grinning as he loaded his bag into the car then climbed in. "Man, that was the best sleep I've had in ages."

"Same," Ashley replied as she did her seatbelt up. "I actually didn't mind that little motel, but I'm still looking forward to getting home."

Driving to the small diner that they'd visited most mornings while in Compton, both agents were silent. Their search for one man had turned into something so much bigger and something unexpected. That was sometimes the way on cases, but this one seemed to have presented a surprise aspect to a whole other level beyond what they'd investigated together before.

When Ashley veered the car into the diner carpark, Tim's phone rang. For several minutes, Ashley heard the words of Tim in response to whatever was being asked or said at the other end of the call. Once again, she was surprised that he didn't just put his phone on speaker, but, hey, that was Tim.

When he hung up, he turned to face her.

"Sounds like it's going to be long days for everyone involved in this one," he said. "Sarah wants us to go and see Kate before we head back to HQ."

"Okay," Ashley replied. "Was there anything else of importance in that call?"

"We'll get a full debrief when we get back," Tim said. "She wanted me to tell *you* that particularly."

"Yeah," Ashley said, chuckling softly. "She knows I usually do a runner as soon as we've finished something. Okay! Okay. This time I'll go for the debrief, but *then* I'm going to take a few days off. There are dozens of crew working on this now. They don't need me there."

Tim only nodded in reply.

"Let's go eat," Ashley said to change the subject. As she opened her door, climbed out, then locked the car, she grinned at him. "Hungry?"

Tim only had to smile at her to give his answer to *that* question.

Pulling up to the workplace of Kate Simpson an hour and a half later, Tim felt a relaxed calm fall over him. Of all the things they'd investigated, finding Kate's grandfather had remained his strongest focal point.

When they walked into the workplace and saw Kate come out to greet them, it was easy to see her emotions.

"Oh, thank you so much!" she exclaimed as she hugged each agent. "I know I won't get to see him for a while, but as soon as I'm allowed to, I'll be going to visit him. I'm going to bring him back to my home. I don't care how much he argues. He's coming home with me."

"I think you might find he'll be glad to do that after all he's been through," Tim said, smiling at her.

Kate looked at each of them. "Was it really that bad?"

Ashley looked at Tim before replying.

"I think your grandfather might tell you a story that could sound unbelievable," she said. "Or he might not want to talk at all."

"He looked so happy when I told him you'd been looking for him. I think that made the difference to him."

"Thank you," said Kate.

Nothing more needed to be said.

CHAPTER 58

On their drive back to HQ, Tim found his emotions pull at him. It was always the way after a case was finished. Ashley usually shut down when they finished something. That was her way. His way was to feel emotions heighten, not diminish.

As he watched the terrain pass outside, he found his thoughts drift to Chris Barnett. Ashley had never mentioned her time being involved with Chris. Tim focused on that for a long time. They'd talked about past romantic involvements on occasion. He couldn't remember anything at all about Chris. He wondered if it was indicative of Ashley having had stronger feelings for Chris than what she'd had for other guys she'd talked about.

Inside his head, Tim told himself to shut up. Whatever had happened between Ashley and any of her past lovers or boyfriends was none of his business. His logic told him that. His brain fought to want to think about her more. It was something that happened so reliably after a case, that Tim knew to try and disregard his feelings on those days. Initially, he'd tried to honestly express his feelings towards Ashley when he felt them. After a couple of times when she'd shot the conversation down, he'd learned that she didn't want to hear what he thought if it involved how he felt about her.

That was wise, anyway. They worked together. Not only that, but they worked *well* together. It would never be worth it to try and push for more than that. They had a perfect balance of friendship. He needed no more.

"Whatcha thinking?" he heard her ask.

When he turned to face her, he saw her glancing at him with a slight look of concern on her face. He liked that, even though he didn't want her to ask about his thoughts at that particular moment. He didn't like lying to her. Experience had proven he wouldn't like the outcome if he told her the truth in that instance, either. Lose-lose. They were always the hardest of scenarios.

He decided that lying would be the lesser of the two options, and probably easiest for Ashley.

"I was thinking about your need for taking time out when we finish cases," he said.

"I know you don't understand it," Ashley replied, smiling at him.

"Actually, I've been thinking it could be something for me to try," said Tim. "When you come back to work after taking a few days to clear your head, you're always so focused and relaxed. That can't be a bad thing."

Ashley studied his face for as long as she dared to take her eyes off the road.

"Are you okay, Partner?" she asked. She knew he always got emotional on their final day of investigations. Even though asking that question could possibly prompt him to give her an answer she didn't want to hear, she didn't like the thought of anything upsetting him or making him unhappy either.

Tim smiled sadly. "Yeah," he replied. "I think I, too, want to get this debrief over with and then take some time at home."

"No hot shags planned then?" Ashley asked, teasing him to lighten the mood.

The look he gave her screamed, 'are we really going there?'. It made Ashley giggle. That, in turn, made Tim chuckle at her.

It wasn't a perfect situation they were in as partners, but it was pretty good. They'd take time out in their solitude, but they'd then move on and solve another case.

CHAPTER 59

"Good job, you two," Sarah said as she faced the two agents in her office. She'd debriefed them on all that had happened since they'd left the island the night before, and all that was currently happening. "There's still much to do to build a case against the Henderson family, but you both deserve a few days off. I have another case for you to look at, but I'd rather you both go and do whatever it is that you do to reset. Come back in next Monday."

"What's the case?" Ashley asked. She needed her time off, but she couldn't help but ask.

"Now that would be telling, wouldn't it, Special Agent Power," Sarah said, delivering a rare smile. "Go! Take your required time to rest and recuperate. The other teams are finishing this one off, and the new one will be sitting here, waiting for you on Monday."

Ashley nodded, smiled, and stood.

"Okay," she said, walking toward the office door. "See you Monday, Boss!"

Tim said his goodbyes to Sarah and then followed Ashley out.

"Come on, Timmy Boy," said Ashley. "I'm going to drop you home and then forget all about you for a few days."

Tim smiled but said nothing. He didn't need time off between cases, but he'd try it. Who knew what could happen.

The End

OTHER BOOKS
BY
ANN M PRATLEY

A POWER MOORE INVESTIGATION TALE
HOONIGAN
ANN M PRATLEY

HOONIGAN

Tristan Clarkson has woken up, over and over, bound to a chair and unable to see. He has no idea where he is, or why he is in the situation he's woken to. His memory is vague, protecting him from recent events that will eventually haunt him for the rest of his life. He wants to remember, but at the same time his mind acts as though he really, really doesn't. Initially he's confused. With each waking, his memory clears that little bit more, as do his senses. He soon becomes aware that the very person who has abducted him, is in the room with him, determined to make Tristan pay for something he cannot even remember.

Meanwhile, in a hospital nearby a patient has been taken. With the help of Special Agents Ashley Power and Tim Moore, an investigation begins into where the man has been taken, and who would have reason to remove him. With the patient having already been weak from time in a coma, time is of the essence in finding him alive.

Hoonigan is a blend of crime and suspense, intermingled with the strength of friendship, and the awakening of one father's realization of just how much his son really means to him.

A POWER MOORE INVESTIGATION TALE
RESOLUTION of HAPPINESS
ANN M PRATLEY

RESOLUTION OF HAPPINESS

Fiona Thompson - better known as Flo to everyone who knew her - took a plunge and stepped out of her comfort zone and into the world of online dating. With persistence she found her prince. He ticked all the boxes. He was handsome. He was financially secure. He loved her. He married her.

She was warned by friends and family that there was something off about him. She didn't listen.

Then she woke up cold, inside the darkness of a wooden box.

Join Special Agents Ashley Power and Tim Moore as they investigate the disappearance of Flo, going on a surprising journey that nobody in Flo's world could possibly anticipate.

TIGER IN OUR HOUSE

TIGER IN OUR HOUSE

When Alana Templeton goes to do the simple task of
hanging her laundry outdoors, she becomes aware that
something is not as it should be in her yard. The sound
she hears is one that many people might not recognize at
first. For Alana, it is, surprisingly, a sound
she's heard before.

Being in the yard, with her toddler in the doorway of
their home, she knows the right thing to do is whatever
she can to save him. The previous time, she
succeeded, but will she this time?

A woman and her infant being put in danger of being
attacked by the large animal that has escaped the local
wildlife park, prompts an investigation into whether
there might be more than just bad luck behind the two
events. It seems unlikely that someone could have used
such a beast for an attempt on someone's life. Then
again, it seems unlikely that the animal would escape its
confine and end up at the same location
two times in a row.

Called in to figure out what might be behind the strange
occurrences, Special Agents Ashley Power and Tim
Moore begin to delve into an elaborate and rather
unconventional scheme to hurt someone
through an act of revenge.